HARVEST OF COURAGE

The daughter of a widowed farmer, Mairi McGloughlin was blissfully happy in the Forfarshire countryside of her birth. A beautiful blessing to Mairi, the land becomes a curse to others. As the schoolteacher's son Robin Morrison proceeds to Edinburgh University and a teaching job in Italy, Mairi's elder brother Ian is denied the opportunities his intelligence deserves. With the outbreak of the Great War, however, two young men could not react more differently. Robin enlists, only for his romantic spirit to be crushed in the horror of Ypres; while Ian, a conscientious objector, sees the world in ways he had never dreamed. Patriots both, they leave Mairi to bring in the harvest, look after her father, and muse upon her future in a world of uncertainty. Why, when she has always despised her brother's academic rival, does Robin's absence make her heart ache quite *so* much?

HARVEST OF COURAGE

Eileen Ramsay

CHIVERS PRESS
BATH

First published 1998
by
Little, Brown and Company
This Large Print edition published by
Chivers Press
by arrangement with
Little, Brown and Company (UK)
1999

ISBN 0 7540 1251 4

British Library Cataloguing in Publication Data available

Printed and bound in Great Britain by
REDWOOD BOOKS, Trowbridge, Wiltshire

For my sisters,
Anne, Nancy and Kathryn

Thank you to my nephew Eli Colner and his friend David Schertzer who rescued this story from the depths of Eli's father's computer—and never once laughed.

CHAPTER ONE

In the spring of 1900 Mairi McGloughlin discovered that she loved the land. She was just nine years old: in fact she had just passed—not celebrated—her ninth birthday. With her best friend, Violet Anderson, she was walking home from the village school. They skipped and walked down Pansy Lane and then Mairi saw the first of the year's snowdrops, virginal white, the lovely heads standing straight and tall on delicate stems, their dark green leaves cradling them protectively.

'Look, Violet,' she said, her voice full of awe, 'snowdrops.'

Violet skipped on the spot, not losing the beat. 'Seventy-eight, seventy-nine—they're jist flooers, Mairi—eighty-four, eighty-five.'

Mairi knelt down in the damp soil beside the flowers and she spoke for herself. 'No, they're not, Violet, they're more, they're harbingers of spring.'

She was top of the class and had seen that posh word in one of the Dominie's reserved books.

'Harbingers of spring,' she said again, liking the sound of the phrase. 'Look at them, Violet. They've come up out of the ground and they're pure white; the muck hasnae stuck to them.'

'Ach, you're daft, so you are, Mairi McGloughlin. Of course dirt doesnae stick to them.'

'Well, why not, since you're so smart, Violet Anderson? Why doesn't muck stick to them?'

For a moment Violet was perplexed. She had not expected to be questioned on something unquestionable, on an irrefutable fact. 'It just

1

disnae because . . . because God made them.'

'Aye, and he made Billy Soutar tae and all the mud in Angus is stuck tae him.'

At the thought of Billy Soutar, the little girls dissolved into laughter and ran giggling down the path, all thoughts of flowers and muck and their place in the great scheme of things gone from their minds.

They parted at the end of the lane. Mairi had to continue another mile to the farmhouse but Violet's father's tied cottage sat four-square to the road almost beside the path. Her mother was in the garden throwing potato peelings to the hens that bustled frenetically around her feet as if terrified that there would not be enough for all.

'There's scones jist oot the oven, lassies,' she called as she went on feeding the hens, 'and a nice jug of fresh milk in the larder, oor Violet.'

Mairi sighed. Pheemie Anderson was a fine baker. 'I cannae the day, Mrs Anderson. I've a pot of soup tae put on for the week.' The pot of soup would have been ready if her brother, Ian, had not let the fire go out. Ian's head was usually busy with anything but what he was supposed to be doing and yesterday he had got so involved watching a blackbird building a nest that he had forgotten not only to keep the range stoked but also to bring in the cows. Mairi had gone for the cows but too late to save her brother from their father's righteous anger. This morning Ian had been too sore to go to the school and Mairi had lied and told the Dominie that he had a cold. Mr Morrison had said nothing but at hometime he had given Mairi a lovely bound Shakespeare.

'If Ian is still unwell tomorrow, tell him to read

2

Richard II and I want him to go on with his history book and the composition he was going to write for me.'

Glowing, Mairi had put the precious book carefully in her bag. She and Ian and the teacher's horrible son, Robin, were the only children who were allowed to read the reserved books. Ian and Robin had fought for the position of top of the class for seven years since the day they had entered the little school together. Sometimes Robin was top, sometimes Ian. Robin always beat Ian in the arithmetic examinations and Ian beat Robin at compositions. Aggregate scores were what counted for top place and Mairi was hoping that Ian would be Dux. Then maybe, just maybe, Father would allow him to stay on at the school beyond the date when most farm boys left.

'He'll need tae count well enough tae buy in seed, no be diddled, and tae pay his men whit they're worth. He doesnae need tae speak poems.' That was Father, who would never understand his son, mainly because he would not try.

Mairi carried on up the road until she reached the farmhouse. The dogs, Dog and Ben, rushed out to meet her and she hugged them both, careless of the fact that they were working dogs and not, according to Father, to be petted like lap dogs. Dogs were the most satisfactory of all animals. They loved totally and without question; everything these strange human creatures did was perfect and Mairi, with her cuddles and scratching of just the right spot under the ears, was the most perfect of all. They even tolerated Ian's forgetfulness and waited patiently when he forgot to feed them. Their master did not have their forgiving nature.

'Oh, you beautiful babies,' crooned Mairi. 'Have you missed me then?'

Their tails wagging vigorously, to show her how much she had been missed, they followed her into the house.

'You'd best lie down in the kitchen while I see where Ian is.'

If they could have, they would have told her that Ian was ploughing with his father. Mr McGloughlin had promised his wife that the children would attend school but here was Ian, perfectly well and doing nothing. He did not have to sit down to help with the plough.

When Mairi realized that the house was empty, she cut herself a slice from a loaf of bread that she had baked herself. She spread it liberally with their own butter and sat down at the scrubbed kitchen table to eat it. Then she changed from her school frock into a working day dress and began to prepare vegetables for the soup: carrots, turnips, leeks and a cabbage all grown either in the garden or on the farm. She washed some of their own barley and left it sitting in a bowl of water while the stock simmered on the range. The stock she had made from the bone of the mutton joint that had been their Sunday and Monday dinner. The soup started, she peeled potatoes and then went out into the garden to gather some of the last of the Brussels sprouts. How good it would be when the spring vegetables began to appear; Brussels sprouts were, unfortunately, such a serviceable vegetable. Mairi could not think of one good thing to say about them and, in fact, sometimes wondered why farmers bothered to grow them. She was only nine years old, not a great age, but, in all that time of

4

living and experiencing, she had never met anyone who admitted to liking them.

'When I'm choosing the garden vegetables,' Mairi informed a particularly tough plant, 'there will be no sprouts.' She sat back on her heels beside the plants. There would be flowers. That's what there would be and something called asparagus that she'd seen in one of the Dominie's books, and strawberries, of course, which grew beautifully in Angus soil under Angus skies, and potatoes, even though Father grew them on the farm. The Dominie had a book about growing vegetables and it said that potatoes cleaned the ground and left it nice and ready for the next crop. Yes, asparagus. Mairi had never eaten, never even seen asparagus, but the gentry liked it and so it must be good. The Laird had a glass house called a succession house and he grew peaches in it. *Peaches*. Mairi had seen them when the Laird had given a picnic for his tenants. Oh, earth, soil, good clean dirt was a marvellous thing; it grew potatoes and peaches both. Even the word peach was good. Peach. When she was a farmer she would have a succession house and she would have a peach tree in it. The Laird would help her. He was a nice old man. He did not chuck her under the chin and expect her to like it as so many elderly and not so elderly men did. He had spoken to her, one gardener to another. Yes, she would not be afraid to ask the Laird. No doubt he had asparagus. She would go to see it at the next picnic.

Mairi jumped up. She had better get the sprouts and the tatties on. If Ian had done nothing to annoy Father they would have a nice time sitting around the table together, even though the soup

5

would not be at its best until tomorrow. But if she made a nice Shepherd's pie and that and the sprouts were ready to be served just as Father walked in from the fields, maybe he would speak to Ian with the soft voice he always used for Mairi and that her brother very rarely heard addressed to himself. She stopped at the back door, her eye caught by a glimpse of white against the garden wall—more snowdrops.

'When I'm the farmer,' began Mairi, and then she stopped, for she would never be the farmer. She was a girl. She would grow up and keep house for her father until Ian married and then, unless she herself married, she would share the chores with her sister-in-law, for it was Ian who would be the farmer, Ian, who was only completely happy when he was reading a story or scribbling away in his secret notebook.

'It's daft,' said nine-year-old Mairi McGloughlin, 'but it's the way it is and there's nout I can do about it.' She thought for a moment and smiled a slow sweet smile that was older than time. 'I'll marry Jack Black and bully him.'

Her future decided, Miss McGloughlin hurried into the kitchen and finished preparing the evening meal. Then there were a few precious minutes to do her homework. She was clever like Ian and the horrible Robin—what a sissy name for a laddie—and so the sums took her no time at all. The parsing and analysis of the three sentences took her a little longer because she was happier just reading and understanding lovely words than cluttering up her mind with parts of speech and suchlike nonsense. Ian now, and that spoiled brat who lived in the Schoolhouse, could happily parse and

6

analyze all the day long. She was about to say that such a failing showed just how horrid was Robin Morrison when she realized that the same label would have to attach itself to her beloved Ian. She vented her spleen on Robin by viciously slicing two sprouts into slivers and tossing them into the soup pot. Father would have been sure to ask her what on earth she was trying to do to his laboriously grown vegetables. Sprouts were cooked whole. Everybody knew that.

Colin McGloughlin and his son, Ian, were welcomed home by the smell of good food beautifully cooked. Ian had managed to keep his mind on his work all afternoon long and so his father was as pleased with him as he ever got. A good hammering had done the boy the world of good, which proved that Ian did not need 'patient understanding' as the Dominie was always saying, but discipline. There was a time for books and a time for remembering to mend the fire and, of the two, the fire was the more important. Without a fire, wee Mairi could not cook and he had never yet seen Ian ready to eat his books instead of a succulent Shepherd's pie. For a moment Colin toyed with the idea of approaching the School Board to allow Mairi to stay at home. There was necessity; he was a widower with two children. Ach no, he had promised Ellen and forbye, the lassie was only nine. She could finish the primary school and then she could stay at home where she belonged and take care of the house. She would not do hard farm work, not his wee lassie. Too much work had killed her mother, a shop girl from the town who should never have married herself on a farmer. But Mairi should be spared the hard work that was the lot of every daughter of the farm and if she did marry, and she had to he supposed, she should marry onto a farm that was owner occupied where there was a bit of extra money for a kitchen maid as well as a dairy maid. But not yet, not for a long time yet.

The little family ate their meal and washed it down with mugs of hot sweet tea. Then Colin went to the fire and sat down, the dogs at his feet. He would sit for an hour or two and then, once he had seen the children to bed, he would take himself off to his lonely room.

Ian too left the table and after assuring himself that his father was safely ensconced in the inglenook, he took the book that Mairi had brought him from the Dominie and carried it with pride and care to a seat on the other side of the roaring fire. He was soon deeply involved in the fourteenth century and totally removed from the world around him. Mairi accepted that she would clear the table and wash the dishes; that she would put the oats to soak for the morning's porridge and that she would fill the stone pigs that warmed the beds. That was woman's work. She could barely keep her eyes open by the time her jobs were finished.

'I'm away tae my bed,' she announced to her father and to her brother but neither heard her. She was not hurt. She did not expect a loving and protracted goodnight ritual. She smiled fondly at her menfolk as if they were her children and took herself off up the oak staircase to her little room under the eaves. She liked her room with its view over the fields towards the Firth of Tay. It was dark and she was tired and cold, but once she was

8

stripped to her vest and knickers she pulled the handmade patchwork quilt from her bed, wrapped it around her shoulders, and sat on the window seat looking out at the night. There were one or two fishing boats on the water. In the moonlight, against the dark sky, they looked like etchings. Mairi waited and waited and there, at last, was the train. It ran like a wheeled jewel box between the fields and the sea. It was going to Dundee, to Edinburgh, to York, maybe even to London itself.

'I'll be on you one day, Train,' she told it. 'Maybe all the way to London, but at least as far as Dundee. You wait and see and I'll have a red coat and a red hat and black leather gloves.'

Satisfied that the nightly ritual had been concluded successfully, she went to bed.

She was able to sleep late for in those days of late February it was still dark at six o'clock. No need to wash in cold water. Was there not always— well, nearly always—a kettle murmuring away beside the soup at the back of the black iron range? She made tea—Father liked a really good strong cup of tea first thing in the morning—before she carried a ewer of hot water back up to the basin that sat on her dresser. She pulled on her petticoats and her hand-knit stockings. It was far too cold to stand there in her knickers just to make sure that her neck was clean.

Ian was coming in from the byre when she went downstairs again to stir the porridge.

'Did you do your composition last night?' she asked him as he slumped tiredly at the table.

His face lit up and he sat up straight, his early morning labours already forgotten. 'Aye, and it's grand. I'll easy beat Robin. I've used near every big word I know.'

'Mr Morrison says whiles a wee word is better nor a big one.'

Ian looked up at her from the superiority of his eleven years. 'You don't know what you're talking about, Mairi McGloughlin. Big words, correctly used, show an educated mind.'

'But you and ratty Robin only look up big words in the Dominie's dictionary. I cannae see much education in that. I think one of thon parrots could do the same.'

Ian refused to answer which was usually a sign that he knew he was beaten but refused to accept it. 'Hurry up with the porridge, Mairi. You still have all the pieces to make.'

'Your wee sister has only the two hands, lad. Get aff your backside and pour the tea.'

The children had not heard their father come in but when they did, they sprang, Ian to do as he was told, Mairi to her brother's defence.

'Ian's jist in from the byre, Dad. We'll have calves and lambs soon. Lambs first, do you think? I hope I can raise one this year. Wouldn't that be nice?'

'No, it wouldn't, lass, because it would mean that I had lost a ewe, most like.'

'Well, if it was like Snowdrop refusing one of her twins again, I could raise that.'

'If she does and if we find it before it starves to death or the crows get it.' Colin turned to his son. 'There's a good job for you on Saturday, Ian. Take the shotgun and get some crows.'

'Teach me to shoot, Dad,' begged Mairi. 'I bet I'd be better than anyone.'

'Shooting's not for girls, lambkin.'

'There were women shooting at the Laird's Ne'erday party.'

'Gentry's different.'

'Women shot in the Wild West, Dad,' put in Ian.

For a moment Colin looked angry and then he started to laugh. 'I'm picturing my wee Mairi like one of they women on the Wild West Show. Who are you going to shoot, Mairi Kathryn McGloughlin, gin your daddy teaches you to shoot?'

Mairi smiled. She had won, as usual. 'Stinky Robin Morrison and even stinkier Billy Soutar.'

'I don't know what you have against Robin. He's really very nice.'

'He's a pain. He thinks he's special jist because his father is the Dominie.'

Ian jumped to the defence of his friend. 'That's not true, Mairi. Robin is great.'

'Robin's great. Robin's great,' Mairi sneered. 'Well, think what you like, Ian McGloughlin, but I don't like him.'

'If the two of you don't get your porridge eaten,' said their father mildly, 'it'll be Robin's father you have to worry about.'

Mairi looked at her father quickly and then at the wag-at-the-wall clock. 'What a fleg you gave me,' she laughed. 'We've hours yet.' She ladled out the porridge and the children sat down and began to eat. Their father took his bowl and ate from it as he walked to the door.

'Straight home the pair of you,' he said, 'and I'll be ready for my tea as soon as the sun goes down. Mind you feed the stirks, our Ian, just as soon as you change out of your school clothes.'

He was gone and Ian breathed a little easier. He

11

was rarely relaxed around his father, unaware that his nervousness communicated itself to the man and made the situation worse. Mairi felt no lightening of the atmosphere. She was a sunny child; she adored her brother and she worshipped her father. She missed her mother who had died three years earlier but time made the pain bearable and because she had been so young when her mother had died, she did not know that she missed certain attentions. If the deficits in her upbringing had been pointed out to her she would have denied their existence vociferously. She had everything she wanted and needed. There were twice-yearly visits from interfering, although well-meaning, relatives but there was, more importantly, Ian and the dogs and occasionally a lamb, and she had, as she knew fine well, big Colin McGloughlin to fight all her battles for her.

Mairi cleared the table, washed the dishes, made up pieces for herself, her brother, and an extra one for daft Billy Soutar who, as usual, would have none, and only then did she pick up her books and leave the house. She did not lock the door. No one apart from their father would enter the house until she and Ian came back from school.

*   *   *

'Robin Morrison, get your head out of that book and fetch some coal. Jack the Carter shovelled it into the shed for me. Your father isn't up to it.'

Lizzie Morrison looked at her son, saw his too-long, too-thin arms sticking out from the ends of his jacket.

'Neither are you, laddie,' she thought, but she

12

said nothing. If she did, he would go out and shovel coal until he was exhausted. 'Just fill the coal scuttle, Robin, and then clear this table so that I can set the tea.'

Robin looked up vaguely at his mother; it took him time to get from 1485 to 1900.

'Coal,' she said again firmly. 'Fill the scuttle and clear the table.'

Robin began to pile the books.

'Coal,' she said again. 'Now. If I don't get coal, you don't get your tea.'

The boy stopped. 'Sorry, Mother, I wasn't really paying attention. Well, I mean, I wasn't *not* paying attention but my mind . . .' He looked at the set of his mother's jaw. 'I'll get the coal.'

He looked regretfully at the book. A few more minutes; if she had only given him a few more minutes. He went outside and the beauty of the night stopped him. He reached up his hands towards the stars. He could touch them if he stretched.

'Maybe that one's dead, laddie.'

His father was standing near the gate that separated school and Schoolhouse.

'Dead? How can it be dead and it shining and twinkling so brightly?'

Robin knew the answer, but he loved allowing his father to show his erudition.

Euan Morrison pointed to a star above the Schoolhouse. 'Perhaps that star has burned itself out but, because it takes the light so long to reach the earth, the only way you can tell if it's dead is to stand right here and watch till the light goes out.'

The door opened and light spilled out from a fire that was still very much alive. So was the voice

13

that floated along on the light and, like the fire, it was warm and welcoming. 'If you two don't stop your star gazing, there'll be no tea for either one of you. Euan, it's near the boy's bedtime and you've been sitting in that cold classroom since four o'clock.'

'Don't fuss, Lizzie. The fire's embers are still sending out warmth. Robin has the coal situation in hand, haven't you, lad, and I'll help with the table. Is that mince and onions I smell?' Deftly he steered his wife away from the steps to give his son time to do his chore.

Robin, the heavy scuttle held before him in both hands, walked stiff-legged into the kitchen a few minutes later. He had overfilled the container so that its weight bent him almost double, and it was impossible for him to bend his knees.

'Laddie, you've too much in there.'

Robin lowered the scuttle to the hearth and stretched thankfully. 'Saves going out again, Dad.' He laughed suddenly. 'We should be like the Romans and put in central heating systems.'

Euan was about to discuss the feasibility of the plan together with the probable objections of the Educational Authorities when his wife interrupted.

'Robin Morrison, there is far too much nonsense in your head. Wash your hands and finish that table. That's not a fitting job for your father.'

Euan winked at his son and went on placing forks and spoons. 'Wee Mairi McGloughlin beat everyone in the big class at spelling today, Lizzie. She's bright.'

'She's a pert wee madam. Her father ruins her.'

'Och, he's doing a grand job raising those bairns since his wife passed away.'

'He's too hard on Ian.'

'No harder than I am on Robin. He just has a wee difficulty coping with a better mind than his own. I wish I'd made more of an effort to get to know the mother, a quiet, shy lassie, never very robust. Perhaps the children, Ian in brains at least, favour her. Colin McGloughlin is an intelligent man but he seems to think intelligence is a weakness in a labourer, as if brains and brawn don't go naturally together.'

'Ian doesn't want to be a farmer, Mother. He wants to travel, see the world, write about it. We're going to go together, to Greece, to Italy . . .'

Euan frowned. 'Fine dreams, Robin, but where would the likes of us find the money for such travel? You might have a chance if you get a place at the university'—he looked at his wife and smiled—'and not get yourself tied up with a wife and a family before you graduate, but Ian. He has no chance of breaking out of his life pattern. In a way he's lucky. His father has a lease on a good farm. The McGloughlins have been tenants on Windydykes farm for three generations. Ian will take over from his father, the fourth generation. Hard work, but he'll have a job for life and a house, a warmer more convenient house than this one.'

'Mairi hates me.'

'No, Robin. She's just protective of her brother. If you were not here, he would be the undisputed top of the class.'

'He's cleverer than I am.'

'You are both intelligent boys. Each of you could go to university but Ian won't need a university education, even if his father could afford it. Now, Mairi's brain is wasted on a girl.' Too late he saw

15

his wife's quick frown of displeasure. 'You have to agree, Lizzie. What use on a farm is a girl who can recite Shakespeare and Milton?'

Lizzie Morrison stood up and the anger emanating from her was almost palpable. It was a sore point with her that almost every female member of the farming community, including nine-year-old Mairi McGloughlin, was a better cook than she was. She had married and set her not inconsiderable intelligence to trying to master all the domestic chores she had never learned as a child, but she was still not satisfied with her achievements. 'So it doesn't take intelligence to run a house on a pittance, Euan Morrison. Well, we all know how intelligent you and Robin are. Fine, there's bread dough proving for tomorrow. It should yield—no, why should I tell you, anyone should be able to work that out. And Colin McGloughlin brought another rabbit. You can work out how to skin it, clean it, and cook it for tomorrow's dinner, and I'll be locking the bedroom door, so work out how the two of you can get yourselves and your amazing intellects into the same wee bed.'

She left the room, slamming the door behind her and Robin looked nervously at his father. Euan smiled.

'Quite a woman, your mother. I could have told her that the Bible says that a woman should do as her husband bids her but I can hear her explaining that since she never had the opportunity to finish at the university she is therefore too stupid to read the good book. If you have finished your meal, away to your bed. I'll crawl in beside you later, when I've figured out how to deal with a dead

16

rabbit.'

Robin said nothing. He would have liked more food but the tension in the air was too threatening. He whispered, 'Goodnight,' and ran up the stairs. When he was washed and in his night shirt he got into his narrow bed and squeezed himself as close to the wall as possible so as to leave room for his father.

But when he woke in the night he was alone in the bed and there was muffled laughter from the bedroom on the other side of the wall. Robin smiled and went back to sleep.

CHAPTER TWO

Jack Black reined in his horse and took in the beauty of the picture in front of him. Sixteen-year-old Mairi McGloughlin was standing on a barrel, her arms stretched above her head towards the kitten that stayed tantalizingly just out of her reach and, every now and again, batted at the outstretched fingers with a soft paw.

Jack stayed looking and appreciating the slim waist, the rounded hips, the swelling breasts against the stuff of her dress. He edged his horse close to the barrel and, reaching up, scooped the kitten from the roof and placed it in her arms. She had been so involved in her battle with her pet that she had not heard him approach and she looked first startled and then pleased.

'Thank you, Jack. Hello, Bluebell.' With her free hand Mairi patted the white nose of the old Bay.

'Let me help you down.'

17

'I can manage.'

He moved the horse away so that she had room to jump and she landed on the ground beside him in a flurry of brown skirts and white petticoats.

Colin McGloughlin watched the encounter from the kitchen window and he put down his pipe, stuck his hat on his head and went out. 'Hello, Jack. You'll have a message from your father?'

'No, Colin, for Mairi, and Ian, of course. There's going to be a dance in the Kirk Hall next Friday. I thought we could make up a table.'

'If you can get Ian to go then Mairi can go, but he's not a lad for the dancing. Prefers to sit under a tree with a book in his hand.'

'I'll make him come, Jack,' said Mairi. 'Is it just for the young farmers?'

'Aye. Will you help with the supper? We thought stovies. Edith is in charge but Robin Morrison will be back from the university and so maybe her head won't be working as well as it normally does.'

Mairi frowned. 'Is his lordship coming then? You'll get Ian. He'll not turn up to dance with your sister but he'll come to swop poetry with his friend.'

'Best not tell Edith that. She's happier thinking the two of them are after her.'

Colin looked at the strong, handsome, young man. 'That's no a respectful way to talk about your sister, Jack.'

'Oh, all the lassies like tae think they're driving us wild, Colin. Do you no mind yourself at our age?'

'I mind myself fine,' said Colin coldly. 'Mairi, it's time there was a meal on the table. Will you join us, Jack?'

'My mother's expecting me, and I still have to go

18

to Peesie Acres.' Jack smiled down at the girl, sure of his looks, his charm, his position as the son of the biggest farmer in the district. 'You'll help in the kitchen then, Mairi, and you'll save the last dance for me.'

'Oh, I don't know, Jack Black. I might be up to my elbows in soap suds like I was at the Ne'erday dance . . .'

'Ach, you were only a wee lassie at the New Year . . .'

'Or I might dance with my brother. Who knows?'

He laughed and turned his horse away. 'Edith'll come by to make lists; she's a grand one for list making. I'll see the two of you next Friday.'

Father and daughter watched him ride away.

'He really fancies himself,' said Mairi and Colin's heart lightened. She would not be the only girl in the district to find Jack Black attractive and, although he knew he would have to give her up some day, he was not yet ready. She was too young. He remembered the picture of blossoming womanhood he had seen on the barrel.

'Don't let me catch you climbing on barrels again. It's not ladylike and, forbye, it's dangerous.'

'I couldn't get the kitten down.'

'I'm over forty years on a farm, lass. I've never yet seen a cat that couldn't get out of the situation it was in, gin it wanted to.'

She tucked her hand into his arm. 'But I wanted him then, Dad,' she told him simply. 'Come on. I've got lettuce soup, a trout Ian caught this morning, new potatoes, and fresh peas just out of their pods. I hear Mrs Morrison is under the weather. She's not over the cold she caught in February. That Schoolhouse needs money spent on it. It's damp.

Robin's nose used to run as often as Billy Soutar's.'

'Robin Morrison's nose never ran in its life.'

'You have an awful respect for education, Dad, if you think that a man is above such things just because he can do the twelve times table faster than anybody else—and besides, he couldn't do it faster than me, if I'd put my mind to it.'

She served the soup and looked at the tureen measuringly. 'I've made an awful lot of this soup. It'll go off since there's cream in it. I know,' she said brightly as if she had just that moment thought of it, 'I'll take what Ian won't eat to Mrs Morrison. That's the first thing that goes when a woman's not feeling her best, her wish to cook. They're probably eating bread and cheese. Who is going to shake off a winter cold eating shop-bought bread?'

If her father thought it strange that she had not expressed concern for their neighbour until she had heard that Mrs Morrison's son was to be at home, he said nothing.

'We're not waiting on your brother then?'

'He's shearing. He has some bread and mutton and can get some water from the burn.'

'Charlie's with him?'

'No, he's taken the extra ewes to the market in Forfar.'

Colin handed her his empty plate for a refill. 'God help my sheep.'

She looked at him, delicate eyebrows raised. 'They're hardly your problem once they're sold, Dad.'

'The ones getting clippit by your forgetful brother, I meant.'

Father and daughter laughed for a moment at their memories of some of Ian's disasters.

'Dad. You're not fair to Ian. He'll do a grand job.'

'Aye, if he keeps his mind on the cutting and doesnae wander away thinking on how beautifully the wool grows from the skin or some daftlike nonsense. I dinnae want them with funny haircuts.'

Mairi laughed. 'He didn't write a poem about sheep shearing, did he?'

Colin watched her deftly bone the trout. 'Sometimes I think it's a wee bit of a shame that you're not a boy, Mairi. I could hae let the laddie go to the university. It would hae been a big sacrifice but we could hae managed and you could hae worked the farm.'

'I can still work the farm, Dad. Charlie promised to teach me to plough since you won't, and I bet I could clip sheep. I've watched you and Charlie often enough.'

'You're a wee bit lassie. You're no built for hauling sheep around or harnessing yourself tae a horse and following a plough. I catch you yoked tae a horse and Charlie'll be at the next hiring fair.'

'Isn't this a grand fish,' she said ignoring his anger. 'Ian should hae been born tae the Schoolhouse and Robin Morrison tae the farm. He's better at tattie howking than Ian, and really enjoys getting his hands mucky.'

'Aye, because he does it once a year tae earn a few bob for his schooling. Day and night, summer and winter, mud and snow, is a different thing. You'll make some farmer a good wife one day.'

'Jack Black for instance?'

'You could dae worse. His father owns his land and it's right beside us. You'd be near me and when I'm ... when Ian is farmer here, you and Jack

21

could keep an eye on him.'

'What eye I had left from watching Jack,' said Mairi drily.

Her father looked at her. Jack, like Ian, was the only son of a farmer and so he had been bred up from the time he could walk to work the land. She could not question his ability. What else did she mean? That rumour that had gone around before the New Year that his mother's kitchen maid had left in tears and disgrace . . . ! How would his sheltered Mairi hear such tales? Ian, even if he was aware of them, would say nothing and Edith would not spread distasteful rumours about her own brother.

'I was talking about the future, lassie. I'm in no hurry to give you up. Ian would need tae marry first.'

'Is that a fact?' asked Mairi laughing. 'Let me tell you, Father dear, I will marry when I choose and so far I haven't seen anyone worth the marrying. I'll away and make you some tea and then I'll take this soup to poor Mrs Morrison.'

'What your mother would say if she could hear the cheeky way you have of talking to your father. Whit a hoyden you would be with a university education.'

'Mrs Morrison has been to the university.'

'Aye, and whit a waste of good money that was. She didn't finish and she never worked a day in her life.'

Mairi sighed. 'That's the kind of marriage I want, Dad. When you see this man and you know he's the one for you and nothing else matters. Forbye, though, she's helped the Dominie times he's been ill and no single woman teacher available. That's been using her education.'

'Education. The woman can talk to you in Latin and Greek and there's the Dominie and Robin thin as two rakes because she can't cook. Do you know what she said to your mother once? "There are more important things in life, Mrs McGloughlin, than recipes for fish."'

'I'll take some of my scones as well,' said Mairi.

'Will I come to meet you, lass?'

'With it as light as day until two o'clock in the morning? I won't be long.'

He said nothing when he noticed that she had changed her dress, but instead took the mug she handed him and went to the fireplace and sat down. He did not pick up a book although there were books in plenty in the house. Reading was something Ian did, and, more often than Colin knew, Mairi. He sat and relaxed into his chair. He scarcely looked up when Ian entered.

'Mairi's left you some tea, lad. Soup's in a tin plate keeping warm in the scullery. Clipping done?'

'Aye. What was Jack Black wanting?'

'You didnae see him?'

'No, but that old horse of his left us a present.'

Colin stood up. 'I didnae notice. I'll away and put it on your sister's flooers. Jack was asking the two of you to a dance at the Kirk Hall.'

'I'm no going to any dance.'

'Aye, you are, for your sister wants tae go and forbye, Robin's going.'

'Robin?' Ian looked around the room as if his sister might be hiding under a cushion. 'Where's Mairi?'

'Away tae the Schoolhouse with some soup for Mistress Morrison.'

'Away tae plague Robin more like. I'll away ben and get my tea.'

*   *   *

Mairi was unsure of her motive in taking soup and scones to the school teacher's wife. Since she had left the small country school she had had little contact with the Morrisons. Ian and Robin had remained friends when they had gone on to secondary school in Arbroath and, even after Robin had won a scholarship to a boarding school, the boys had continued to see one another, at least when Robin was at home. But Mairi resented Robin who was having the chance that she knew her brother deserved. Sometimes she felt that, had the Dominie tried harder, her father might have relented and allowed Ian to continue his formal education. But Mr Morrison had accepted the status quo and Ian had left school on his fourteenth birthday. His sole contact with books and learning seemed to be Robin's periodic visits but Mairi suspected that the Dominie loaned her brother books and discussed them with him whenever there was an opportunity. For most of the year there was no time for long chats but in the winter when there was little light for working, as long as the inbye animals were fed and watered and their bedding changed regularly, Colin had no objection to his son's visits to the Schoolhouse. But Mairi had no reason to visit her former teacher and, until tonight, no intention of doing so.

She walked carefully up the farm road, taking time to admire the beauty of the briar roses and the honeysuckle twining in the hedges. She was conscious of the indescribable and ethereally beautiful Scottish summer evening light when a lilac blueness seems to hang over everything and, if she had not been carrying a pail of soup in her hands, she would have raised them in supplication to the self same sky to show her awareness of her oneness with the world around her.

'How can he say he wants to leave this? How could anyone ever want to live anywhere else?'

Mairi was well aware of the struggle for survival that her father and brother fought almost every day of their lives. She had seen them return from the fields too tired from hours of back-breaking labour even to eat. She knew too that Colin had never considered living in any other way. Ian loved the land; he saw beauty in an unfolding leaf, the innocence in the play of a young animal. Had he not written poem after poem to those same delights and yet, when he spoke at all about himself, it was always to say how much he wanted to get away, away from the things he loved.

How strange. Mairi loved the land and her love made her want to cleave even closer to it. How was it possible to love something and to want desperately to go away from it?

The Dominie was in his garden and, as he stood up from his hoeing, his face expressed his delight and surprise at seeing her.

'Soup, Mairi, how very thoughtful of you. Mrs Morrison enjoys lettuce soup but just hasn't had the energy for cooking this summer.'

'Goodness, Dominie, it cooks itself. I'll take it into the back kitchen.'

He put down his hoe, obviously glad of an opportunity to rest. 'No, no, lass. Let me take you

25

in the front door. Mrs Morrison will be overjoyed to have a visitor and, as for me, a wee crack with a former star pupil is always a delight. You're enjoying being the mistress of the farm? Your brother tells me you rule with a rod of iron.'

Mairi blushed to the roots of her hair and vowed silently to make Ian regret his flippancy. She made her menfolk do only what was good for them. 'Ian's a blether. Hello, Mrs Morrison. I hope you don't mind, but I made too much soup for the three of us.'

Lizzie Morrison rose with a smile of welcome and Mairi had to stifle a gasp at the difference a few months had made. The Dominie's wife had always been slim, but now she was almost emaciated. Her face was thin and pale and her great eyes looked too big for their sockets. Her hair, which had always curled around her head in soft feathery curls, was dry and lifeless. Her voice, too, was lifeless but she did try to make it bright and there was no doubt about the warmth of her welcome.

'Oh, Mairi, how very kind of you. We have missed seeing Ian this past summer. The Dominie misses Robin so much and Ian is almost as dear to him. But come, my dear, sit down and tell me what you are doing.'

Mr Morrison, with a murmured, 'I'll move the kettle onto the fire,' took the pail and the plate of scones and went off to the scullery and Mairi was forced to sit down. She felt stupid and awkward. What had she been doing? Nothing. Nothing but washing, ironing, cooking, cleaning. What was there of interest in that?

'I grew roses this summer,' she said, 'Bourbons

26

and gallicas . . .'

Mrs Morrison sniffed, her eyes closed. What a strange way for a grown woman to behave.

'Oh, I can almost smell them, Mairi,' she said, 'and what else did you grow?'

'Canterbury Bells and Hollyhocks.'

'I should like to see your garden, Mairi. I suppose you have no need to grow vegetables?'

'But I do, to get them young and sweet. Even potatoes.'

'Your father keeps us in potatoes and cabbages, carrots and turnips in season. He's a fine man and Ian is very like him.'

'Ian? But Ian is nothing like our father, Mrs Morrison. Why, Ian is a . . . a poet.'

'And your father isn't? I think all men who work with the land are poets, Mairi, especially the big, gentle ones like your father.' For a moment she looked embarrassed but was saved by her husband's entrance.

'Have you made us tea, Euan? And here's a poet can make a cup of tea, Mairi.'

'But not scones, my dear. The scones are Mairi's.'

Mairi looked up and her eye was caught by a sepia portrait of Robin, so starched, so formal. He did not look like the boy who had plagued her in the playground. Or had he ever plagued her? Was it not Ian who had said, 'Go away, Mairi. This is a boys' game.'

'How is Robin?' she asked politely. 'I hear he is enjoying the university.'

'He is a very new student, my dear,' said the Dominie, 'and like many new students has made his share of mistakes but he ended his first year

27

well and, having managed to just scrape through his examinations, is vowing to do better next year.'

'And what will he do with this fine education?' asked Mairi and surprised herself by the bitterness in her voice.

If the Morrisons noticed, and probably they were too innocent and gentle to believe they had heard it, they said nothing except, 'Well, here is his mother who would like to see her son a doctor or a lawyer, but would you believe, Mairi, our Robin wants to teach.'

'To teach?' Mairi almost screeched. 'Not here surely?'

'He has fallen in love with our magnificent capital city. Perhaps his future lies there, but he will start in Angus, probably in Arbroath since that is where the nearest secondary school is. Robin will teach Latin and Greek. There is little need for Latin and Greek here.'

'Latin and Greek. I would have liked fine to learn those languages, Dominie. One day, I'm thinking, farm girls will learn them.'

The Morrisons laughed politely and Mairi, a picture in her head of herself reciting Homer to a milk cow, laughed with them.

'Pigs might fly, as Bridie O'Sullivan is always saying,' she said, and stood up to go.

'Wait, child. I'll put the soup into a pot and give you back your pail.'

'No matter, Mrs Morrison, I'll drop in when I'm passing.'

'Or Robin could bring it over some evening when Ian is at home,' suggested Mrs Morrison.

'Aye, he could do that. Ian's in most nights and if he's out, he's lying by the burn with a book, probably one of yours, Dominie.'

They saw her to the gate and Mairi turned when she reached the entrance to Pansy Lane. They were standing watching her, the Dominie's arm around his wife.

'Aye,' thought Mairi again. 'That's the kind of marriage I want,' and she raised her arm in salute before picking up her skirts and running like a child down the path to the farm.

CHAPTER THREE

The band was ready: Edith on the piano, George Trace on the fiddle and Maggie McLeod on the accordion. Maggie looked a bit awkward, she so wee and the accordion so big, but nobody laughed because everyone in the Kirk Hall had seen her throw bags of tatties on to her father's cart. A feisty wee soul was Maggie and it was a brave man who would meddle with her.

Mairi McGloughlin found her toes tapping in anticipation and she had no idea how her vitality and eagerness transmitted themselves to the watching farm boys. She had made her dress and she was pleased with the soft frill around her throat, at the end of each narrow wrist-length sleeve, and around the whirling hem. Green was a colour that suited her burnished auburn curls and large green eyes, and well she knew it.

'You'll save a dance for me, Mairi,' and there was Robin.

If only he had asked properly and humbly like the rest of the boys—except Ian—in the hall.

'I don't know that I have a space left, Robin Morrison.'

He laughed. 'Duty done, Mairi,' he teased and sauntered off over to where Ian stood awkwardly, obviously wishing he were anywhere else.

Mairi tossed her curls with vexation. Robin was not quite so good-looking as Jack but he was a better, more courteous dancer, and what was more, he seemed unaware of his attractiveness. All the girls in the room wanted to dance with him.

'Only because he's a good dancer,' said Mairi angrily to herself, 'and a girl who hasn't had too much practice looks better when she's dancing with someone who knows what he's doing.'

'Don't tell me I heard you turn down Robin Morrison, Mairi?' Edith, released from the piano for a moment, was at her elbow. 'You must be daft. He is the best dancer in the hall, apart from our Jack and I can't imagine why anyone would want to dance with him.'

Mairi looked over to where Robin and Ian were standing, their faces animated with their interest in each other and in their discussion. She tried to see them objectively. Robin was too tall, too thin, and his too-long dark hair hung dejectedly around his ears. Ian was his father's son, with the strong legs and broad shoulders of a working farmer. His skin was weatherbeaten and his eyes shone out a brilliant blue against the tanned skin. They were fine-looking men, Robin perhaps a slightly poetic, Byronic figure, although she would die a thousand deaths before she would let him know she thought so. Ian looked . . . trustworthy, capable, kind: fine-looking young men, both of them. A girl could count herself lucky to attract either one of them.

30

'And doesn't Robin know it?'

She turned and looked across the hall to where Jack was sitting, one girl, who should have known better, on his lap and another sitting in a chair gazing at him as if every word that fell from his lips was gold.

'We don't see our brothers the way other girls see them, Edith. Your Jack is very handsome.'

'Oh, he's not on a par with your Ian, or Robin. Robin's beautiful, don't you think?'

'I think he looks as if he could use a few plates of stovies,' said Mairi disparagingly. Ian was a big man and every inch on him solid muscle. No one would ever say Mairi McGloughlin didn't know how to feed her men.

Edith looked hopefully at the clock on the wall and sighed. 'It's too early for supper. You'd better get a dance or two first.'

'Unfortunately girls have to be asked.'

'Goodness, Mairi, you're not one of those awful modern women who think they should do the asking?'

'I don't care who does the asking; it's having to smile sweetly and say yes to every corrie-footed farmer who asks that bothers me.'

Edith looked at her and laughed slyly. 'I didn't notice you smiling sweetly at Robin.'

'Och, he's not a man . . . well, I mean it's different with Robin and I didn't exactly say no, I just said maybe.'

He would not ask again, she knew that. She knew too that even if he did ask, something in her would make her say no.

Mairi McGloughlin was beginning to wish that she had stayed at home.

'I'd better get back to the piano. Pity you can't play, Mairi. Boys love it and besides, I'm dying to dance.'

For years, sitting in the schoolroom, Mairi had envied Edith with a longing that was almost palpable. Imagine being able to sit in front of a piano, look at a page of funny little black squiggles, and begin to make music, music that could make you dream, music that could make you cry, music that could make you dance. But, yes, if you were sitting up there at the piano, you could hardly be whirling and twirling around on the floor. She smiled and the smile caught at Jack Black's notoriously unselective heart. He dumped the girl from his knee, crossed the floor and presented himself to Mairi.

'I'm sure you said yes to Broon's Reel, Mairi. Let's get ourselves into a decent set.'

Mairi went, conscious that most girls were looking at her with envy and completely unconcerned about the young man whose name was already on her card. To give her her due, she had not looked at her card and had forgotten completely about him.

Sinclair, the Minister's son, saw Mairi's rejection as just one more cross on his troubled way and would have accepted it. Not so Violet, Mairi's one-time best friend.

'Sinclair, did you not say you had this dance with Mairi McGloughlin?'

Her young clear voice carried across the hall. Mairi stopped in mid-step and blushed to the roots of her hair but Jack laughed and, grabbing her arm, whirled her around in a proprietary way that annoyed Ian. Everything about Jack Black annoyed

32

Ian.

He walked across the hall to Sinclair. 'Did she promise this dance, Sinclair?'

Sinclair blushed like Mairi. 'It's not worth making anything of it, Ian. She forgot, that's all. Can't expect a beautiful girl like Mairi to—'

'My father would expect his daughter to dance with Billy Soutar if she's given her word. I'll stop the dance.'

Robin, who had followed his friend across the floor, put a restraining hand on Ian's arm. 'Don't make a scene, Ian. She's thoughtless; that's hardly a crime.'

'My father spoils her but he'd not allow her to be rude.'

'Would he prefer his son embarrass her in front of a roomful of people? Sweet little Violet has already done that.'

'Embarrass her? Our Mairi?'

'She's desperately sorry.'

'That's why she's dancing like one of them dervishes with her skirts flying higher than any decent girl's should?'

'Exactly and forbye, she's only a lassie. Leave her alone and she'll apologize to Sinclair. If you do the big brother routine she'll stick her heels in like Carrie Kennedy's old goat and not be moved for love nor money.'

Ian looked at his friend and then back at Sinclair. 'Is that enough, Sinclair? Will I leave her to say she's sorry?'

'I'm so surprised she agreed to dance with me anyway. I can understand her preferring Jack.'

'For God's sake, man, stand up for yourself.'

Sinclair winced at his language. 'I'll stand up for

what I feel is important, Ian, like taking the Lord's name in vain.'

Ian looked down and had the feeling that subtly Sinclair had changed and then, before he could analyze the change, the feeling was gone and once more timid, harmless Sinclair was there.

He turned away. 'Let me know if she doesn't apologize.'

Followed by Robin he walked back to their chairs against the wall. 'Look at her,' he fumed as he watched his sister sail, like a beautiful yacht, down the length of the hall, her energetic steps allowing her to keep pace easily with Jack's longer strides.

Robin was looking and what he saw was confusing him. 'She's grown up, Ian. When did your wee Mairi grow up?'

Ian looked at his friend in disgust. 'For Heaven's sake, Robin, it's just Mairi. Anyone would think you were St Paul on the road to Damascus with your tongue hanging out like an old dog needing a drink. Come on outside for a while.'

'I want to ask Mairi to dance.'

'You did.'

'I know but I didn't really mean it and now I do.'

'And you think she'll say yes? You'll never learn about women, Robin. Mairi can't abide you. And even if she did, she'd die rather than dance with you now.'

Robin looked at his friend in stunned silence. Mairi disliked him? He had known that she resented the times when he had beaten her beloved brother, but that she disliked him . . . No, surely not. Well, she would never know how much her dislike hurt him.

'You know Edith will be taking a break in a while and she's got awfully pretty, don't you think?'

'Well, she's certainly prettier than Maggie McLeod.'

'You are turning into an old grouch, Ian. Why on earth did you come to the dance if you're not going to enjoy yourself?'

'I came to see you,' said Ian angrily, and then added the second truth. 'My faither made me come to look after our Mairi. I doubt he could, the mood she's in.'

'Well, there's the end of the dance. I'm away to talk to Edith.'

Ian stood angrily and watched his friend cross the hall. He saw the way everyone, boys and girls alike, smiled and nodded as the Dominie's son passed them. He had always been popular, his position as the teacher's son and brightest pupil rarely held against him. In fact, everyone in the world, with the exception of Mairi McGloughlin, recognized the worth that was Robin.

*   *   *

'I'll thank you not to make a talking point of my sister.' The words were out before Ian thought. His fist connected with Jack's jaw before the other boy had even had a chance to protect himself. In amazement, horror, and some pride, Ian looked down at the sprawled figure of his sister's dancing partner. But not for long. With an oath that easily drowned out the squeals of excitement from various young ladies and words of encouragement from several farm boys, Jack had jumped again to his feet and thrown himself at Ian.

They went at one another with strength but without skill. The other boys formed a circle around them and the girls stood squacking outside that.

Robin jumped down from the platform where he had begun to ask Edith for a dance and pushed his way through the excited young people.

'Stop it,' he yelled but neither of the opponents heard him.

'Come on, Ian, it's the Kirk Hall.'

It's doubtful that they would have paid attention had he told them they were in the Kirk itself. Robin grabbed Jack and pulled him back just as Ian swung a blow at Jack's jaw. It connected, of course, with Robin and sent him to the floor in a crowd of multicoloured stars.

The shrieking stopped, the shouts of enthusiastic encouragement died away as the young people looked down at Robin.

'Now look at what you made me do.' Poor Robin heard Ian's voice yelling at Mairi and he smiled as he pulled himself to his feet. Edith was there to help him stand up.

'Oh, Robin, you poor lamb. I'll make you a nice cup of tea. And you'd best away home, our Jack, afore I tell Faither.'

'You too, Mairi,' Robin heard Ian say and he looked back to see Mairi, her face white with fear and embarrassment, burst into tears and run from the room followed by her brother. He would have gone after them but it was remarkably comfortable being propped up by Edith. Was she aware of how close her well-formed bosom was to his swollen jaw? He hoped not for he would have hated for her to move away.

She did though while she made him tea, having first given him a wet cloth to hold to his face.

'You're going to have a magnificent black eye,' she said. 'You were so brave, Robin, to get between Ian and Jack like that.'

'Stupid, more like,' groaned Robin who was beginning to wonder how he would explain his bruises to his parents.

He was not, of course, the only young man with explanations to manufacture. Colin McGloughlin was not at all pleased to have his daughter return home in tears and when he heard the story, told reluctantly by his son and somewhat hysterically by his daughter, was unsure as to which of his offspring he should berate first. As usual he chose Ian, only to have Mairi—as usual—jump to her brother's defence.

'Don't yell at Ian. It was my fault. I did promise Sinclair but I had forgotten until Violet reminded me.'

Colin looked at his dishevelled offspring. 'Oh, go to bed, the pair of you,' he said and went back to his account books.

*   *   *

It was several days before Robin showed his face outside the Schoolhouse. He had been concussed when his head hit the floor—not, he assured his father, when Ian's fist hit his jaw—and he suffered from headaches for a few days. When his rather splendid black and purple bruising had changed to an unfortunate bilious yellow he made his way to the farmhouse with the pot in which Mairi had carried the soup. Ian and Colin were not yet home from the fields and Mairi was in the kitchen preparing their evening meal. She flushed when she saw Robin standing there.

He had known that she would be alone and he had known that she would be embarrassed and possibly annoyed to see him and yet he had been unable to prevent himself from coming. Why did she dislike him? What had he ever done to deserve her animosity? The questions rankled.

'Ian's still in the fields,' she said angrily. 'A farmer uses all the hours God gives him in the summer. Even a brilliant Greek and Latin scholar should know that.'

'Take your pot, Mairi McGloughlin, before I put your head in it.' Robin was well and truly fed up. He had had a painful and ignominious few days; his mother had been distressed and all for the sake of this Madam. He thrust the pot at her. 'It's a pity your father never gave you a few of the skelps he was so keen to give Ian; it would have been the making of you.'

For the second time in less than a week Robin found himself on the receiving end of a McGloughlin fist but this time he saw it coming. He grabbed her hand and pulled her forward, fully intending to slap her with his other hand and found to his surprise that he had pulled her into his arms. Her beautiful green eyes sparkled up at him like those of a furious wildcat and he bent his head and kissed her full on her soft yielding lips. Stunned, she stayed quiet for a second and then Robin felt her respond.

He was eighteen years old and had never kissed anyone except his mother and he had not done that for several years. This was very different. It was

38

wonderful until Mairi came to her senses. She kicked him hard in the shins and when he released her with a yelp of pain she pushed him as hard as she could. He stumbled backwards and fell over the theekit pump that stood just outside the scullery door.

It was painful and it was humiliating. He looked up at her. One minute she had been kissing him so that every nerve-ending in his body tingled with the hints of unknown delights and the next she was kicking and slapping him.

'That's it,' he yelled. 'Edith's right, Mairi McGloughlin. You'll end up an old maid and serve you right.'

She stood above him, her face red with fury, her eyes full of unshed tears, and then as suddenly as she had become a fury she deflated.

'I hate you, Robin Morrison, and I'd choose to be an old maid rather than have anything to do with the likes of a Mammy's boy like you.'

Then she burst into tears and fled back into the farmhouse, slamming the door so hard behind her that the old stone house seemed to rock on its foundations.

CHAPTER FOUR

Robin Morrison, after promising faithfully to write to Edith Black, returned to the University of Edinburgh and decided to get a very good degree.

'And that'll show her,' he announced to his suitcase as he tightened the extra leather strap he had fastened around it, the catch not being reliable.

He had little desire to 'show' Edith anything. Edith was a clinger and there were times when a chap wanted to cling and times when he wanted to be clung to, but pleasant as a little dalliance was, there were other things in life.

After his first year, Robin did not usually return home for the university holidays since jobs were more readily available in the city, but he did return in the summer of 1910. Robin Morrison was going abroad, to Florence, to study for a year in the places he had read and dreamed about since he first learned to read.

Ian had the news first.

He was sitting at the fireside waiting for Mairi to bring the soup to the table. He and his father and their hired men had been ploughing all day and they were dirty and exhausted. Ian had been slumped in his chair almost too tired to eat and forgetting completely that it was four weeks since he had heard from Robin who was normally a faithful correspondent. Mairi had put the letter up on the fireplace propped against the Wallie dug, that bone china ornament no self-respecting Edwardian household would have been without and, softened by her brother's obvious exhaustion, she brought it to him.

'This came today, Ian; it's from Robin.'

Immediately Ian brightened. These letters were his passport to a world in which he should belong but from which he was barred by poverty. Robin told him everything: classes, professors, university social events, opinions, political, religious, whatever ... Robin shared with his friend. Ian never once complained of how much he missed their meetings and had taken to going to the

Schoolhouse once a week, where he discussed the world past, present and future with the Dominie, and which he used as a library.

Now he carefully opened the letter and read the closely written thin sheets again and again and just this once allowed his heart to fill with grief that he too should not see Rome and Florence or one day, maybe next summer, ancient Greece.

'Dad, Mairi,' he called. 'Come and hear this. Is it not wonderful? Robin's won a scholarship to the University of Florence. A whole year, Mairi! He's going to Italy for a whole year. He's studying his daft old Romans, of course, but he plans to go on walking tours, to Venice, Mairi, and to Rome and, would you believe, Dad, Greece. He hopes, if he can save enough on his food, to get to Greece before he comes home for his last year in Edinburgh. What I would do to go with him!'

He handed Mairi the letter to read and sat back down in his seat. 'He'll send me postcards and he'll sketch.'

Colin looked at his son and not for the first time wondered if he had done the wrong thing by forcing the boy on to the land. No, no, no. The land was constant. People needed food. Therefore, although he would have to work all the hours God gave him, Ian had a job, a life. How many young people in this glorious new century could say the same with any security? Weren't machines taking jobs every day, even on farms? Hadn't he seen a bit in the paper about a machine cried a tractor? Couldn't it plough an entire farm in a meenit with just the one driver?

'All well and good, lad,' said Colin as he moved to his place at the head of the scrubbed table, 'and

41

I'll like fine tae see his postcards, but whit kind of a job is he going tae have at the end of all this?'

'Teaching, Dad, but that's not important. He'll have seen things, maybe even put his hand on stones touched by Cicero and Plato and . . .'

'If you want ancient stones, laddie, there's plenty here on the farm. The Picts is as ancient as your Romans and Greeks and forbye they spoke decent Scots.'

Ian stood up angrily. 'We don't know what they spoke, because we're none of us clever enough to read their stones.'

'Soup,' Mairi almost yelled. Ian must be distressed. He rarely argued with his father and certainly not over education and learning. She pushed him gently towards his seat. 'I'm glad Robin's coming home afore he goes gallivanting. I doubt his mother'll live through many more winters in that draughty old house. The doctor's bike's fair worn a new path to the Schoolhouse.'

'Aye, I think from the tone of Robin's letters that his father isn't telling him the whole truth; he knows his mother's poorly but I doubt he knows how often she's really ill.'

'Why has he no been home lately, lad?'

'Work, Dad. He's worked as a postie and he's worked . . . he's worked in a bar. Not everyone who goes in a bar gets drunk, you know,' he added defensively, 'and he needs money since his father makes next to nothing as a Dominie.'

'Then why in the name of heaven is the laddie set to be a teacher? Forbye there's only about two bairns at the most that wants tae learn Latin and Greek.'

'Robin sees teaching as a calling, like to the

42

Church. Teachers want to make the world a better place.'

'So do farmers, but we want a decent wage for it.'

'You'll be glad to see Robin, Ian,' broke in Mairi. 'Goodness, have you spoken to him since that awful dance?'

'The dance wasn't awful, Mairi McGloughlin, you were,' said Ian with his rare smile.

'Stop it, you two. Sometimes I think you're getting younger instead of older. This is grand soup, lass. I'll have another bowl.'

Mairi picked up her father's plate and went through to the scullery. Rome, Florence, maybe even Athens. Robin would see all of them and she would stay at home content to see Dundee. No, she would not. She could live nowhere else but, oh, to see somewhere else, Edinburgh even, or London. It would be grand to look at famous buildings that sometimes seemed to exist only in books. Robin would see the wonders of the ancient world; he would speak in a language that she could not understand.

'What are you thinking about, Mairi? Here's Faither wondering if you've burned the soup.'

Ian was behind her, his bowl in his hand, Oliver Twist begging.

'Aren't you jealous, Ian? Robin away to Italy and you, that's just as clever, stuck behind a plough.'

'Jealous, no. Unhappy, yes. But I'll go abroad one day, Mairi, and I'll relish every minute the more for having been denied. And in the meantime Robin will share.'

'Oh, aye, Lord Bountiful. He'll send you a postcard and not feel guilty.'

'Good Heavens, lassie, why should Robin feel guilty? It's no his fault I couldnae stay on at the school, that I wasnae born rich. One day people will want to read the words I write and they'll pay to read them and I'll go to France and see castles and vineyards. Will I take you with me, my wee sister?'

Mairi did not doubt him. 'Will you come back? I'll go with you but I'd need to come back.'

'Of course I'll come back, especially if I'm not forced to stay, but first we'd better get the dinner on the table or neither one of us will be going anywhere.'

*   *   *

Robin came home but he was rarely at the farm. Ian was too busy and besides Robin wanted to spend time with his parents.

'Robin'll be away abroad afore I've had a chance to talk to him,' Ian complained to his sister, when he finally came in, exhausted. It was very late but still daylight and Mairi had been ironing while she waited for her menfolk to come home from harvesting.

'You'll be through by Sunday if this fine spell holds,' Mairi heard herself saying. 'Invite them back after Church for their dinner.'

Ian hugged her in one of his rare gestures of affection. 'You're sweet, Mairi McGloughlin, and I'll run away down to the Schoolhouse afore I eat and ask them.'

Then he spoiled it. 'You'll be nice, won't you, to Robin?'

Mairi stamped the hot iron down on his shirt as

if she wished her brother were still inside it. 'I hope I know how to behave in my father's house, polite and . . . and ladylike.'

'Och, Mairi, can you no just be yourself?' He stared at her aghast but she smiled.

'Away afore you hang yourself,' she said and, with a sigh of relief, Ian stuck his cap on his head and went back out.

It was nearly an hour later when he returned and his father had already eaten.

'I'm sorry I took so long,' Ian apologized. 'Robin and I got talking about the Romantics and the Realists. I fair enjoy a chat like that, Mairi, and Mrs Morrison offered to make me a piece . . .' He looked up at his frowning sister. 'But, of course, I couldn't stay and miss this.'

Mairi still held on to the plate of delicious-smelling rabbit pie. Harvest was a good time to make easy catches. She struggled with inclination and desire and then capitulated and sat down, after giving her starving brother his plate.

'Come on, tell me, what's Romantics and Realists?'

Ian's eyes twinkled at her over the top of a full fork and when he had finished chewing and savouring he told her.

'Realists is people like Hardy and Wells, and a French fellow, Emile Zola, and they write about life as it really is. You know, you see the dirt swept under the carpet, and then the Romantics are writers like Lord Tennyson and Rudyard Kipling, softer stuff, poems and such like, "Come into the garden, Maud."'

'Surely poets are Realists?'

'Yes and no. They paint the world as they see it

45

and that might not be the way you see it. And it's the subject as well. You wouldn't write a poem about anything nasty, like wringing a hen's neck, or a scuffle in Arbroath on a Saturday night.'

'Your friend Tennyson wrote about war. I cannae think of a less romantic subject.'

'That was then. We're civilized. War's a thing of the past.'

'If women were runnng the world it would be,' snapped Mairi and went off to put the oats on to soak for the morning.

*   *   *

Robin Morrison went to Italy and Mairi found herself, like Ian, looking for his letters. Not that she cared a fig for Robin but a first-hand account of foreign travel was interesting and educational. But there was more to life than watching for the postman's bike. The farming year turned unrelentingly on its axis from one harvest and immediate ploughing and planting to the next. By October the harvest was over and the fields were being readied for the next year's crops. Turnips were piled for winter feed and the constant repairing of binders and tack and the thousand other things that were indispensable occupied Colin and Ian indoors during the long winter nights.

They had a break at New Year and Colin kept an open door for any of the neighbours who wanted to come in for a dram and a bit of Mairi's Black Bun or the more delicate shortbread she baked. It was the only day of the year that the McGloughlins saw their father the worse for wear. He drank dram for dram with his neighbours and grew maudlin and sentimental until he fell asleep in his chair by the fire and was carried up to bed by his son, no longer Colin's laddie but a man, suddenly grown bigger and stronger than his father. In the morning Colin was up as usual and if his mouth was dry and his skull a throbbing mass he said nothing and no one, not even Mairi, dared ask him how he fared.

Soon after Ne'erday came the seedtime, the sowing of oats and spring barley. Then, without drawing a breath, it was time to prepare the ground for the root crops, especially the potatoes. The farmers painted a living picture on the soil with little awareness of the beauty they were creating but still with an appreciation of the world around them and even big men like Colin McGloughlin would stop and admire the delicacy of the primroses that peeped out from every turn. He would tell his horses to stop while he pulled a bunch, roots and all, for his daughter's garden.

Then the weather turned warm enough for Colin to roll up his sleeves and unbutton his shirt, not to the waist, merely a decorous button or two—had his daughter not been nearby he would have liked fine often to remove shirt and singlet both—and get on with thinning out the turnips. And always, always the farmer watched the progress of the grain. The seeds were sown and the fields were watched for the magical overnight when thousands of little green soldiers suddenly appeared above the ground. They did not spring into action like those of the Greek hero . . . but bided their time growing taller until the summer sun turned their heads gold. Then Colin and other farmers like him all over Angus and further afield would lean over a fence and look and swither about whether or not to cut now—could they not hear the grains rustling and whispering in their silken beds, and surely this fine spell could not last?—or should they pray for good weather and wait another five or maybe six days?

And then the word miraculously went round that the harvest was ready and McGloughlin was hiring. Men and women, but not his wee lassie, could work ten or even twelve hours a day, stopping at noon for a piece and a cup of tea. Colin did not give ale, not until the day's work was done, and then he and Ian would dish it out from a pail to men and women both, and Mairi would watch from her bedroom window and wish that she could run like the children among their elders and listen to the stories, often bawdy, always funny.

Robin had seen a different harvest in Italy, the grape, but the camaraderie had been the same, and oh, how Mairi Kathryn McGloughlin would have liked to kirtle her skirts above her knees and stamp those grapes, but wild horses could not have pulled that admission from her.

When the haystacks were standing in the fields it was time to dig the potatoes and to find time to laugh at the fat bellies of the golden turnips that vigorously pushed themselves from their earthy bed; they could wait there until the frost and no harm done. And the work filled days, and nights marched on and at the end of the harvest when September was telling the trees that it was time to wind down in preparation for winter, Robin Morrison returned home from Italy and he brought Mairi a small glass fish from a fabled city where there were no streets and the buildings floated in water like the lilies on the duckpond.

Mairi was amazed. No one outside her

48

immediate family had ever given her a gift before. In fact she could count on the fingers of one hand the presents she had had in her entire life: a cloth doll, a book, ribbons when the tinkers came with their wares, a peach from the Laird at the picnic, wonderful but not much, oh, and primroses still wet with dew.

She looked at the little fish with its golden tail defiantly flipping and its little pink body shimmering in the afternoon sunlight and she knew that it was the most beautiful thing that anyone would ever give her and, while her heart melted inside her, she frowned.

'Why, Robin?'

He did not misunderstand. 'Because it reminded me of you.'

She blushed. It was so achingly delicate and lovely. 'Of me?'

'Yes. Look at it. It's saying, "Here I am, ready to take on the world." I saw it and I thought of you.'

Her fingers clenched themselves around the tiny work of art and she seemed to feel the little heart beat and she could not hurl it at him because it would break.

'I hate you, Robin Morrison,' she said and once again slammed the door in his face.

CHAPTER FIVE

There was a harvest dance in the village hall. The hairst was over and the fruit of several months of back-breaking labour—with some help from the variable Scottish climate—was gathered in. It had

49

been a good harvest and grain and seed potatoes had been sent south on the train, that same train which Mairi watched from her bedroom window.

Colin added his figures and then added them again. Yes, it had been a good harvest.

'Here, Mairi,' he said as he turned from his chair at the table to where his children stood watching and waiting breathlessly for the smile or the frown that would tell all. 'Buy a new frock for the harvest dance. You could do with a new shirt, our Ian, but I'm sure you'll find a book.'

Buy? A dress from a shop? Wordlessly Mairi clutched the coins to her and thought delightedly of which shop should be honoured by her patronage. She would put on her Sunday coat and hat and—she would take the train to Dundee! One of the big shops would be sure to have the dress that would make Robin Morrison regret that he saw her as a feisty termagant.

'Dundee?' bawled Colin. 'On the train on your ane? You shall not and I can't go with you because of the cattle sales. Ian, you'll take your sister into Dundee on Saturday and make sure she sticks to the High Street ... maybe Reform Street, at a pinch.'

Ian groaned and Mairi grinned. She could handle Ian.

She turned from her brother with a swish of skirts. 'You can away and find yourself a bookshop. With a big publisher in Dundee, there's bound to be a bookshop for brainy folk, or were you planning on buying that new shirt you need?' she teased as she slipped into the kitchen. If she was going into a shop she would need to make sure she had on the cleanest underwear that the sales lady

50

had ever seen. She would wash her gloves too and maybe her Sunday frock. If the weather held she could get it out and dried and ironed tomorrow.

*　　　*　　　*

'Don't let her out of your sight, lad,' warned Colin on the Saturday morning. 'Didn't I see the smile of pure mischief she gave when she heard me say I was busy. If there's enough money left after the train fares, take her to Lamb's restaurant at the top of Reform Street for her dinner, or Draffen's if she gets stuck there in the dress department.'

'Don't you want to take her, Dad?'

Colin turned from the pegs at the door with his cap in his hand. His face and voice were serious. 'More than anything, laddie, but you've not experience enough for the sales and besides, I ken fine you're dying to buy yourself your own book.'

Ian flushed and Colin laughed but it was a gentle, understanding laugh. 'You've my frame, Ian, but your mother's brain and I'm pleased that you're clever. Write your poems if you like. I've nae objections whiles if the work's done properly.'

He had said more than he meant to say and he was embarrassed. Daft saft gowk that he was. He took refuge in simulated annoyance. 'Are you going then or do you plan tae walk sixteen miles?'

Mairi squeaked with nervousness. She had rushed downstairs in a flurry of skirts and a too-generous application of bottled toilet water. Now she looked at the clock and at her father. 'You have the worst sense of humour in the whole of Angus,' she told him.

'Jist as well I've the worst nose as well,' he said

51

drily. 'You've as much scent on as would dae five lassies.'

He wished he had said nothing—it would have blown out the train windows on the way to Dundee—for here was Mairi squeaking again and rushing back upstairs to scrub her neck and behind her ears.

'I'll need tae take the pair of you in to Arbroath,' he told Ian who had resettled himself with the paper. 'Serves me right for getting between a woman and the impression she wants to make.'

Ian looked up. 'A woman? It's only Mairi.'

'Exactly,' said Colin and went out to hitch up his horse.

When his sister, now smelling slightly of carbolic soap, joined him on the cart Ian took a good look at her. Goodness, she was even sitting differently, her back straight, her knees together, her cotton-gloved hands demurely in her lap. Ian watched the hands. They did not look as if they could deal the unwary a sharp blow but he knew to his cost that they could.

Her eyes were shining with excitement and it was obvious that she wanted to forget that she was this mysterious creature called *woman* and jump up and down with joy on the bench the way she would have done—yesterday. He was more full of trepidation himself but he was looking forward to being on the train and to taking Mairi for a meal at a real restaurant. He lifted his own chin a little.

Colin left them at the station. He did not promise to meet them on their return; a new dress and a book would hardly weigh his children down on the four-mile walk home. Mairi and Ian, in their turn, could barely wait for him to go. This was their adventure and they met it unflinchingly in their different ways.

Ian bought the tickets, trying to sound as if he bought tickets for train journeys every other day. Mairi sat on the very edge of the wooden seat and then almost jumped up and began to pace the platform and then, at last, at last, the train came steaming and snorting and roaring around the corner and by some miracle hissed itself to a halt right in front of the platform. For a moment Ian panicked. How did the doors open?—but the guard was there and when he and Mairi were seated on a hard bench across from two elderly ladies who smiled at Mairi's dancing eyes, the guard waved his little green flag and the train wound itself up and belched out of the station.

And there was the sea, and, oh look, our farm and our house and there's my window and today the train can see *me* and I can't see it because I am inside it and I am going to Dundee where I will buy a ready-made dress for a dance.

Carnoustie came rushing to meet them with its magnificent golf course and beautiful hotel.

'Look, Ian, look. I'm sure you have to be a millionaire to stay there.'

And there was Monifieth and Broughty Ferry with houses like palaces—and then Dundee. The noise, the smell, was overwhelming.

'What do I smell, Ian?'

'Fish and, I don't know, beer, I think.'

'Can I smell jute?'

Ian frowned and tried the air like a dog on the scent. 'I don't know what jute smells like. Now come on, Mairi, take my hand crossing the road. I've never seen so many carts and, look at the carriages! They cannae be going to the Kirk on a Saturday.'

'It's ladies going shopping—like me,' laughed Mairi and, ignoring his hand, she danced away from him. He cursed under his breath and followed her.

How did she know so unerringly where she was going? They were on the High Street where the smell of fish from open shop fronts was more pervasive.

'Now Draffen's is just down there, Ian. You go and find a bookshop and then come back for me and we'll go for our tea like jute barons.'

He did as he was bid. He wanted to go but it would have been useless to argue anyway and so Mairi Kathryn McGloughlin found herself in the middle of Dundee on a Saturday afternoon with nearly three pounds in her purse. She would not go into the shop, not just yet. She would walk and she would look and she would remember.

The first thing Mairi noticed was that most of the women who were shopping were extremely well dressed. She would see a carriage draw up at the front of a shop; the door would open and first a highly polished boot of the finest soft leather would emerge, to be followed by yards of the best material excellently tailored. On top of all would be a hat—and such a hat! Perhaps there was a large brim—Mairi favoured them—and piled around the crown and trailing over the brim would be yards of fine tulle or silk or feathers. Superb. One hat made her laugh. For all the world, the elderly lady who was wearing it looked as if she had balanced on her head one of Father's finest cabbages.

'And she had to pay a lot more than Dad gets for

his cabbages,' Mairi said to herself as she stored the memory to share later with her brother.

A sudden gust of wind reminded her that it was almost October, by blowing some leaves along the gutter, and Mairi, in her best coat, shivered. And that was when she noticed the children. Children of all ages and sizes, all of them dirty and all of them without shoes. They did not seem to care as they ran in and out among the shoppers, getting in the way, their shabby clothes doing little to protect them from the elements.

'Noo watch oot for some of that lot, hen,' advised a portly middle-aged woman who had come out of one of the fish shops. 'They're nae better than they should be and they'll hae your purse if you're no careful. Just come in from the country, have you? They'll have you marked.'

She bustled off and Mairi tightly clutched her purse with its precious coins and sighed at the knowledge that she did not look nearly so sophisticated as she had hoped. Then she brightened. She was going to buy a shop-made dress. No one would mistake her for a country girl then. She turned and hurried off to Draffen's.

And there at the door was one of the children, a girl with uncombed, tangled hair and the loveliest blue eyes peeping out from a grimy tear-streaked face.

'Got a ha'penny, Miss?' she whined, rubbing one bare foot against the other leg as if to warm it.

Mairi had the woman's words of warning in her head and so she did not reach for her purse immediately.

'And if I have and I give it to you, what will you do with it?'

'Gie it tae meh mam for some bread,' came the answer. The girl looked up at Mairi and opened those incredible blue eyes even wider.

Mairi loosened the string on her purse. 'And where's your mother?'

The girl lowered her head. Mairi saw the thin shoulders shake and she heard a sniff. 'In her bed, Miss, coughing and sneezing and that weak she cannae lift her heid.'

'Tuberculosis?'

'We cannae afford the doctor, Miss, but if you gie me a penny I can get her some food.'

Mairi knew that tuberculosis was one of the diseases that was prevalent in Dundee. The conditions in which many of the poorest people lived, herded into tenements that were damp and vermin-infested, encouraged such illnesses.

She looked at the girl who was once more staring at her with those eyes that said, never in my life have I told an untruth.

'If I give you some money will you buy your mother some nourishing broth?'

The tangled mop of hair nodded vigorously.

Mairi took out a shilling. She could still afford a store-bought dress. She looked down into the child's eager, hungry eyes. Perhaps she was lying but her body could not lie. It told a tale of hunger and perhaps abuse. She thrust the purse at the girl.

'Here, take it, get your mother a doctor and buy yourself some hot food.'

The girl grabbed the purse and stood for a moment poised like a little bird for flight. 'You mean it? You'll no yell that I robbed you?'

'No.'

The girl began to back slowly away from Mairi as

if she did not quite believe her and then when she was some few feet away she turned and disappeared into the Saturday shoppers and Mairi was left alone on the pavement. She shrugged her shoulders. Maybe the girl was lying but she, Mairi McGloughlin, had three frocks in her cupboard and good food on the table every day of her life.

'I can look at the dresses in Draffen's and make something over,' she told herself and feeling thoroughly depressed—is virtue really its own reward?—she went into the hallowed sanctuary that until today she had only read about.

The shop smelled of perfume, expensive perfume, quite a difference from the street outside, and Mairi's heart lifted. There were more important things in life than new dresses and many of them were free. She pretended that she was the daughter of one of the jute barons and that a little maid walked behind her ready to carry any parcels lest *Madame* exhaust herself. This was such a strange picture even to Madame that she laughed out loud and was frowned upon by several of the extremely superior-looking sales assistants.

Mairi walked up several flights of stairs and lost herself in china and hats and materials and lingerie. She stood close to an elderly lady who was buying a dinner service for her daughter. Several attendants scurried around with different patterns and at last *the* pattern was selected.

'Everything,' ordered the customer.

'For eight, Madam?' asked the senior sales assistant solicitously.

'Good gracious, no. For twelve,' said the dowager and Mairi noticed that apart from her signature in a little book she was required to give no further information.

'They must know her,' thought Mairi. 'I bet she owns the shop but if I did I'd be nicer to the hired help.'

She stayed in the china department long enough to choose her own pattern, lots and lots of delicate flowers on white china so fragile that Mairi feared her work-worn hands might break it.

She found a sales assistant in hats who knew perfectly well that her young customer could not afford her models but who was obviously tired of putting hats on imperfect heads. Mairi found herself glad that she had given away her money, for a totally impractical summer model—greatly reduced to three shillings and ninepence, *'and maybe they'd take the ninepence off too'*—was perfect on Miss McGloughlin's auburn curls.

'Those yellow roses do suit you,' said the assistant and Mairi, looking at the wide-brimmed hat with its huge cabbage roses, was forced to agree.

'Such a shame I didn't see it a few months ago,' said Miss McGloughlin shamelessly and the girls parted company, both delighted with the past half hour.

She did not venture into gowns but went instead to look at materials while she congratulated herself that really to make one's own clothes was so much more sensible and original. She finished with a visit to the overly modest lingerie department where she asked to see a satin chemise and smiled at the sales girl who could not make up her mind whether the girl on the other side of the counter could or could not afford any of her delicate frivolities.

'Too chilly in the country,' Mairi dismissed the

expensive nothings and went to meet her brother.

At first he did not notice her empty hands, being too busy with his own brand-new book on whose fly leaf he had already written *Ian Colin McGloughlin.*

'Look, Mairi, Palgrave's *Golden Treasury*, first published in 1871 and this edition with additional poems reprinted every year since 1907. Come on, we'll go to Lamb's because I didn't spend all the money Dad gave me and I'll let you read a few of the poems.'

They were in the restaurant and seated at a table before Ian noticed that there was no precious parcel.

'Och, Mairi, you couldn't make up your mind. Do you want to get a later train?'

'I gave the money away.'

At the sound of the words, Mairi's heart began to thud rapidly. She had given away all of Dad's hard-earned money, Ian's too, of course.

'Dad'll kill me,' she whispered.

Ian looked at her. She had done some pretty appalling things for which Colin had scolded her severely but nothing so stupid as this.

'No, he won't. Come on,' he said, standing up, 'we'll use the tea money for a frock.'

Mairi looked at him and smiled. He was the world's very nicest young man, easily. 'No, we won't,' she said. 'It was to a poor wee girl whose mother's got a terrible disease.'

'Och, Mairi, a terrible drink problem, more like,' said Ian when she had finished telling him the tale. 'You found yourself another Billy Soutar. You shouldnae be let out without a keeper.'

'Would you care to order?' asked a refined voice above them.

'Yes,' said Ian, 'please. Two haddock and chips with bread and butter and tea, and two cakes please, a yellow one and a pink one.'

At the thought of a pink cake Mairi sat back and looked ten years old again. Ian stared at her, wondering at the strange ways of women, and knew that if Colin was angry, his anger would be directed against his son.

But apart from vowing that if his children were ever let loose in a city again, he and his hired man would both be with them, Colin said nothing.

CHAPTER SIX

The weather broke on the day of the harvest dance and rain clouds scudded down from the North and vented their anger on Forfarshire.

Colin looked out of the window at an already darkened afternoon and watched the great beeches bending and bowing before the fury of the wind. 'You'd be better tae stay by the fire the night, lassie. It's no weather tae let a dog out in.'

'I am not a dog,' smiled his daughter as she pirouetted before him in the dress she had just turned up. 'And I am going to dance every dance tonight. I'll wear my coat, Dad, and my boots—till I get there.'

Colin smiled at the picture of his daughter dancing with her great, heavy, but very necessary, boots.

'I'll take you in the trap and come back for the pair of you. I'm no leaving one of my horses oot in weather like this.'

Mairi chose not to argue. She would not win and so the effort would have been wasted. She just prayed that no one else would be arriving at the same time to see her being brought to the party like a little girl.

Five of her friends and acquaintances turned up at the same moment, the Blacks driven by Jack himself, and Robin, who had been given a lift by a young married couple from a farm nearer to the village and the Schoolhouse. This was no night to stand around greeting one another and Mairi was delighted since she had no wish to even speak to Robin Morrison. She had, however, a lowering suspicion that he felt exactly the same way about her and she determined to show him that she cared nothing for him or his opinions.

She filled her card with initials, mostly J.B., and knew without a doubt that she was the most popular and therefore envied young girl at the dance. She danced too with Sinclair who was also enjoying his last few days at home before the university term began. When Robin and his partner were near her in the course of a dance she could hear her own laughter, louder and sillier than anyone else's, and she hated herself.

'You sound like auld Agnes Dalrymple when she gets a dram at Ne'erday,' remonstrated Ian. 'What's bothering you?'

'Nothing,' said Mairi and danced past him laughing louder than ever.

At the second interval several of the young men went outside 'to see if it's still raining'.

'They're away for a smoke,' complained Edith. 'I've tried it, have you, Mairi? I've stopped though because Robin says it's a terrible unfeminine smell.

I wouldn't like to be thought unfeminine. Would you?'

'I don't care what Mister Morrison thinks about me.'

'That's obvious, if you don't mind my saying so, or the other boys either. One or two of them were giving you . . . knowing looks.'

Mairi gasped. She would die of embarrassment; she prayed for the ground to open and swallow her up, or for the roof to be blown off, anything that might make this dreadful evening end.

'You have a foul mouth, Edith Black, and just mind that no one washes it out with carbolic soap.'

Trembling, Mairi turned away and hurried outside. Edith must not see how much she had hurt her. The men were huddled under a tree and so Mairi slipped out and ran around the corner to the back of the hall to the ruins of the old church. She leaned against a broken stone pillar and began to cry, until eventually the peace of the building stole over her and she relaxed, stopped sobbing, and wiped her nose.

'Oh, I hate you, Robin Morrison,' she breathed into the silence.

'I know.' The voice was sad. 'You've been telling me for years and I keep asking myself why?'

Robin emerged from behind another pile of stone. He looked wary. 'Don't yell at me, Mairi. I only followed you because one or two of the lads have had a dram or two—they brought flasks—and a man with a drink can be awful silly.'

'Not half so silly as some women without drink,' sniffed Mairi.

He came closer and she saw that he had her coat. 'You'll catch your death,' he said as he slipped it around her shoulders.

She could not thank him. Instead she asked him how his mother was keeping.

'I see an awful difference in her since I went away,' he said sadly. 'Her letters were always so brave, so full of me and what I was doing, and when I asked her how she was, she ignored that bit and I let myself think that was because it was so inconsequential, her health, I mean.'

What could she say? They stood silently together listening to rainwater running off the broken roof and dropping from sightless windows.

'Could I ask you to keep an eye on her for me, Mairi? Ian doesn't notice; he's not really too interested in people he doesn't love. He notices your dad and you—his letters are full of you—and he sees me but . . .'

'Everyone else he cares about is a dead poet,' Mairi finished for him and they both laughed.

'I don't think that's strictly true but it's near enough.' He straightened up off the pillar against which he had been leaning. 'We'd better go in or we'll be talked about.'

She walked ahead of him back around the hall and at the door she stopped. 'If I think there's a change I'll make sure Ian tells you.'

The door opened and there stood Jack. 'Well, where have you been, Mairi? The dance has started and since my partner was missing, I couldn't get into a set.'

'I don't think I have to tell you anything about my activities, Jack, but I'm sorry if I've missed the dance. I was talking to . . . an old friend.' She could almost feel Robin relax behind her as she took Jack's arm and went into the hall with him.

For the rest of the evening she was a model of propriety, dancing with all the young men to whom she had promised a dance, saying little and laughing less. Sometimes she saw Robin across the hall but he avoided her eyes and she turned away from him too. He was her old enemy; she had disliked him all her life and nothing had changed. But it had. He had cared enough for her—or for Ian—to watch over her and he had shared his worry about his mother's health. Little things? Major things? She did not know. She welcomed her father so heartily that he worried and could hardly wait to get her off to bed so that he could quiz his son.

'Mairi? She had a great time. Danced every dance. She was pleased tae see you because she was ready for her bed and maybe she was pleased to have half the men in the area miserable because she left early. Don't ask me about women. I just let her get on with it and stay out of her way.'

Colin stood up and Ian remembered how his father had towered above him when he was a child, terrifying him into stupidity.

'You didn't let anybody bother her?'

'Dad, she had every able-bodied man in the area wanting tae dance with her. She was even outside with Robin for a few minutes.'

Colin relaxed. Robin? She would be all right with Robin. 'I don't want her outside with Jack Black.'

'I think she'll make her own mind up about Jack, Dad. You're the one reminded me she's no a wee lassie. She's near twenty. She'll be worrying soon that she's an auld maid.'

'An auld maid, my Mairi, never! Mind you, I'm in no hurry tae let some man have her and you watch her with Jack Black.'

He stomped off up the stairs leaving Ian to lock the doors and mend the fires. Ian looked around the comfortable homely room when he had finished, picked up his precious book, and followed his father upstairs.

Suddenly his father had faith in him? Misguided or was it just that the older man had no real notion of what a single-minded young woman could do? In his own room he looked at his strong farmer's hands.

'I couldnae begin to keep an eye on our wee Mairi but I can make sure Jack Black knows I'll break every bone in his body if any harm comes near her.'

*   *   *

Jack Black, of course, had no intention of harming Miss McGloughlin in any way. He had become quite used to being the most sought-after young man in the area and he did not much like it when the Dominie's son came home for holidays. This had been a very pleasant year with him off stravaiging all over Europe. But he had come back and he and Mairi had been outside together during the dance. If a girl was not loose, and Mairi was certainly not that, she went outside only with someone very special, someone with whom she was walking out. Jack had got used to thinking of Mairi as Ian's wee sister who would be there whenever he sought her out and here she was outside with Robin Morrison. He thought long and hard about his plan of campaign.

He had been told often enough by the females of

65

his acquaintance that a well-set-up man on a horse was a splendid and even exciting sight.

On the day after the dance, after the church service and the ritual of Sunday dinner was over and all the elders were snoring gently by the fire, hands resting on well-fed stomachs, he saddled Bluebell, still handsome in spite of his advanced age, and rode slowly over to the McGloughlins' farm. He carried with him the first of the autumn's brambles, picked by Edith and ready for a pie.

In answer to his prayers, Mairi was outside surveying the damage done to her flowers by the storm.

'Can I help you tie them up, Mairi?' he asked in a sympathetic voice. 'I just rode over with these brambles I picked before church but I'll be happy to help you repair the damage.'

Mairi had looked up at the sound of his voice and now she smiled as she took Edith's hard-won brambles. 'How lovely, Jack, we'll have these with cream tonight. None of ours are ripe enough yet. Where did these come from? That sheltered spot by the burn, I suppose.'

Jack had absolutely no idea and so he mumbled and stayed on his horse.

'I'll take these inside,' Mairi said. 'Come in and have a cup of tea with us, Jack.'

Jack was aware of exactly where he stood with Mairi's father and he knew why. He hesitated. 'If you bring the twine . . .' he began.

'Not on a Sunday, Jack. It's only necessary work that gets done here on the Sabbath. Look, Dad,' she said as Colin appeared in the doorway, 'look at these lovely berries Jack picked. I've asked him in for a cup of tea with us.'

Colin looked from the berries to their donor. 'You have early brambles, Jack. Kind of you to share. I take it your mother has as many as she needs.'

'Oh, aye, and it's Edith makes the jellies in our house. A grand hand with jam and jelly is our Edith.'

Colin grunted. 'Well, tie up Bluebell, and come in for a cuppa. Ian's away tae the Schoolhouse if you wanted a crack with him.'

'Who would want to talk to Ian when Mairi was in the same room, Colin,' said Jack and Mairi blushed while Colin watched her with trepidation clutching his insides.

'Talking's fine,' he said and led the way into the farmhouse.

Jack sat down at the fireside across from Colin while Mairi made some tea and buttered scones. She had been happy all day notwithstanding the devastation wrought in her flower garden by the wind, and the men could hear her singing.

'Pretty sound,' said Jack gingerly.

Colin was none too fond of Jack. He had watched him grow, a wild, spoiled young lad, and he knew the truth in some of the rumours that sometimes swept the area, but he found himself smiling at the young man who relaxed perceptibly. 'Aye, she has a sweet voice. A woman singing at her work is a comfortable sound.'

'You wouldn't say that if you could hear our Edith,' said Jack. 'If she would just stick to the piano playing we'd be happier.'

They laughed together companionably and Mairi saw them and the dull day brightened further.

'It was good of the wind to stay away till the

hairst was over,' she said as she encouraged the men to eat. 'The shepherds say we're in for a bad winter.'

'Ach, if there's anyone with more gloom and doom in him than an Angus farmer,' laughed Jack, 'it's an Angus shepherd.'

'I wouldn't like to be marooned up past Hunter's Path with snow up to the window sills,' said Mairi as she poured Jack a second cup of tea, giving him, at the same time, her most devastating smile.

There was more than one handsome young shepherd up in the hills. Jack suddenly realized that he would have to be more careful with Miss McGloughlin.

'No reason for you ever tae be that far up the Glen, is there, Mairi?' he asked anxiously. She had danced with two of the boys from the Glen, now that he minded.

'A bad snow comes,' said Colin, 'she'll be snug and safe by my fireside.'

Jack heard the unspoken warning and applied himself to his scones. They were delicious, as was the home-made jam. The room was clean and tidy, not nearly so luxurious as his father's own much grander farmhouse, but it was rather pleasant to sit across the table from a very pretty girl even with her father glowering at him from beneath shaggy eyebrows.

He did not outstay his welcome. He complimented his host on the warmth of his fire and his hostess on the lightness of her scones and then he left. Mairi saw him to the door.

'I could come by and tie up those flowers for you tomorrow, Mairi,' he offered as they stood together beside the placid Bluebell.

68

'Ian or my dad'll do it, Jack. They have me fair spoiled between them.'

'Will you walk home from church with me next Sunday—if the weather's fine?'

He had not meant to say it. He had no real idea of why he had come; he knew only that it was suddenly very important that he did come and that Mairi begin to walk out with him.

Mairi looked up at him and wondered if he would bring her a coat on a cold night.

Jack turned from her and easily climbed into his saddle.

A good-looking man on a fine-looking horse is ... pleasant to look at, thought Miss McGloughlin, and agreed to walk with him— depending on the state of the weather.

'Walking home with Jack Black, lass? Ian'll walk too,' decided Colin. He did not want his daughter's name linked with that of the handsome young farmer.

Mairi looked at her father in exasperation. 'Ian will not either, Dad. This isn't a declaration. It's just a walk; two people walking home from church together.'

'Your brother likes a walk.'

'Then he can walk in the other direction. Dad, Jack and I will walk home from church. Half of Angus is on that road on a Sunday morning. What in the name of Heaven do you think we're going to do?'

Embarrassed, Colin blustered, 'What a way to talk to your father? What do you think we're going to do, indeed. Jack Black has not the best reputation, Mairi, and I don't want my daughter's name mixed with his.'

'That old story about his mother's kitchen lassie having a baby? Honestly, Dad. If you could see the way the girls hang on poor Jack. He just attracts gossip.'

'I don't want mud attaching itself tae my lassie. Jack's dad owns his farm. He's a good-looking laddie and knows it. He's spoiled, Mairi, used tae getting what he wants.'

'Me too, Dad,' laughed Mairi and almost danced past him into the kitchen where she began to wash dishes. Once again she was singing.

Colin sat down by the fire with his paper but no matter how he tried he could not follow the news. Instead he saw all the advantages to be gained from having Jack Black as a son-in-law. If anyone could tame him, Mairi could.

'But not yet,' said Colin fiercely to the column that reported the disgraceful price of potatoes by the ton. 'No, my wee lassie.'

*   *   *

His wee lassie went for her walk watched over by all her elders and betters and it was seen that Jack never so much as laid a hand on Colin's lassie but instead watched her solicitously as she walked demurely beside him—but not too close.

And the young couple walked home every Sunday after that when the weather was fine. And then one day Jack asked Colin if he might drop by the farm and sit with Mairi in the front room and Colin agreed. Next they went by train to Dundee where they watched a theatrical performance. Jack was bored to tears but Mairi was enchanted by the whole thing and he found himself thinking that he

70

could watch her face, as she watched the actors, for the rest of his life. He planned to kiss her when he walked her home from the station; he could feel excitement building up inside him and he was terrified that it would show, but Mairi noticed nothing and when she saw her father with his trap at the station she ran to him in excitement and not in disappointment.

'There's snow threatening, Jack, and she has on her light shoes,' explained Colin as he avoided the young man's eyes.

'Oh, Dad, it was wonderful,' sang Mairi, completely unaware of the undercurrent. 'I think I will leave home and become an actress. Don't you think that must be the most wonderful . . . well, you can hardly call it a job, can you?'

'You'll dae fine looking after the house and the family, Mairi,' said Colin gruffly but Jack calculated that if he took Mairi's side—and he was sure she had no real desire to leave home—he would rise in her estimation.

'I think she'd make a wonderful actress, Colin, in fact I bet you could do anything you wanted to do, Mairi.'

'Until tonight all I've ever wanted to do is be a farmer.'

Both men hooted with laughter, drawn together by their patient tolerance of the silly twittering of their women. 'A farmer? Surely you mean a farmer's wife?'

'No, I don't,' said Mairi angrily as they trotted along. 'I've far more interest in the farm than Ian and maybe even you, Jack, and I wouldn't be the first woman to run a farm.'

'Ach, women forced by circumstance, lassie, and

71

that end up mare man than woman. I'll no have my wee lassie knocked aboot by life, no while I can help it.'

Jack took his courage in both hands and pressed Mairi's hands into her lap. 'I'll make sure life delivers no blows either,' the pressure and his smile said and Mairi found herself getting warmer and wishing, for the first time, that Colin had not met them at the station.

'The fire'll need a shovel of coal,' said Colin as he jumped down from the trap at the door of the farmhouse. 'I'll away and tend tae it and then I'll put the horse away.'

Suddenly shy, they watched him walk into the house.

'It was a lovely . . .' they began together.

'I really enjoyed the play, Jack,' said Mairi. 'It was kind of you to buy the tickets.'

'You don't really want to be an actress, do you, Mairi?'

'It must be a lovely glamorous life. Staying in hotels, having all your meals cooked, and people bringing you flowers.'

'I'll bring you flowers,' he offered, and pressed his lips to hers.

Miss McGloughlin was surprised but not frightened; she had expected to be kissed at least twice before. Since she did not struggle and, in fact, returned some of the pressure, Jack became a little more demanding. He had kissed girls before. Mairi sensed that he was no amateur and the effect he was having on her was not unpleasant, so she cooperated.

'I'll away and untack the horse,' they heard Colin bellow from the house in warning. Mairi laughed.

There was no one in the house—Ian was at the Schoolhouse for his weekly meeting with the Dominie—but Jack drew away from her just as she was prepared to become even more enthusiastic. Regrettable but there would be another time.

For the first time she sensed her power. Oh, yes, there would be another time.

By the end of the year everyone knew that Mairi McGloughlin and Jack Black were walking out. He had even been seen buying a bouquet in the town's flower shop.

'Perfect for Mairi,' said the neighbours. 'Jack'll heir that farm and Mairi'll be near her faither. Who could ask for anything more?'

Mairi herself asked that question more than once. When Jack was with her she was excited and happy. His kisses set her body in a whirl of sensations and it was he and not she who put limits on their experimentation. But when she was alone in the house, doing her chores, preparing vegetables, washing clothes, completing one of the thousand tasks that had to be done every day, she would sometimes find herself full of a longing for something she could not understand.

'I want . . . more,' sighed Mairi, but more of what she did not know.

CHAPTER SEVEN

Snow fell. Mairi stood in the silence and let the weightless flakes melt on her hands. Such incredible beauty, but what chaos it caused. The school was closed. No children could walk through

73

that relentless accumulation. Colin and Ian worked for hours clearing paths to the animals and as soon as they had cleared a way another fall mocked their attempts to master the elements.

'Where's it coming from?' an exhausted Colin asked no one in particular, but his son said *Russia* and was told to keep his smart remarks to himself.

Unlike many of their neighbours, the little family were snug and warm in their kitchen. Ian had cut logs in every spare minute for months past and there was a huge pile keeping dry under an old canvas just at the back door. The cellar still had some good lumps of coal and plenty of dross that could go on the back of the fire to keep it in during the longest and coldest nights.

'They'll be struggling at the Schoolhouse,' said Ian. 'I cut logs for them and *I* know they had half a cart of coal the last time the boat came in but the place is that draughty.'

'How is Mrs Morrison?' Mairi asked, suddenly mindful of her promise to Robin.

'She never complains and she wouldn't let me tell Robin. Nothing is to disturb his chance of a good degree.'

'Gin his mother dies this winter, whit are his chances of finishing?' asked Colin and Mairi, stricken, looked from one to the other.

'She's not dying, is she?' she asked. 'I promised Robin I'd make sure you told him, Ian.'

'I wish you'd spoken to me, Mairi. I wrote to him just before Ne'erday with her usual story that she was fine.'

Guiltily, Mairi remembered how absorbed she had been and still was in her meetings with Jack. 'I've been . . . busy,' she said. She got up and went to the window and looked out at the snow-covered fields. So beautiful. So dangerous.

'I think I'll walk over to the Schoolhouse and see how she is. I promised Robin and I haven't kept my promise.'

'You're going nowhere in weather like this, Mairi,' said Colin from the fireside. 'Some drifts could swallow up a wee thing like you.'

'I'll go with her, Dad, and see to the cattle when we get back.'

Colin looked at them steadily for a moment and then turned back to the fire. 'See if they're needing ocht we can help them with, and dinnae let your wee sister fall in the burn.'

'He always has to have the last word,' said Mairi to her brother as, well wrapped up against the cold, they set off for the Schoolhouse.

Ian glanced at her but said nothing. If he said what he was thinking she would only yell at him, little shrew that she was. He pushed her gently as if to knock her off balance and she picked up some snow and threw it at him and together they began to run or wade as quickly as they could through the drifts towards the school road. Mairi's face was soon rosy with cold and effort and she felt so hot that she unwound the thick scarf she had wrapped around her neck.

Ian examined her critically when she was so involved with keeping her feet that she had no time to wonder what her brother was thinking.

'Why, our Mairi is pretty,' Ian thought to himself. 'Her eyes are sparkling like the frost on the burn and the sun is turning her hair to copper.' Then he spoiled it by deciding that his sister looked about ten years old.

'You're seeing an awful lot of Jack these days, Mairi, what with the dancing and the theatre.'

'So?'

'Nothing. Just that it's hard to think of you being married to someone and not being at home with Dad and me.'

'Married? Who said anything about being married?'

'It's what usually happens around here when people walk out together.'

'Does it happen because it's expected by the neighbours? I certainly won't do anything just because that's the way it's done. Jack and I are . . . friends.'

'Is that all? I mean, do you let him kiss you?' asked Ian bravely. 'I hear he's kissed every girl in Angus.'

'Is that so?'

Colin recognized danger but had no idea how to extricate himself from it. 'There's been talk,' he began and he would have done better to keep quiet.

'He's told me all about it, Mr Perfect. Just because a man is handsome and his father owns his own land . . . girls chase him, Ian, and it's not fair. That girl was no better than she should be and was walking out with two of their men. No doubt one of them is the father.'

Ian blushed. 'You shouldn't speak of such things.'

'Oh, what hypocrites men are. Jack told me before he asked me to walk out with him. He said it was only fair and it's only fair that he should be judged innocent until someone finds him guilty and, as far as I know, he's never even been

76

accused . . . out loud that is, by the girl herself, or her family.'

Since it was rumoured in the countryside that Jack's father had withdrawn a great deal of money—over a hundred pounds—on the day the servant girl left his wife's employ, Ian said nothing. Arguing against his sister's involvement with the young farmer seemed only to make her more anxious to defend him and, to be fair, Jack had been a model of decorum since he started courting Mairi McGloughlin. He was pleased that the difficulty of walking made it easy to remain quiet, involved in the business of putting one foot in front of the other and pulling it out again. Several times Mairi stumbled and would have fallen but for his strong arms and although she pushed him away and told him roundly what she thought of men who considered women weak, helpless creatures to be cosseted, she was smiling.

'Women,' he thought. 'Just when you think you've got their measure they change completely.'

They had reached the Schoolhouse where a slender column of grey smoke showed that someone was trying to keep a fire alight.

'They're a handless pair,' said Ian. 'They fall apart when Robin's not here. I think they're only beginning to realize just how much of the practical work he did around the house.'

'It's a son's place,' said Mairi. She would find no praise for Robin Morrison.

The Dominie greeted them at the door with his usual charm and with obvious delight at seeing them.

'Come in, come in,' he said. 'What a great pleasure. Mrs Morrison will be delighted. She's not too well, you know, but you two are the tonic she needs.'

They followed his gaunt figure into the front room where Mrs Morrison was sitting in a chair by the fire whose feeble flame tried to do battle with the cold and damp of the old house.

'It's not drawing very well, Dominie,' said Ian. 'When was the chimney swept last?'

'The School Board takes care of things like that, Ian. They're very good, you know.'

'Well, let me see if I can get a better blaze for you.'

'And you sit by me, Mairi, while Euan makes us a nice cup of tea. You bring the sun into a room with you, child. Is it just that burnished head or is it personality too?'

Embarrassed, Mairi took refuge in laughter. She well knew that she had never been a great favourite of Robin's mother. She must indeed be sick to find Mairi McGloughlin a welcome tonic.

'I'm glad we've had such a fall, Mairi. Euan needs a rest. The school takes all his energy and then he has to come home to a useless wife. We have enjoyed today, sitting together and talking. He's been reading to me.' Her eyes fell on the book turned upside down on a chair. Euclid.

'She actually likes Euclid,' thought Mairi and wondered a little about the life of these two people in this cold inhospitable house, so much grander than the farmhouse but so much colder. But there was a warmth, an atmosphere, and when Mairi saw the sick woman smile at her husband as he came in with a tray of ill-assorted cups and saucers, weak tea, and stale biscuits, she realized that the warmth was love.

'They don't notice the cold and the damp, not when they're together. They probably sit here, read Euclid to one another, and talk about Robin,' she thought.

'Have you heard from Robin recently?'

'Oh yes,' the Dominie answered. 'He writes every week. Can you believe, Mairi, that he is in his final year? In June he graduates with a Masters degree.'

'That's what I'm waiting for,' smiled Mrs Morrison. 'June, when all the roses are out, we will take the train to Edinburgh to see our boy become a Master of Arts, just like his dear father.'

'That will be a lovely day,' said Mairi but she saw the look that passed between husband and wife and knew that though they hoped for a fine June day, they were almost sure that only one of them would see it.

She was quiet as they walked home, retracing their own footsteps in the bright moonlight. When they reached the farm, Ian turned to go off to feed the cattle.

'You'll write to Robin tonight, Ian.'

'She looked better as we were leaving.'

'She knows she's dying and she wants her son. She'll not see the spring flowers, never mind the roses.'

'I'll write.'

She heard a sob as he turned and stumbled to the byre and, for the first time, Mairi wondered if her brother remembered their own mother.

'He must remember; he had been old enough. Poor Ian and now poor Robin.'

Ian wrote the letter and, next morning, he walked through the snow to Arbroath to post it.

*   *   *

Robin and another, even fiercer, snowstorm arrived together.

The McGloughlins were in their front room; the fire blazed brightly, sending odd shadows dancing and gyrating on the walls.

'Remember when we were wee,' Mairi spoke into the silence. 'You used to make up stories about the shadow men, scary ones.'

Her brother did not answer and she looked at him. He sat in his chair with his head cocked like a pointer dog.

'Can you hear something?'

'If Robin came in on the train he'll get lost on the way from Arbroath.'

'He'll hardly have got your letter yet.'

'He wouldn't wait for the weekend, Mairi. He would come as soon as he read the letter. I have an awful feeling.' He jumped up. 'I'm going to walk to Arbroath to meet the train.'

'You're out of your mind, lad. This is no a night for a dog tae be out.' Colin stood up as if he would physically prevent his son from going out into the snow.

'I'll take a lantern, Dad. Robin has no sense of direction, never has had. If he steps into a ditch he'll lose his way.'

'You're an idiot, laddie. You're going out to walk five miles to meet someone who is probably sitting on his backside by his fire in Edinburgh reading one of they great books.'

'If he's out there, he'll die.'

Colin reached for his coat. 'Hap up the fire, lass,

and keep it going all night if you have to. I'll need to go with him. He'll start thinking how beautiful the moonlight is on the snow and freeze tae death in a ditch while he's thinking on a poem.'

Mairi said nothing. She looked from one to the other as they wrapped themselves up. She believed that Ian's instincts were right. Robin Morrison was out there in the storm. Whether Colin believed or not, she could not tell, but something was telling the older man to go.

'We'll take the dog,' said Colin, 'and the crook tae fish your daft brother out of the drifts and then I'll belt him with it when we get hame. Cat got your tongue, lassie? It's got my brains, both of them.'

The door closed behind them and Mairi ran to the window and pushed aside the curtain. She could see two large huddled shapes and a small bobbing light and she watched them until they disappeared into the swirling snow.

'I'll make soup. I can't sit by the fire and imagine them out there. Oh, Robin Morrison, if anything happens to them because of you . . .'

She forced herself to concentrate on cutting woody carrots and turnips meant for the cattle into perfect shapes. She would not think, she would not.

And outside in the storm Ian and Colin struggled together unerringly towards Arbroath. The dog followed in their footsteps. He did not question, merely accepted, as always, the strange conduct of these Gods who ruled his life. If he was called upon to die for them he would do so without thinking. They were the reason for his existence and although he would have been more comfortable by the fire, he was happier here.

'I couldn't manage without you, Dad,' said Ian as

his father's strong arms pulled him for more than the first time from a drift. Colin had walked this way for over forty years in every weather. He knew where they were by the feel of the stone of a wall, by the texture of the gnarled trunk of a tree. He thought his son was a fool and he looked forward, with pleasure, to telling him so when they got home. Imagining the words he would use almost made him smile as he wiped the freezing snow from his eyes. But there was no time to smile, time only to struggle on, to keep the boy on the path, to pray that the snow would stop.

'Where is it coming from?' he asked as they helped one another up after losing their balance once more in a drift that looked a few inches deep and turned out to be at least three feet.

Exhausted they clung together, too tired even to push themselves apart.

'Canada?' croaked Ian and was delighted to hear his father's laugh.

What if Robin wasn't out here? What would his father say if Robin was snug and warm in his Edinburgh boarding house?

'He'll kill me,' he said as he had said a thousand times through his childhood and then he realized that his father would say nothing. He wished he could say, *I love you, Dad*, but he never had said it before and during a snow storm when they had to fight for their lives was hardly the time to start.

They reached what passed for a main road and the way was clearer because there was some shelter from an avenue of trees. Colin stood for a moment to get his bearings and then, unhesitatingly, pressed on and Ian and the dog went with him. Because the going was easier they both became aware of how

82

wet and cold they now were. More than once each had stepped up to his waist in a drift and the snow now made itself felt as it invaded every inch of the material that covered the lower half of their bodies.

'We'll have to go all the way into town,' thought Ian. 'Otherwise we'll never know if we've missed him.' For a moment he lifted his head to look before him into the swirling snow instead of at the road just ahead of his feet. 'I have no idea where I am. It must be worse for Robin. Is he out here somewhere?'

At that moment Colin plunged up to his neck in a drift and Ian turned swiftly to pull the older man up.

'I'm sorry, Dad, I'm sorry; this is madness.'

'Aye, but the right kind, laddie,' gasped Colin and shaking off his son's hand he went on. He was happy, unbelievably happy. He had worked with his son in all weathers and they had shared a kind of companionship but this, this struggle with the elements, was different. He had the greater guile; the lad had the greater strength. 'Comes tae us all, tae tak a back seat to our own lads.' He wished he could tell the boy, say, *We're a great pair*, but he didn't know how.

They found Robin less than a mile from the town. He had fallen into a ditch and lost, not only his balance, but also his sense of direction and had, in fact, just realized that he was struggling back into the town. The snow had taken pity on him and had, for a moment, abated to show the lights of Arbroath.

They helped him take off his rubber boots and empty out the snow and freezing water.

'Good job nane of yer professors can see you

now, Robin. You look like a drowned rat.'

'Thanks a lot.' Robin tried to smile between teeth that were chattering together with cold.

'We'll need tae mak you run, Robin laddie, or you'll tak your death,' said Colin. 'Ian'll tak the one arm and I'll tak the other. You wouldnae think on coming back tae the farm afore you go home? Mairi aye has water on and she'll be making soup tae keep her mind busy.'

Robin shook his head and tried to get going under his own steam. He would love to go to the cosy little farmhouse, where a pretty girl would be waiting with hot food and maybe a warm welcome. Knowing Mairi though, he assumed she would be furious with him because her father and brother were in danger, but at least she would feed him and dry him off. He well knew that had the McGloughlins been a few minutes later he would have died out here so close to the town and yet so far away from safety. What friends they were. He did not ask them what had brought them out. It would be days before his mind would work on that. He accepted their presence, their strength, and thanked God for them. One day, when his body and mind were once more functioning properly, he would thank them too.

They said no more as they struggled the rest of the way. The snowfall had stopped and it was fatigue that was their enemy now, but doggedly the farmers plodded on, holding the slighter man between them and, at last, when all three were deciding that they could take not one more step, they saw the Schoolhouse with one little lamp shining from an upstairs window.

Ian was the one with enough strength left to

84

raise the knocker and they waited for several minutes until at last the door was opened. Mr Morrison stood in the doorway, a candle in his hand. He saw his son and, with a cry of joy, clasped the soaked young man to his heart.

'She knew you'd come. "I'm waiting for my Robin," she said. Take off your coat and go straight upstairs. Come in, Mr McGloughlin, and you too, Ian.'

'I've left my lassie, Dominie,' began Colin.

'Mairi will understand. She's going, you see, and I don't know what to do.'

Colin had lived through this night years before.

'Go to your sister, Ian. I'll stay here and see to what needs to be done.'

He put his arm around the man he had always respected and of whom he had often been in awe. Tonight it was the man of learning who was so sadly in need of the man of the soil.

'We'll be fine the night, laddie,' he said to Ian who had reached the gate. 'Come back the morn and you'll know what to bring.'

Ian nodded. 'Mairi,' he said to himself. 'I'll bring Mairi.'

CHAPTER EIGHT

Farmers from all over the area came to dig out the road for Mrs Morrison's hearse. Robin, looking out of the Schoolhouse window at the dawn spreading over a frozen landscape, was startled to see small moving black dots and, as he watched, the dots became larger and he saw that they were men, men and boys and even women, each with a shovel.

Nature had not helped. It was as frozen as Robin's heart and the roads were impassable. At first he did not realize why so many people were struggling through the deep frozen drifts and then when he saw the shovels he knew. Somehow the word had spread through the farms that the Dominie's wife was dead and that the Schoolhouse was cut off from the roads.

'We'll dig her oot,' someone had said.

The local carpenter-cum-undertaker had dug his dignified way in and made the simple coffin in the front room. It was cold in there; even the usual feeble fire had been allowed to go out for the body was there and, had the weather been kind, would have been buried days ago. But the other downstairs rooms were warm and cosy. Had they ever been so cosy? Robin thought as he watched a silent Mairi McGloughlin cut large slices of bread to make sandwiches for the people who were digging the path from house to gate and the road from the Schoolhouse to the Kirk yard. The doctor had managed to get through almost twenty-four hours after his mother had died peacefully in her husband's arms and the Minister, too old and frail to be safe far from his own fireside, had arrived on the back of Charlie Thomson's biggest Clydesdale. The horse had managed only part of the way. Even with his great feet wrapped in sacks, not to pay silent homage to the dead but to prevent him slipping, the animal was unsafe on the road.

'Do ye ken, I walked clear across the dyke,' Robin heard one farm lad say to another. 'The drifts are that high the dyke's buried and I knew I'd lost my way when I ended up to my neck in snaw.

Luckily oor Bob was with me and pulled me oot, and him laughing like a loon. When this is feenished I'll see how he likes freezin snaw doon the back of his neck.'

'My mother is dead,' thought Robin, 'and they can dig through appalling conditions and still have fun.' He had been to school with the lads and knew that they could find joy in almost anything. But they had not found joy in school and none at all in his mother who had had few of the skills of which their mothers were justifiably proud. 'I'd dig for them,' he thought, 'but would they ask me or would I even find out that they needed help?'

He looked across at Mairi who smiled at him. 'They're good people,' she said. 'They mean no disrespect by laughing.'

'Mum would like to hear them laugh. She always regretted that she couldn't communicate well.'

Mairi turned away, embarrassed. Some of the children had thought that the Dominie's wife believed herself a cut above them because of her education. Many had revered her just because of it. Probably she would have preferred something in between.

'How is your father this morning?'

'She had prepared him,' said Robin bitterly. 'I should have been here.'

'She was so proud of you, Robin. She wanted nothing to get in the way of your education, your degree. She'll be there with you, when the roses bloom, always.'

She had no idea why she had said that but she knew it was true. When Robin Morrison stood up at the grand university of Edinburgh in his cap and gown, when the roses bloomed in voluptuous abandon all over the country, his mother would be there.

'Robin, Robin, laddie.' It was the Dominie. 'Have you seen them? Boys—and girls—I taught, now grown men and women, are here with us, caring, helping.'

Robin suddenly pulled himself out of his daze. 'And I'm in here, warm. I'll away out to help, and I'll send your dad in, Mairi. He's worked like three men, the past few days.'

Mairi smiled. 'That's the way he always works,' she said and went back to her sandwiches.

Edith came later, and Mrs Black, and they made soup and Edith's famous stovies, and the men and women of the farms sat quietly, ill at ease in the Schoolhouse, and ate their dinner, and then went back to work again. The older men struggled back to their own yards to feed animals but at last the work was done.

'It'll be the morn's morn, Dominie,' said Charlie Thomson. 'There's more snow coming and we'd best get her buried.'

'Thank you, Mr Thomson. I appreciate all your efforts. And you, Robin, my boy, I want you on the first train to Edinburgh after we've said goodbye to her.'

'I can't leave you, Dad, not yet, not alone.'

'I'm not alone, laddie, and the children will be back as soon as the roads are passable.' He put his hand gently on his son's shoulder. 'Who can give up with a school full of children to teach? You're going back to work for your degree; that's the only thing in the world she wanted.'

*   *   *

Robin did return to Edinburgh on the first train to get through and in June he graduated with First Class honours. Mairi and Ian read about it in the local paper under the heading: LOCAL BOY'S SUCCESS.

Mairi looked out on her patch of garden where the roses danced in all their splendour. 'What now?' she asked her brother.

'Oxford. Can you imagine, Mairi? Robin's going to Oxford, and then probably a fine job in a great school somewhere in the city. The Dominie's so proud. He wanted me to go with him, you know, to the graduation, and if I could have got to Edinburgh and back all in the one day . . .'

'With two rivers to cross? There's a dream to write a poem about, Ian. Eighty miles and two rivers and back in your own bed on the same day. Pigs might fly.'

They laughed at the old childhood joke.

'I'll go to Oxford,' said Ian. 'I'll stand there and I'll touch the stones and I'll breathe in the poetry. You can come too, Mairi. I bet Robin would like that.'

Mairi turned away. Robin had said nothing to her since he had stood watching her cut the sandwiches. She had known that he was too distressed, too incapable of thinking, and he had walked away from the Kirk yard without turning back.

'Jack's asked me to marry him,' she said. 'I doubt he'd be keen on his wife going off to some English city to see another man.' She turned on Ian angrily as he looked as if he was about to question her further. 'Away out from under my feet, you and your local boy's success story.'

When he was gone she picked up the paper and read the item through again. There was even a picture of Robin, even more formal and somehow remote than the one she had seen in the front room of the Schoolhouse. 'I'd like fine to go to Oxford, Robin, but would it be to see you or to see the city?'

She put the paper away and hurried on with her tasks, for Jack was coming and they were going to a tennis party, and she knew that he would find a way to get her on her own to ask her again, and she would go because being with Jack was exciting.

He arrived just as she was finishing washing up the dishes from their evening meal and was forced to sit in the front room with Colin while she hurried upstairs to put on her tennis dress of heavy white cotton. She had altered an old one the better to resemble the lovely dress worn by the celebrated Mrs Mavrogordato during her mixed doubles match on the hallowed greens of the All England Tennis Club.

'It's a wonder she could play, let alone win,' mused Mairi as she buttoned hundreds of little white buttons, down the front and on the cuffs of her dress. 'At least I look nice and it's not so hot in the evenings.' She blew her damp hair up from her forehead, wished desperately that she had some lip rouge and then descended the staircase. Well she knew the effect she was creating, but if she had expected to captivate her father as well as Jack, he gave her no satisfaction, telling her only that it would be impossible to get the dress clean if the courts were dusty.

'No one will be able to play for looking at you,

Mairi,' breathed Jack, getting as close to her as he dared. 'You're beautiful.'

'She's well enough,' said Colin, 'And she's to be back by eleven at the latest. It's early up these mornings.'

'I may not bring her back at all,' said Jack daringly.

Colin looked at him for a long cold moment that made Jack sweat in his long-sleeved white flannel shirt.

'Then it's me will be after you with a shotgun, not that I'll need it.'

'Och, Dad, Jack's only joking. We'll see you later,' said Mairi crossly and almost pulled Jack out of the door.

'I don't know that I am, joking I mean,' said Jack and he in turn pulled Mairi into his arms and kissed her firmly, his tongue trying gently to force open her lips.

She pulled away. 'Don't be silly, Jack, not here, at the very window.'

'I'll wait until after the tea,' promised Jack, 'and then I want an answer, Mairi McGloughlin.'

She looked at him provocatively and took to her heels like a hoyden as he came after her and it was two rather breathless tennis players who arrived at the little local club.

'You didn't get chased by Tyler's bull, did you?' asked Sinclair, who was chairman. 'You'd best sit down and draw your breath and hope you're not on first.'

They played singles and doubles and enjoyed themselves heartily until ten o'clock. The long evening still stretched clear before them but most of the young men were ruled by the soil and their animals and knew that they would have to be up early next morning.

'We'll have our tea now,' decided the chairman and Mairi was delegated to pouring, not tea, but the cool and refreshing barley water made by the minister's wife.

'I told Robin all about you and Jack,' smiled Edith. 'I thought it only right to wish him well at Oxford and to bring him up to date with local gossip.'

'That was kind.' Mairi forced a smile. 'But you can't have given him gossip about me, Edith, because there is no gossip to tell.'

Edith laughed archly. 'I know my brother. He always gets what he wants and . . . so do I.' She danced off to press sandwiches on the other players leaving Mairi to fume with rage.

'What have you been saying to Edith about me?' she asked Jack furiously when he came to sit beside her. She flushed as she thought of things that Jack might have said, private things between two people who cared for one another.

'Just that I'm mad about you,' said Jack. 'What else is there to tell?'

'Nothing, and that's how it will stay.' Mairi got up and went to do her share of the dish washing. She wanted to go home and she wanted to go alone.

Jack followed her. 'Mairi, wait. What's Edith been saying to upset you?'

What had Edith said? Nothing really. Except that she had been writing to Robin Morrison.

'I don't like being gossiped about.'

'Gossip? My dad says if I don't stop talking about you he'll move into the barn for some peace.

Is that gossip? Edith's jealous because I'm always talking about your hair or your scones, or your light hand with a sponge. Come on, let me walk you home.'

Mairi hesitated. She liked Jack. She liked walking home with him and stopping in the shade of some great tree where they could sit for a few minutes until Jack's lips and hands became too demanding. It was exciting, a little naughty, but nothing wrong. 'I don't know, Jack. I did want to, very much, but now I don't want you to ask me to marry you again. I'm not ready.'

'Oh, you're ready all right,' laughed Jack and it was not a pleasant sound. 'Let me show you just how ready you are.'

She pushed him away and he made to catch her, then he thought of her father's eyes when he had said, *I won't need a gun*, and he let her go.

'Don't think I'll hang around waiting. There's a wheen of girls ready and willing to take your place.'

'Then let them,' said Mairi coldly.

She hurried home up the lovely country lane, taking no pleasure in the briar roses intertwined among the hedges. She went over and over the evening in her mind.

'Robin Morrison,' she said out loud. 'The evening went wrong when Edith talked about horrible, nasty Robin Morrison.'

She managed to let herself into the farmhouse and up to her room without disturbing her father or her brother.

As usual she stood at the window to watch the train.

She played her game. 'I'll be on you one day. I'll go to Edinburgh, to London, maybe even to

93

Oxford. And what will I do in Oxford? I'll walk in the sunshine and I'll pretend I don't see the imploring eyes of Robin Morrison.'

But why that thought should make her cry, she did not know.

CHAPTER NINE

'It's not right,' said Ian quietly. The words fell into the hot air that had been flying around the room and hung there like grubby washing on a line. No one wanted to look at them.

'War's not right either,' said his father quietly, 'but there is a war and we're in it whether we like it or not.'

'Kier Hardie says we should be for peace not for war.'

'Aye, and he chose to make his peace speech from the plinth of Nelson's column. That's whit clever fellows like you and Robin would cry. Irony, is it no, him being such a great fighting sailor?'

'Why can't you ever say, "Clever fellows like me", Dad. Everyone else, according to you, is clever but you're the one that's saying it. There's nout wrong with your brain.'

'There something up with yours if you think that helping the oppressed is wrong.'

Ian stood up, his huge frame sending the room scurrying into its own shadows. 'That's not what I said and tell me, Mister Clever, who's the faither that skelped me for fighting with Robin at the primary school? Violence doesn't solve anything, Dad.'

'I walloped you because you were bigger and stronger than Robin and wrong into the bargain. Belgium's wee. Germany's big and needs skelping.'

'Your argument is too simple, Dad,' Ian started again but Mairi interrupted. She was tired of this war that had been raging since some prince or other had been assassinated in a place called Sarajevo and by a boy scarce nineteen years old.

'It really doesn't matter,' she said, 'since neither of you will be involved; you're needed here on the land.'

That was true but many, many young men from the area had already enlisted, anxious to be part of what they saw as an exciting moment in history. By September of 1914 the Scottish Division of Lord Kitchener's First 100,000 or K1 as they were called, had begun to assemble. They were sent away from the hills and glens of Scotland to Bordon, near Aldershot in the south of England. They had thought to win the war quickly, whip the Germans, and return home, with medals for bravery, to their sweethearts, their mothers, their wives. But too many were already dead in places called Ypres, the Marne . . . One farm boy had been on a ship, a submarine, that had dived under five rows of mines, torpedoed a Turkish battleship, *Messudiyeh*, and got back safely. The news that he had been killed not by the enemy but in a freak accident had reached his elderly parents on the same day that a letter had informed them that he had won this brand new medal, the Distinguished Service Medal, that the King himself had established.

'Where in the name o' God is the Dardanelles and whit guid is a medal gan tae dae his mam at her age?' had been the feeling of many of his friends who had stayed at home on the land.

The Earl of Dalhousie, whose family had owned or still owned the land that most of them farmed, was injured by a bursting shell while he saw action with the Scots Guards.

'Aye, his legs and arms baith hit by shrapnel,' was the chatter in the bothies. 'He's a guid man and oor ain. We wish him well.'

Every Friday the muster roll of those who had answered the call grew longer and longer in the pages of the *Herald*, among them the names of the one or two who thought that a certain young lady's eyes might light up with pleasure at the sight of a young man who sported a shiny new medal. For different reasons they went. But not Ian McGloughlin.

And night after night Ian lay awake and worried, for he knew that farming would not keep him safe much longer. He had never believed that the war would be over quickly. In fact he could not see how it would ever end. What would he say when the letter came, this year, next year, for the huge open maw of the great war machine would never close and would devour more and more of Scotland's finest and, one day, one day very soon, there would be Conscription?

'I cannot agree that the way to solve our problems is to take up arms against some other farmer's son.'

Wars should be fought around a table, with these great powerful men sitting there and arguing until they agreed on what was right for all. What good did blowing a country to bits, destroying cities, farms, rivers do? He could not believe that French farmers wanted to fight. He shuddered at the

96

thought of the devastation of the land. How long would it take the fields, that were today running with blood, to recover? Where would next year's wheat grow? What about the Germans? Did they like fighting? He had never met a German but in the paper they looked much like him. The Dominie had told him of great poets who spoke German, of great musicians who spoke German. There had to be farmers among these Germans too.

'Fightin's no the way to handle this,' he said again into the silence.

'You'd better no let anybody in the village hear you talk like that, Ian. They'll be crying you a coward.'

Ian looked at his father in surprise. He had never considered that. A coward? Was he a coward?

He felt an icy hand clutch his heart. 'You don't think I'm feart?'

Colin looked up at him. 'No, laddie,' he said and his voice was sincere, 'but then, I'm your daddy.'

Mairi threw her mending down on the rag rug before the fire. 'Enough,' she said. 'It's Christmas, the birthday of the Prince of Peace. There's hypocrisy for you. Now, we'll have no more talk of war, or cowards or anything else in this house. The war is nothing to do with us.'

Ian smiled sadly at her. 'Not talking about it won't make it go away, Mairi. Sinclair's joined up; his mother's devastated. And we'll have Robin in afore too long.'

Robin. Mairi deliberately kept her face turned to the fire. Robin. How little they had seen of him since his mother's death. He had gained a second degree at Oxford University and was now teaching in Rome. The Dominie had gone with him for a holiday and had returned, refreshed but alone, to the Schoolhouse. Robin's letters to Ian arrived religiously and so she supposed that his father must hear often too. And Edith, did she receive letters from Italy? Now that she was no longer walking out with Jack, Mairi's path seldom crossed Edith's. Both young women were polite to one another but at a distance.

'I don't care if he's writing to her,' Mairi thought while she made herself pretend an interest in the Minister's son. 'Sinclair Sutherland in the Army? But Sinclair wouldn't hurt a fly.'

'It'll be mair nor flies he'll be hurtin,' said Colin but Ian said nothing at all.

He did not know that, that very year, a No-Conscription fellowship had been formed and that there were already 16,000 members. He did not hear that the Anabaptists and the Quakers had adopted a completely Pacifist Doctrine. Had Robin been at home, no doubt he would have told him and they would have discussed and argued as they had done all their lives, but Robin was not at home.

*   *   *

When he did come home, the young men did not debate pacifism.

The first they knew that Robin was back was when Colin went to answer a knocking at the door and found the young schoolmaster on his step. He had not seen Robin for some time and was surprised at how the boy had grown, filled out, matured. He was as handsome as ever, his dark hair falling untidily about his lean scholarly face.

98

'Can't I come in, Mr McGloughlin?' said Robin at last into the silence.

Colin grabbed him. 'Laddie, laddie, I near didn't recognize you. Come away in. Goodness, you're near as big as my Ian.'

Robin laughed. 'It's the sun. It pulled me up.'

'Aye,' said Colin seriously. 'I'll bet it pulls the crops and all. Will you have had time to look at the fields?'

'Rome's not the best place to study agriculture, Mr McGloughlin, although I've seen oranges and lemons growing on trees, would you believe.'

Robin had taken off his coat and was seated at the fire when Mairi came in from the kitchen. She had been baking and her hair was escaping from its pins, her face was red from the heat of the ovens, and her hands were covered in flour. But this handsome man of the world was only Robin, the bane of her childhood. Impulsively she hurried forward and then when she went to touch him, she saw her flour-covered hands and drew back.

'Robin,' she said and was aware of her flying hair and her apron over her oldest, dullest dress.

'Mairi, how good to see you. I hope you don't mind my dropping in.'

'No, no. You'll stay to supper? You just missed Ian, but he'll be back soon.' She was sounding like all the dizzy girls she disliked; all of a flutter because a handsome man had come in—and Robin was handsome. He looked nothing at all like the boy she had quarrelled with all her life, but then he smiled at her, his shy sweet smile, and he was Robin, and she wondered why she had ever believed that she disliked him.

'Gosh, it's wonderful to see you, Mairi,' he said.

99

'You're like a breath of fresh air.'

A breath of fresh air? Not very romantic but why on earth was she coupling Robin Morrison and romance? One had nothing to do with the other.

'You're home, Robin? We didn't expect you until the summer. Do they take days off at Christmas in Italy?'

'I've resigned. I came home to tell my father and then, of course, my oldest friend. I'm enlisting at the start of the year.'

'Well done, lad,' said Colin and he shook Robin's hand.

Mairi stared at them aghast. They were grinning, well pleased with one another. 'I'll go and finish my pie,' she said and doubted that they had even noticed that she had left the room.

In the kitchen she put another plate to warm, and then finished her pastry. Her hands continued to perform their tasks automatically although her mind was busy with Robin and with what she had just learned as she had stood in that comfortable, friendly little room. No, not that Robin was going off to war. That was vitally important and would certainly affect her later. No, no. This was knowledge that was much more important in the great scheme of things, if indeed, there was a Divine plan, and how could there be if selfish men were allowed to maim and mutilate all in the name of achieving a lasting peace?

'I love him,' said Mairi McGloughlin to the pie crust that hid the mortal remains of an old hen. 'I have loved him all my life, and I have fought with him and driven him away and now he is going to war and it's all such a stupid waste.'

She did not know that she was crying until she

100

heard Ian's gentle voice from the door. 'Mairi, love, that's not onions. What is it?'

She gulped and wiped her nose with her oven cloth. 'Nothing,' she said, opening the clothes boiler and throwing in the cloth. 'Nothing except that stupid friend of yours coming just at dinner time.'

His eyes lit up. 'Robin, you can't mean Robin.' He was already pulling off his wet clothes. 'Don't worry, Mairi, he can have half mine,' he said and he was gone into the front room.

'Stupid man,' seethed Mairi. 'Even the best of them, thick as a barn door. As if I couldn't add a tattie or two, and look at me in my old frock and Robin's been in Rome, Rome, the Eternal City, whatever that means, but Italian women are beautiful.'

Robin explained why Rome had been called the Eternal City as he devoured a plate of her chicken pie. 'Boy, that was good,' he said as he handed her his empty plate for a small second helping, the portion he did have to share with Ian. 'I really liked Italian food but home food is better.'

'Your father?' asked Mairi, suddenly feeling guilty. 'You should have brought him, Robin.'

'He's never been fussy about food. My mum wasn't the best cook in the world and his mind is too full at the moment to be good company, but I'd appreciate it if you'd go to see him now and again while I'm away. You're too necessary on the land, I suppose, Ian. Bad luck.'

'Ian, don't,' said Mairi but Ian was too honest ever to dissemble.

'I don't believe this is the right way to go about it, Robin. I wouldn't go to war even if I could.'

101

Both young men had gone white and they avoided looking at one another.

'He'll see sense in a month or two,' said Colin jovially, 'if it's not all over by then.'

'I won't see sense then, Dad, because I see it perfectly clearly now. You're a scholar, Robin. You should be in your classroom teaching the bairns about the stupidity of war.'

'There won't be bairns anywhere in Europe for me to teach if I don't go now. It won't be over in a few months, Mr McGloughlin. It'll take years, so the sooner I go and do my bit the better for everyone.' He stood up. 'Thank you for the pie, Mairi. It was delicious. Mr McGloughlin.'

He said nothing to Ian; he did not even look at him. He walked to the door, took his coat and hat from the peg and walked out into the night. When the door closed behind him the family sat still in their chairs at the table. At last Ian spoke. 'He thinks I'm a shirker. He knows me better than anyone else in the entire world and he thinks I'm a shirker.' He pushed back his chair so that its legs protested, shrieking along the floor, and then stumbled from the room.

'Robin couldn't think Ian's scared, Dad. He couldn't.'

' "There won't be bairns anywhere in Europe to teach." Did you hear him, lassie? Here was me thinking jist of us, but there's bairns all over Europe affected by this. If I wasn't an auld man, I'd away and fight with Robin. Ian's no feart. It's all that poetry the Dominie stuffed in his heid when he should have been working on the farm with me. What bluidy good did education do my boy?'

Mairi found herself alone with the remains of

the meal. She sat for a while looking at the gravy congealing on the plates and then she stood up stiffly, like an aged crone, and began to clear up.

'Dear God, where is it written that women are doomed to do nothing but clean up the messes men leave behind them? It's women who will clean up the mess from this war.'

She ran to the door, picked up her heavy old tweed coat and let herself out into the night after Robin. All evening she had been doing things automatically. Now, in the dark and the rain that lashed at her remorselessly, she found her way automatically to the Schoolhouse.

Robin was sitting hunched over an excuse for a fire when he heard her knocking and he opened the door just as she realized what she was doing and was turning to run back to the farm.

'Mairi, what on earth are you doing? You look like a drowned rat. Come on in,' he finished, dragging her inside and closing the door behind her. 'Damn it, you shouldn't be here. My father has gone to bed. What will people think?'

'I don't care what people think. I care what you think about Ian.'

He took her wet coat and hung it up on a peg by the door. 'Come and sit by the fire. Does your father know you're here . . . no, he can't know. This was silly, Mairi. What if anyone saw you? There are people in the village with nothing better to do than peep out from behind their curtains.'

She ignored that. It was unimportant. 'Ian's not a coward,' she burst out.

He laughed. 'God, will you ever grow up or are you going to spend your entire life fighting your brother's battles, real and imaginary.'

She slapped him hard and they were children again. He grabbed her arms and shook her and looked down into her angry face. 'I had almost forgotten how pretty you are,' he said and kissed her.

For a lovely moment Mairi felt herself relax and the pressure on her lips became harder and then she remembered what he had just said and she pulled herself free and swung her arm back. He caught it easily before she could hit him.

'Ian and I were always sure we would never make a lady out of you,' he said and then was sorry when he saw the tears spring into her lovely eyes.

She turned and stumbled to the door, grabbed her wet coat and ran out. He followed her but slipped on wet moss that had been allowed to grow on the top step and hurtled ignominiously to the ground. Mairi heard him cry out and stopped for a moment in her pell-mell flight but when she turned round he was pulling himself to his feet and so she turned again and ran into the darkness.

Robin stood tentatively for a moment looking after her. He had to have broken something with a fall like that but although his right ankle hurt badly when he put his weight on his foot, he was able to walk. He stopped at the top of the short flight of stairs to ease the pain and suddenly he remembered standing there with his father half a lifetime ago, watching the stars.

How simple life had been then: lessons, exploring the natural world with Ian, the unwanted Mairi constantly tagging along behind, reading poetry, trying to write some and discovering with excitement and pleasure that this was where Ian definitely had the greater gift. Mother had been here then with her inability to bake a cake and her ability to help with Latin homework when Dad wasn't looking. Now she was gone, Dad was becoming more and more of a recluse. Mairi was a woman and one who disturbed him—he remembered the warm softness of her lips—and Ian. What was Ian?

'He's my friend,' decided Robin as he hobbled into the house, 'and that is all that matters.'

CHAPTER TEN

Early in January Robin went off to Dundee to join the army. He was, his father told Colin and Ian with a mixture of pride and sadness, *officer material.*

'But that's good, Dominie.' Colin, with his own son safe beside him, tried to cheer him up. 'They'll get the best of everything, the officers.'

'Certainly,' agreed the Dominie. 'Including the best chance of being shot.'

What could one say to a response like that? Colin, out of his depth, muttered something innocuous, and hurried off to look after his cattle.

'He'll be well trained, Dominie,' said Ian.

'Oh, aye, laddie, but read your history books; you always liked history, Ian. You'll find it's the boy officers who are first in the firing line. I shall trust in God, lad.' He looked at Ian shrewdly. 'He told me of your decision. He respects it, you know. Doesn't understand it but he respects it. He'll need letters from friends more than ever. Don't let his initial reaction spoil a lifetime of friendship.'

Ian smiled. His heart felt lighter. It would have been unbearable to have Robin hate him. 'Thanks, Dominie. I've promised my dad that I'll keep my mouth shut for now, but, gin anyone asks me, I'll have to say what I think.'

'Don't court disaster, lad. I'm glad you've never been one for the pub on a Saturday night; drink's a sure fly way of loosening the tongue. Keep your own counsel and pray for a just ending to this war, for all our sakes.'

He turned and Ian watched him walk off to a house that would be cold and damp and empty. He could not remember that his home had been damp and cold and cheerless after the death of his mother but then his father was practical and there had been family and neighbours. Had the Dominie no one now that his wife was dead and his son had gone to war? The Minister, surely? They would be the same class. But Robin, his friend, the one person in the world who believed that Ian McGloughlin could become a writer, had gone off to war and wanted letters from his friends.

'He doesn't hate me; he respects my decision. I'll write and tell him what that means to me.'

Then there was the Dominie. Robin would be concerned for his father's well-being.

'I'll maybe ask Mairi to make him scones now and again and maybe some soup.'

Mairi had no objections to helping the schoolmaster. 'But he doesn't need charity, Ian. He won't want me going in there with food and surely he can afford to get someone in from one of the cottages.'

'He'd maybe never think on it.'

'Well, if I talk to anyone who might do for him
106

I'll let you know,' said Mairi and put the Dominie out of her head. Robin refused to leave her thoughts though. She was glad that his fall had not injured him but she regretted slapping him. Too often her mind seemed to dwell on that kiss. It had not been the same as a kiss from Jack which had excited and terrified at one and the same time. This had been gentle.

'Oh, I will waste no more of my time on Robin Morrison. Goodness, I doubt we'll see him here for a year or two and then it will be off again to Rome or Athens. He'll have no time for a tiny village school in Scotland. And besides, I have more than enough to worry about here.'

As the spring slowly pushed the winter away, the routine of the farmhouse followed what it had been for years and years, as long as anyone could remember. Up at first light, a full day of endless back-breaking chores, home with the setting sun for a meal and a wash, and then, if there was any energy left, reading and his almost secret writing for Ian, clerical chores for Colin, and the occasional visit to friends. For Mairi there was constant work to keep the family fed and clean. There was her garden to tend, and her chickens, and with the spring, a lamb, sometimes two, to bottle feed. She loved this time-consuming chore and enjoyed leaning back in an old chair while the small white bundle at her feet sucked vigorously from an old baby bottle.

'If you'd stop wiggling that ridiculous tail,' she would tell the lamb, 'you would have more energy for eating,' but it paid no attention and went on sucking and wiggling in a twinned ecstasy.

The Dominie reported, through Ian, that Robin was training near Dundee. He was learning to march, and to salute.

'The Dominie's no sure how much his learning will help him fight the Hun,' reported Ian, 'but he's learning to dig trenches or to order other folk to dig them while he learns all about sending messages. Have you thought of that, Dad? If you're a General sitting in one hole, how do you tell the General in a hole five miles away that you're running out of ammunition?'

'It'll be a boy on a bike,' suggested Colin. 'It's aye a boy on a bike.'

'I hope they're teaching him to shoot,' said Mairi quietly.

'I wish them luck,' laughed Colin. 'Goodness knows I tried and that boy couldnae hit the barn door. You should be there looking out for him . . .' he began and then, appalled at what he was saying, he turned away in embarrassment.

'We cannae hide from this, Dad, at least not here by ourselves. I'd look out for Robin; I always have. But where do I stop?'

'Whit aboot Mairi? How far would you go for Mairi?'

'Ach, Dad, that's different.'

'Stop it, both of you. I can take care of myself, thank you, and both of you into the bargain, great lumps that you are. Now go, get to bed for you have to be up at the crack tomorrow.'

They went sheepishly, almost happy to be bullied, and Mairi watched them and then sank into her chair by the fire. She sat for a while just watching the sparks jump from one piece of wood to another and then she slipped out of the chair and knelt down beside it.

'Don't let him be killed,' she prayed, but to whom was she praying and who was the subject of her prayer?

Wearily she picked herself up and climbed the stairs after her father and brother.

'I'll look in on the Dominie,' she promised herself. 'There'll be someone in the farms happy to make a little extra money by doing for him. One fewer thing for Robin . . . or anyone else to worry over.'

*   *   *

The whole town of Dundee turned out to watch their men march away, and countless people from the farms and glens too. Impossible to tell a farmer from a fisherman in a kilt. They were all the same and the women of the town gave their kisses and hugs freely to all unless, of course, they had a man of their own to cling to, a husband, a son, a brother. Mairi stood on the street outside the West Station and remembered the first time she had seen the place when she had come to buy a dress with Ian and had given her money away to a little beggar girl. She looked around. Maybe that girl, grown older, was somewhere in this hysterical crowd. She could hear the pipes as the Battalion marched out of Dudhope Castle, that ancient fortress that had once been the home of John Graham, Bonnie Dundee, the best of all the bonnie fechters. The bands were playing 'Bonnie Dundee'. She recognized the tune as did the huge throng, the cheery cheeky notes brightening the heart and lifting the spirits. Were there braver, finer soldiers anywhere than these lads?

'Goodness, they must fairly be skipping if they have to march to that,' thought Mairi and in a wee while noticed that the tune had changed, to give the pipers, or the soldiers, a slight rest. It was 'Scotland the Brave' that rang out and then again the music changed to a pibroch, a series of musical variations that Mairi did not know.

A bent, gnarled old man beside her enlightened her. 'Isn't it the Pibroch of Donnil Dhu.' He smiled up at her through blackened teeth as he began to caper around in the cold. 'Does it not ever make you want to dance, lassie?' and Mairi watched him jigging away among the crowds. She laughed, for a second forgetting why she was here and then she remembered that Robin was going away to war and she had to see him, had to.

But she could not. She was too small and the crowds were too dense. She pushed and shoved and managed to force herself through the mass to see the men march into the station. He was tall, not so tall as Ian but taller than average. She should spot him easily but there were so many tall strapping men among those men of the Fourth Battalion, the Black Watch. She waited until the troop train had pulled out of the station and then she felt such a sense of loss, of desolation, that she put her head down and began to cry.

'Your sweetheart gone, my child?' asked a gentle voice and she looked up through tear-filled eyes to see a clergyman peering solicitously down at her.

Sweetheart? What could she say?

She shook her head. 'It was Robin,' she said,

110

'just Robin, and I couldn't see him.'

'No doubt he saw you, my dear, and that surely is the more important thing. He knew you were here?'

'No.'

'If you were anywhere near the front of the crowd he saw you. Think of that and go home and write the first of many letters.'

Mairi smiled a wavery smile as she decided to walk into the town to look at the shops. Her train would not be leaving for another hour and by the time she got home, Colin and Ian would be in from the fields reading a note that said: *Soup keeping hot on the grate.*

She had better have some purchases to explain her trip to Dundee. But they saw her face and asked no questions.

*   *   *

By mid-September 1915, the Fourth Battalion, the Black Watch, were down to some four hundred men and twenty-one officers. Second lieutenant Robin Morrison was still alive, at least his body moved and did as it was asked to do, but he himself was gone. He had come under fire first at a place called Neuve-Chapelle, and then there had been Ypres where the Germans had used poison gas as a weapon.

April, and instead of a sky full of larks there had been a sky full of choking, burning yellow smoke. He had remembered Ian's first letter in which he had tried to explain his position and he had scoffed. But now, after six months that had changed him from a loving, cheerful boy to an automaton, he did not scoff. He could not think; he could not pray. He had even stopped worrying that he might disgrace himself by showing fear. For the first few months that real terror had marched or crawled through the trenches beside him. He did not want to die but he was not afraid of death and he did not fear pain. He had met pain before and conquered it but he was afraid and he did not know what he feared.

Perhaps it was the noise. Noise was constant, whining, shrieking, thudding, swishing, screaming, sobbing. But worse than the noise was that endless fraction of a second of utter stillness between the dull thud that said a shell had landed and the appalling roar it made when it exploded. Robin had prayed once that a shell might put an end to this misery but instead he endured the silent eternity, then the roar, then he felt his head almost jerked from his shoulders and he picked himself up out of the muddy blood bath or the bloody mud bath, face scorched, hair singed and he screamed *why* but no sound came from his mouth.

Would it never end? They were all dead. He looked around and the carnage made him vomit and that dry retching only made him feel worse. Surely, surely he was not alone; far better to be honourably dead than to be here in Hell alone.

'Whit did you cry this place?' a cheery voice asked behind him, adding *Sir*, as an evident afterthought.

Robin looked through the blood that was pouring down his face into the dirty but unmarked face of his corporal, a regular soldier who had run away from the jute mills twelve years before because soldiering was at least a regular job.

Robin found a fairly clean handkerchief in his pocket and wiped the blood from his eyes, anything to stop him throwing his arms around the older man for comfort. 'Loos,' he said at last. 'As in "All Hell's let, et cetera, et cetera,"' and they laughed together for a moment as only soldiers can.

'You're no hurt, sir?' asked Corporal Wallace. 'Bad, I mean, for I think it's jist the two of us in here.'

Tentatively Robin felt his head, his ears. No holes that he could find. 'No,' he said. 'Surface stuff, I think. The head always bleeds like mad.'

He was himself again and he was responsible for this man and this trench, or what was left of it. He would not lose his nerve again.

Of the twenty-one officers of the Fourth Battalion, the Black Watch, twenty were killed or wounded at Loos together with two hundred and thirty-five of the enlisted men. It was the end of the Battalion which was forced to amalgamate with the Fifth Battalion. For Dundee and parts of Angus and Fife it was also an end, for almost every home, from closes in the city itself to stately homes in the countryside around, was affected. Death had no favourites. His selection was catholic, indiscriminate. He did not ask, *Is there anyone at home to feed the children left behind?* He spared no thought for the old mother left alone with no child to succour her last years. He did not care how many prayed to join their loved ones soon.

But on a wee farm near Dundee in the lovely fertile Angus countryside the Dominie proudly told Mairi that Robin was now a Captain.

'He says because no one else was left alive, Mairi. What sights my boy has seen. You will write

113

to him, Mairi, keep him normal. He must know there is some point to this.'

'But there isn't,' said Ian and turned away from his sister and his former schoolmaster, the father of his friend, who sadly watched him go.

CHAPTER ELEVEN

Hard work, good weather, and better luck brought in a good harvest in 1915. While Robin was suffering in France, Ian suffered, in a different way, in Scotland. He knew that 1916 would not bring the end of the war. He read every paper he could get his hands on, talked with the Dominie, and could see no end at all. He kept away from the village as much as possible but Colin insisted on Sunday morning appearances at the wee Kirk in the village and that was where everyone met in the pleasant sunshine to talk about, not the harvest, but the war.

And the talk was always the same.

'Did you hear that Jimmy Simpson frae the Knock, him that's married on Bert Thomson's eldest lassie, has joined the Navy?'

'And Angus Watson's twa eldest boys have gone tae try fer the Airforce. Seems auld Angus can manage fine with his youngest and the wife.'

And the lads from . . . here, there, and everywhere in between. War was exciting, better than following the back end of a horse up and down the fields in the same old monotonous way. Soldiers, sailors, and these brand-new exciting airmen got regular wages which were sent back to mothers and wives at home.

And at last the question that had worried some for a time was uttered aloud. 'You'll be going now, Ian. Yer dad and auld Charlie and Mairi can manage. You'll be wanting the Black Watch like the Dominie's Robin. You were aye as thick as thieves.'

'I won't be joining the Black Watch,' answered Ian quietly and felt his father tense beside him.

'Don't say you fancy flying through the air in a wee bit machine? Raither you than me, laddie.'

'I won't be joining anything.'

'Ach away. Your auld man's no needing you and your country is.'

Colin tried but to no avail. Ian had wanted to utter the words for months, had longed to hear them said aloud so that he and everyone else could adjust.

'I don't believe in war as an answer to international problems,' he said quietly and then he looked squarely at his interrogator. 'I won't go, even when they tell me to go.'

No one knew what to say. They stood edging from foot to foot, coughing discreetly, and then found an excuse to hurry away. And then one turned, spat in the road, and uttered one word.

'Scrimshanker.'

'What the Hell does that mean?' asked Colin furiously. He did not know the word but he certainly recognized the tone in which it was said.

'Let's get home, Dad, Mairi,' said Ian. 'It's just ignorance. I'm not a coward and some people are saying that people like me are cowards, shirkers, scrimshankers.'

Mairi had been avoiding Edith since she had stopped walking out with Jack but now she saw the look of disdain that passed between Edith and her

115

mother and it made her very angry. She hurried after her brother and slipped her hand into his. He smiled down at her.

'Brave wee Mairi,' he said. 'I'm not a coward. I thought all this out independently of anyone and now I have to act fearlessly on my own moral convictions. It is wrong to kill another human being. Men are making money out of death. There's men all over Europe retiring as millionaires on the money they're making out of misery. That's wrong, that profiteers, safe and warm far from the battlefields, should make money while men die in horror.'

He stopped talking, the longest speech he had ever made in his entire life, and Mairi could only squeeze his arm in comfort and support.

Colin caught up with them. 'Can you thole it, laddie?'

'Aye, Dad. The question is, can you?'

'No more, no more,' begged Mairi. 'Listen, Dad. Did you hear Willie Webster's Clydesdale made eighty pounds at the sale yesterday?'

Colin was so shocked that he stopped walking. 'Away! It never did. That's twice the annual wage of the man that looks efter it.'

'A good Clydesdale is irreplaceable, Dad. Men are expendable.'

Was there nothing they could talk about that would keep this hideous war away?

'Mr Morrison missed the Kirk this morning,' said Mairi after a while.

'I meant to tell you,' said Ian. 'An old friend of his has come out of retirement to teach in Dundee. The Dominie's away through for the weekend. That's a nice wee break for him.'

'More than profiteers doing well out of the war then,' said Mairi. 'If more men join up they'll be desperate enough to have married women teaching in the schools.'

'Ach, it'll never get that bad, lassie,' laughed Colin and lightened the atmosphere. 'Noo, let's have oor dinner and then I have a wheen paper work to do. You should maybe have a look at it with me, Ian, and you too, lassie. I'm bringing my rotation records up to date because we're due for a new seven-year lease and I want the Factor tae see that everything's been done right. The war's good for farmers, Ian. I can sell as much food as I can grow. We'll maybe look into getting a bit more land. My best field has tae lie fallow this next season.'

'Maybe the government will lighten the rules, Dad. Isn't producing food more important just now than letting the land rest?'

'Short-sighted, lass. You have tae look ahead on a farm, no just what's growing this year but what the land will bear in ten years.'

When they reached the farmhouse, Mairi hurried upstairs to change out of her best Sunday dress and then came downstairs to dish up the scalding hot soup made from the carcass of the old hen that would provide the second course. Sunday dinner was always the same: soup, then a roast of some kind with homegrown vegetables, followed by heavy pudding in the cold months and lighter milk puddings in the summer.

'Isn't it a shame the strawberrries and rasps are over?' said Mairi to her father who was sitting at the fireside, his fingers scratching the ears of the dog who lay devotedly at his feet. 'There was that much fruit I've way too many jars of jam in the store cupboard.'

'Aye, but you're right, lassie, soft fruits are better the way God made them. There's nothing better than fresh fruit.'

'I had raspberries in white wine at the Big House last year at the picnic,' Ian announced as he came in from the steading.

His father and sister looked at him, one in awe, the other in amazement.

'What did they taste like?' asked Mairi.

'How did they get you to drink sich a daft thing as wine, and white at that?'

Ian laughed. 'There's some as doesn't see a great country yokel when they look at me.'

Colin looked at his son and saw a tall, well-formed and yes, a good-looking young man, with wide clear eyes, and a firm well-shaped mouth.

'The Laird's niece? It was her, wasn't it? Oh, you sly old thing, Ian McGloughlin.'

'They asked for you, Mairi. The Laird had peaches in his wine; he said you would have liked that, rather than the strawberries. He gave me a peach for you but I put it down somewhere and forgot it.'

Over a year it had taken him to tell her. Typical. Mairi smiled as she turned away to attend to her sauce. This strong brave Ian was still her brother who could forget everything if his mind was stirred by something beautiful. Miss Arabella Huntingdon was beautiful. Ian and a lassie? No. He had never been interested in the lasses.

'Come on, let's have dinner and this year I'll go and get my own peach.'

'The picnic is usually in August and here we are

118

at the beginning of October. Maybe there won't be one this year, not with the war.'

But there was and neither Mairi nor Ian realized that it was because Miss Huntingdon had persuaded her uncle, much against his better judgement.

It was to be different. In former years everything had been provided free for the tenants but in 1915 the Laird charged a shilling for each family and a halfpenny entrance to all the games. All monies collected were to go to war charities.

'You go, Mairi, and pay our shilling. I don't think it's a good idea for Ian and me to go and there's too much work here.'

'I'm going, Dad,' said Ian. 'I'll do all my chores before I go but I'm not ashamed of my stance and people can say what they like.'

Colin looked out of his windows, windows that Mairi kept clear and shining, no matter how dusty or dirty the steading became. 'I don't want to provoke anything, not in the Laird's grounds. Some of the ither tenants have already lost kin.'

'I won't provoke anything, Dad, and I'm happy to explain my point of view to anyone that wants to talk to me.'

'We must go, Dad, and you have to enter the shooting and throwing the hay bale and you too, Ian. It's for the war effort. We can't have our neighbours saying we're not doing our part. The Blacks will be there and the Sutherlands and the Dominie. It'd be a good time to talk to him about taking a lassie into service if he's needing help.'

'Won't the lasses all be working on the land, Mairi?'

'There's still plenty in the tied cottages with

119

more mouths to feed than money coming in, Dad.'

'Well, we can hope for a bad day and a cancellation,' sighed Colin and his children looked at him, Ian with a heart full of guilt.

It is difficult to be noble if your nobility causes distress to the people you love. Ian decided to be very circumspect. He would be a good and dutiful son. He would take part in all the competitions, even the shooting, and if he shot well and Miss Huntingdon saw his success, no doubt Colin would be pleased.

Ian was not the only one who was making resolutions about the Tenants' picnic. Because it was to be held in October which can be a lovely month in Angus or a wild one, depending on its mood, Mairi decided to buy a light-weight woollen suit that she had seen advertised in the *Courier* for three guineas. D. M. Brown's was offering the suit in blue, green, or a light grey and so Miss McGloughlin took the train into Dundee with not three but four guineas in her purse. The suit, which she wanted in green, had a very masculine line and needed, she decided, a soft feminine blouse to make it just perfect. This time she allowed nothing to dissuade her from her self-appointed task and a very happy young lady swept, with head held high, from the Dundee shop a mere two hours after entering it. Buying the suit, although she had tried on one in each of the colours, had taken only thirty minutes but oh, the difficulty of buying a blouse.

She sat on the train and looked, not at the countryside, but at the two brown paper parcels on her tweed-covered lap. She could hardly wait to show off her purchases. The McGloughlins would present a united, and even elegant, front to their neighbours.

And so they did, for Colin and his son were both well-set-up men who wore their Sunday suits with easy assurance, and Mairi looked lovely both because she was pretty and perhaps more importantly because she felt good.

Her pleasure in her suit was diminished a little when she saw the ravishing outfits worn by the Laird's wife and niece. A three-guinea off-the-peg suit is no match for haute couture when it is worn by elegant women and Arabella Huntingdon and her aunt were both tall and slender. They greeted their guests politely although Mairi felt sure that Miss Huntingdon's eyes grew warmer when she addressed Ian.

'They would make a lovely couple,' thought Mairi but sensibly kept her opinions to herself.

Even if Ian had wished, they could not linger and the family went off to enter the competitions and to wander around the gardens, no longer in full flower, but tidied and prepared for winter.

'Sir Humphrey is such a good gardener,' sighed Mairi as she bent down to smell some of the bushes that had replaced the summer flowers. 'The last time I was here, this garden was an orgy of colour. Now look, it's all green, or bits of yellow, but it's still lovely and some of these leaves have a pleasant smell. I bet they would be especially nice after rain.'

She looked up and saw Edith, Jack, and their parents walking towards them.

The families saw one another at the same time but it was too late to pretend that they had not. The two farmers, of course, felt no qualms about greeting one another. The fact that their children were no longer friends meant nothing.

'Nice to see you, Mairi,' said Jack. 'I like your new costume, you look very . . .'

'Nice,' said Edith, waspishly.

'I was going to say, sophisticated,' said Jack and then turned to Ian. 'Haven't seen you in ages, Ian. Come on and I'll take you on at the shooting.'

'It's only men I have a problem shooting, Jack, if you were looking for an easy prize. I hae nae qualms about targets.'

Jack blushed to the roots of his hair. 'I wasn't thinking about your politics, more whit you were like when we left the school.'

'I've improved,' said Ian simply. 'Come on then. Sorry I was so touchy. Are you going to watch us, girls?'

'Rupert Grey-Watson is home on leave,' said Edith. 'Mother and I were on our way to pay our respects.'

'Away you go then, Edith,' said her loving brother. 'But he'll not look at a bean pole like you when the juicy Arabella is around,' he added unkindly.

'Are you coming, Mairi, or do you want to swoon over the delicate Rupert?'

'She'd much rather swoon over his father,' teased Ian. 'Isn't that right, Mairi. Unless of course, young Rupert can grow peaches.'

Mairi fell into step beside them. 'I don't know why you men have to pretend to be so tough all the time. And Rupert isn't delicate,' she added as she caught a glimpse of the young cavalry officer who was walking with his mother and cousin on the other side of the garden. Edith and her mother were hurrying towards them and, for a moment,

Mairi thought that Rupert might pull his mother and cousin into a path that would take them away from the advancing women but, if he had considered it, he changed his mind and bravely stood his ground and waited.

'Captain Grey-Watson, we are so proud of you.' She could hear Mrs Black's voice. So too could Jack who was looking extremely uncomfortable.

'Our Edith's given up hope of catching Robin Morrison; he hasn't written to her in months. Now she's after bigger game.'

Ian stopped and turned Jack around to face him. 'Jack, if you can't stop being nasty, find yourself someone else to play with,' he said and stalked off in the direction of the shooting range.

'Touchy, touchy,' said Jack. 'Come on, Mairi. I'll take you for tea and scones.'

'Thanks, Jack, but I'm having tea with my dad.'

She went to walk off after her brother but Jack looked so lost and he had once, after all, been quite dear to her. She took pity on him. 'How have you been though? I haven't seen you for ages.'

'Fine, but I'm thinking of joining up. It'd be great to see a foreign country and hae a crack at Jerry. I'm nearly twenty-five, Mairi, and I'm still living with my parents, being told what to do.'

'You're a partner now?'

'Name only. My dad is so used to being the boss, it never occurs to him to ask anyone else for advice. Truth is, he's usually right.'

Mairi thought of her father and brother who worked harmoniously together season after season. Any blemishes in their relationship had been smoothed out long since and even Ian's pacifism would not change their respect for one another.

'It would be worse to be the younger Harper though, Jack, wouldn't it? It must be awful to have your brother tell you what to do all day.'

Jack looked round and saw an ironwork garden seat. 'Come and sit down for a bit,' and when Mairi did so he added, 'you haven't heard then?'

'Heard what?'

'Tam's gone for a soldier. Left Jim as tenant. Wanted to get away from his wife, I think.'

Mairi ignored that reflection on domestic harmony. Every farm was changing. Who would have thought that Tam Harper, thirty if he was a day, would have enlisted?

'It'll just be the Blacks and the McGloughlins without serving soldiers,' she said.

'Not if I go and, besides, two of our lads have gone since the news of Loos came through. They were so angry at our losses they just disappeared overnight. My dad'll keep their jobs for them. He'll be decent that way. Mairi, if I go, will you write to me? Everyone else I know is keeping company or married.'

Mairi laughed. 'That's hardly a compliment, Jack.'

'Ach, you know fine what I mean and we always got on.'

'If you go, Jack, I'll think about it.' She got up from the seat. 'Come on. Ian will be waiting to take your money.'

'All prizes to our brave lads in uniform,' smiled Jack and he took her arm.

They walked off between the beech hedges and came face to face with Rupert and Arabella. Rupert smiled and stepped back to let them walk before him and Arabella said, 'Are you enjoying the

124

picnic, Miss McGloughlin?'

Mairi blushed. It had not occurred to her that the young aristocrat would remember her among so many tenants, but before she could answer Arabella showed who was really remembered by adding, 'My cousin here tells me that Mr McGloughlin is the finest shot in the area. We hoped to see him compete, perhaps against Rupert.'

'My father and brother are both excellent shots, Miss Huntingdon, and so too is Mr Black.'

'Then we'll have a wager, Bella,' said Rupert. 'Five guineas tells me that I can beat either Mr McGloughlin.'

'Done,' said Arabella, clapping her gloved hands together. 'Either way the Charity will profit. Come along, Miss McGloughlin; let us find your brother and, of course, your father.'

CHAPTER TWELVE

Afterwards Mairi could never remember how a day that had started so agreeably could have ended in such an unpleasant way. She went with Arabella past the front of the great house and into the side gardens, followed by Rupert Grey-Watson who was making heavy weather of light chit-chat with the nervous Jack, until they came to the area that had been set as a shooting range.

Two of the Laird's grooms were in charge of the guns, the shot, and the targets which were old chipped plates and saucers that had been collected for weeks by the children of the local primary school. The younger undergardeners took turns throwing a target into the air; it was all very light-hearted because, while most of the boys had no skill in throwing, one of them was the leading light of the local cricket team. His plates went higher and wider than those thrown by the others and were usually harder to hit because he threw as he bowled, a different route every time.

First Ian shot against Jack. They appeared to be evenly matched and Mairi stood beside Miss Arabella and watched her as she, with shining eyes, watched Ian.

'This,' Mairi decided, 'is a very unexpected and exciting new development.'

'Mr McGloughlin is very good, isn't he?' breathed Arabella.

'He gets lots of practice shooting crows.'

'No doubt harder to hit than pheasant, Bella,' said Rupert. 'I think I may lose my bet.'

Ian won the first match and then Rupert shot against Jack, who was so nervous at having been singled out for attention by the local aristocracy that all his shots went wide.

'Bad luck,' said Rupert generously. 'It's that gun, you know. I meant to tell my father to have it looked at. We'll have another go after your friend has trounced me.'

Rupert looked around at the crowd who were gathering to watch the excitement. 'Where's the senior Mr McGloughlin?' he asked. 'I'd like to shoot against him.'

But Colin had wanted no part of a sideshow in which he was a component of the entertainment and had gone off to throw horseshoes with several other farmers.

'Bad show,' smiled Rupert. 'One hears what a first-rate shot he is; it would have been jolly good fun to shoot against him.'

'I'm sure Mr Ian McGloughlin is just as good,' said Arabella, looking at Mairi for confirmation.

'I don't know,' said Mairi simply. 'Shooting crows is just part of his job.'

'Like being a soldier,' said an unknown voice from the crowd.

Rupert laughed. 'I do hope there's more to soldiering than shooting. Will you shoot against me, McGloughlin?'

'Aye, sir, for the Charity.'

'Splendid. We'll have ten plates each, and we'll have Gus throw for us.'

Mairi could tell nothing of what Ian was thinking from his face, which was set and almost cold.

The first plate was thrown—and was immediately shot out of the sky. The second, the third. On and on it went and the crowd grew louder and louder as they cheered, but it soon became obvious that they were shouting only for Rupert Grey-Watson.

Mairi, who had been standing quietly beside Miss Huntingdon, her fingernails digging into the palms of her hands, began to shout encouragement to her brother, and then Arabella, too, dropped all pretence of being neutral and joined her. The girls forgot for a moment that they were aristocrat and peasant and they yelled naturally for the young man in whom each had an interest. They looked at one another and laughed.

The first match was a draw.

'Shall we try again, McGloughlin?'

'There's many here could give you a good match,

127

sir,' said Ian, who hated being in the limelight, today more than ever.

Rupert looked at the young farmer shrewdly. 'There's more going on here than a shooting match. Why is no one, apart from my cousin and your charming sister, cheering you on?'

'Never mind,' he added quickly as Ian struggled for a truthful answer. 'I need to beat you.' He turned to one of the undergardeners. 'Run up to the house and ask Mrs Potter for some kitchen cups; the plates are too easy.'

The cups were brought by Rupert's parents and the crowd moved back respectfully. Sir Humphrey was a popular landlord.

'I'm putting a wager on McGloughlin,' he told his son, 'and Mama is backing you. We have twenty-four cups; Mrs Potter won't let you have any more but I have brought these in case we have a second draw.' He took two tiny bone-china egg cups out of his jacket pocket. 'Think you can hit that, young Ian?'

'He can hit onything bar a Hun,' came that voice from the crowd and Mairi gasped.

Ian stood stock-still and looked into his landlord's eyes.

'That the way the wind blows, is it?' asked Sir Humphrey. 'Well, I'm sure you have your reasons. Let the match begin.'

Rupert had lowered his gun and was looking at it as it pointed to the ground as if it was the most important thing he had ever examined.

'Rupert,' said his father.

Rupert looked from his father to his mother who was pointedly looking into the distance, then back to his cousin who was white and shaking, and then

128

to Ian.

'C.O.?' he asked.

'I believe this war to be wrong, sir.'

'And what will you say when we come for you, because we will, you know?'

'I will say what I have just said.'

'That'll take guts, McGloughlin. You shoot first.'

He stepped back and Ian moved forward to the firing line and then, with a soft rustle of silk petticoats, Miss Arabella Huntingdon ran forward and spoke softly to Ian. He smiled at her but said nothing and she stepped back beside Mairi.

Ian missed the first cup and the crowd went wild with enthusiasm. Rupert fired and scored. Ian then hit three in a row and Rupert hit two and missed his fourth. Three all.

Five all. Seven six to Ian. Nine seven to Rupert. Nine eight. Nine all. Ten all. Eleven ten. Twelve eleven to Ian and Rupert still to fire.

'Save the last shell for the coward,' yelled that horrid hidden voice.

Ian turned white, but not with fear, and Rupert stepped forward.

'I see no cowards on this side of the line,' he said. 'I do not agree with Mr McGloughlin's views but I am prepared to fight for his right to express them, not only with the enemy but with anyone here who dares to show his face and make his challenge.'

There was muttering from the crowd but for once it was not against Ian.

'Throw your egg cups, Father,' said Rupert, and, as Sir Humphrey did so, both young men fired and the shattered china fell to the ground.

They stood looking at one another. Ian held out

his hand. Rupert looked at it until Ian flushed and withdrew it.

'I have lost too many friends,' said Rupert. 'We should have met in happier times,' and he turned and walked away.

Arabella stood looking after him. Her aunt and uncle still stood, obviously disagreeing, and then Lady Grey-Watson called, 'Arabella,' and, without waiting, began to walk after her son.

Mairi was with Ian who was now white with distress.

'Well done, lad,' said Sir Humphrey. 'Forgive my son.'

'Forgive him, sir, for what?'

'You have chosen a hard path, young man. There will be Conscription within the next few months. If you need help, at any time, don't hesitate to use my name.'

'I'll plough my own furrow, Sir Humphrey, but thank you, sir.'

This time it was Sir Humphrey who extended his hand and Ian took it and found his fingers grasped in a hand that reminded him uncomfortably of his father's.

'Bella,' said Sir Humphrey as he turned away.

She stood for a moment and then she turned again to Ian. 'I do think you're perfectly splendid. I should like to give you my scarf but . . . I suppose that's quite silly.'

'Not silly,' said Ian. 'I am going into battle, Miss Huntingdon.'

Her scarf was of the finest silk and must have cost more than Mairi's entire outfit but Bella slipped it from her neck and held it out to Ian, and Mairi saw her shy, gawky brother take the scarf, kiss it gently, and slip it inside his shirt.

*　　　*　　　*

'Well, we'd better go and find Dad afore he hears all about this little fracas from someone else,' said Ian, as if the most momentous event in his life had not just occurred.

Mairi went with him and they followed in the wake of the crowd. She was frightened and exhilarated. Ian had won, or at least, since Rupert had not tried to hit his last cup, he had equalled the shooting of the young army officer; that was gratifying. Then there were Arabella's muttered words—how she would love to know what they were, but knew that she could not ask—and the giving of the favour. But there had been Rupert's reaction to the news that Ian was a conscientious objector, and more horrifying, for Rupert had behaved with gentlemanly self-control throughout, the shouted words from the heckler.

'Save the last shot for the coward.' Surely no one would want to kill Ian for his stance? Rupert was prepared to fight for Ian's beliefs, which was amusing in a twisted kind of way since Ian, who was the stronger of the two, would not fight for himself. But the man in the crowd had to be someone known to them, someone who had perhaps shared their table or their fireside at some time over the years.

'I won't think about it. The war will be over, it will, and Arabella Huntingdon has given Ian her scarf.'

Arabella. What a beautiful name, so much more glamorous and sophisticated than Mairi. Could she

131

mention the scarf to Ian? The days when she could tease him and worry him like an annoying fly that buzzed constantly just out of reach were over.

'Here's Dad. And by the look on his face, he knows.'

'I hear you won the shooting. Good lad. It's a lot of money for the Charity and here's the Laird told me that if you weren't to tenant one of the best farms he'd have you for gamekeeper.'

So he would, when the time came, be given the tenancy. Even conscientious objectors could be good farmers. But what if Rupert was the Laird by that time? Colin was younger than Sir Humphrey.

'He's a good man, the Laird,' said Ian.

'There's at least three people told me about Sam Jarvie heckling you—' began Colin when Mairi interrupted.

'Sam Jarvie? Him that has taken his dinner with us near once a week for years?'

'He's not been himself since he lost his boy, Mairi.'

'You're always too ready to make excuses, Dad. It was horrible the way they muttered at Ian, like dogs when the biggest one's got a bone they want, all ready to nip in at the right minute.'

'Let's go home, Dad. We did what we came to do. I'm sorry you didn't get your tea, Mairi.'

'Tea? There's nobody bakes better than me anyway,' said Miss McGloughlin saucily and they walked home together, with Ian and Colin teasing her by going through a long litany of local bakers— 'except for Pheemie Anderson, except for Betty Starkie . . .'

*　　　*　　　*

Ian was quieter than usual that evening and went upstairs early.

'He'll be away to write a poem, or maybe a letter to Robin,' said Colin, and Mairi, who felt sure that her brother was sitting at his window looking towards the big house and holding a delicate silk scarf between hard, work-worn fingers, smiled and said nothing.

They were both right and both wrong. Ian did spend a lot of time holding the scarf, sniffing its faint perfume, holding its softness against his weather-beaten face. He tried to write a poem but all he could write was one word: Arabella. He tore the poem out of his notebook and folded it with the scarf which he replaced inside his shirt. Then he wrote to Robin.

I want to do it now, to get it over, but that would hurt my father and Mairi, but as soon as Conscription is announced, and that must be soon, I will do it.

We did not speak to your father, and Mairi wanted to see if he needed somebody to help in the house, not her, but some other woman in the farm toon. I'm sure she'll see to it soon, if you want her to do so.

The news from the War Front is more horrific than ever, and we pray for you. The Minister leads prayers for servicemen each Sunday. He must think, especially, of Sinclair; Sinclair who, at school, was terrified of both you and me and, even more, of Mairi, and who has now been decorated for 'conspicuous gallantry in the face of the enemy'.

He did not write of his embarrassment when Rupert Grey-Watson had refused to shake hands with him, and he did not write of the scarf.

CHAPTER THIRTEEN

The war was no closer to ending. It was escalating. By the end of 1915, Britain, France, and Italy had declared war on Bulgaria and by the end of March 1916, when Colin was looking forward to the springtime lambing, Albania and Romania had opened up hostilities against Austria, Germany was at war with Poland, and Great Britain had instituted a conscription policy.

'I can't keep who's fighting with who straight in my mind,' said Colin. 'Have you ever heard of half these wee places, Ian?'

Ian was staring into the fire and seemed not to hear and with an exasperated shrug Colin went back to his newspaper.

Ian stared on as if the answers to the questions that plagued him and would not let him sleep were to be found in the flames. Then abruptly he stood up and looked down at his father.

Colin lowered the paper. 'Well, laddie? Something on your mind?'

Still Ian stood and Colin looked at his tall young son with all the marks of manhood on him and he smiled up at the boy. 'Cat got your tongue, laddie?'

Ian returned the smile but did not answer. 'Goodnight, Dad,' he said and Colin heard him walk to the door, open it, and then climb the stairs to his room.

'Damn and blast the bluidy Kaiser,' Colin said and returned to his paper where he saw that the Canadian Pacific Railway was advertising for farm hands and domestic servants to travel from Liverpool to Canada in search of a better life, and that it was expected that trade sheep would fetch at least forty shillings per live hundredweight in the Forfar Sales.

'We'll hope there's still some farmhands around in April tae sell the beasts,' mused Colin and set his mind to pondering if there was anything left in the house fit to donate to the Queen Mary's Needlework Guild's appeal for donations.

Upstairs Mairi slept and Ian sat at his table in his nightshirt and set about writing a difficult letter. He had tried, several times, to find both the time and the words to tell his father everything that was in his heart but the words would not come. Now he sat with his pen in his hand and watched the ink drip from the nib back into the old inkwell. He took a deep breath and began to write and this time the words flowed from his brain, from his heart, on to the paper.

It's a matter of a few weeks, a few months before they find they need agricultural labourers too, Dad. I'm a strong, healthy man and they will come soon and tell me, 'Your country needs you.' And I will tell them that I will not fight, I will not take the life of another man. They will say, 'Would you protect your wee sister, by force, if she were attacked?' and I will have to say, 'Yes, I would do everything in my power to keep her from harm,' and so they will tell me that I have

135

no right to object to war, for surely it is only a matter of degree.

But what I say is, 'If someone asked me to murder a child, what would God and my fellow man expect me to do or say? No, and again No. But asking me to join the army and to kill children legally is barbaric. In war it is always the innocent who suffer. War brings starvation, poverty, illness, deformities, disease, and it brutalizes. Decent human beings become brutalized by the very brutality they practise and I know they cannot change back.'

I have gone into Dundee to tell the recruiting sergeant that I will not fight but I will cook food, or cut down trees, or drive wagons, or whatever kind of job they can find for me. I will let you know what happens as soon as I can. Don't worry about me. I have to do what my conscience tells me is right. Ask Mairi to tell her I have taken her favour into battle.

Your loving son,
Ian

The recruiting sergeant had no idea what to do with Ian McGloughlin.

'Laddie, there's Boards being set up all over the place tae hear them as has been called and disnae want tae go. Whit the Hell am I supposed tae dae with you?'

'I thought you would know,' said Ian.

'Why don't you away hame tae your ferm and maybe this bluidy war'll be over afore we get to the M's.'

'I can't do that. It's now a point of honour.'

The sergeant looked at him. 'Honour's got

precious little tae dae with onything, laddie. Away hame.'

'I've come to join up. There must be somewhere for me to go.'

The sergeant was saved from the effort of answering by the entrance of an officer. 'New recruit? Well-set-up lad. Just what we need.'

'He's C.O., sir.'

'Not on my patch he isn't. Got your papers?'

'I haven't been conscripted,' said Ian and deliberately left out the sir. 'I'm here to enlist.'

'In what, the ruddy ballet corps? If you haven't been conscripted and you're a shrinking violet, get the hell out of this office.'

He turned away but Ian stood stock-still and waited. His stomach was churning, just as it had countless times in his childhood when he knew that his father had gone for the shaving strap that hung by the fire. But he had gone too far to back down now.

'Surely I'm not the only man who's come in here and said he was a conscientious objector. There must be somewhere for me to go.'

'Man?' The officer turned and looked vaguely around the room. 'Man? Do you see a man, besides ourselves, in here, Sergeant?'

Ian would not be cowed and he would not be angered. 'I am fit and healthy and have worked on a farm since I was a wee boy. There must be something I can do.'

'You can go to jail for the night at least, you useless scrimshanker. Put him in a cell, Sergeant, and I'll see what Major Graham has to say in the morning.'

Whatever Ian had expected, it was not to find

137

himself in a narrow prison cell. There was a rather dubious-looking mattress on the floor, a threadbare blanket and a hard pillow. Ian poked the mattress gingerly with his foot and then decided to remain standing for what was left of the day.

It was the longest day he had ever lived through. He could hear vague noises from the office but no one came near him for hours. At a few minutes past seven in the evening the sergeant came in with a cheese sandwich and a mug of hot, sweet tea.

'The Major's a decent man and he'll ken how tae handle this,' he said. 'I'll bring you a po for your convenience and you can empty it the morn's morn when I come back. Ye fancy a jam butty for your breakfast—ma missus'll mak ye one.'

He was gone and Ian, for the first time in his entire life, was completely alone and in complete darkness. He crouched down against a corner of his cell, wrapped the blanket around his shoulders, and waited for the morning.

It was a long time coming. Every hour or so Ian stood up and slapped his arms against his body in a futile attempt to keep the circulation going. He was stiff and cold and hungry and he thought he could almost smell Mairi's soup simmering away on the back of the fire. It would be warm there in the kitchen with the firelight throwing shadows on the walls. Mairi might be singing or humming as she went about her countless jobs; his father's long legs would be stretched out to the warmth of the fire and he would sigh now and again as he thought of his son.

'I'll be able to tell you the morn, Dad,' he said into the darkness, and his voice startled him as it exploded the silence. He crouched down again against the wall and tried to recall the words of Arnold's 'The Scholar Gypsy' that he and Robin had tried to learn one summer so long ago as they sat under a tree by the stream. He recalled the first ten lines and then another ten and then the lines began to run together in his head and he fell asleep, only to wake later colder and stiffer than before. He was on his feet walking around the perimeter of the cell when he heard the door open.

It was the sergeant. 'We're out of jam, lad, but there's some dripping in the bap. I'll make you a cup of tea. Looks like you could do with being warmed up.'

Gratefully Ian took the soft roll and ate it quickly. He would have liked to wash too and to shave but there was no water and his bag with his razor and his change of clothes was still in the office.

'Why didn't you just wait for call-up, lad?' asked the sergeant when he came back. 'You'd have saved the both of us a lot of trouble and Captain McNeil's a right bugger when he's crossed.'

'Surely not all jobs in the Army are done by fighting men? There must be non-combatant groups.'

'Aye, there are, but they had the decency to wait till they were called up. Why couldn't you wait and go before the Board according to regulations. Regulations make life easier for everybody.'

Ian had never expected to feel sorry for the military. 'I'm sorry, but I couldn't live any longer with the threat of Conscription hanging over my head. It's just a matter of time.'

'Hell of a lot can happen in a few weeks, laddie, even in a few hours. I got hit two days after I

139

reached Belgium; was hardly worth being that bluidy sea sick. And now you're upsetting this nice little job.'

They heard the office door open and the sergeant turned to leave. 'That'll be his nibs. We'll see what he's come up with during the night.'

But the immaculately dressed officer who came into the little cell was not Captain McNeil but Major Graham. And the Major was very angry.

'What is this man's crime, Sergeant?'

'He's a C.O., sir.'

'I wasn't aware that that was a crime. Why are you here, boy?' he asked, turning to Ian.

'I came to enlist in some kind of non-combative corps, sir.'

'Been conscripted?'

'No, sir, not yet. I'm a farmer. Well, I'm working with my father.'

'And why do you want to enlist?'

'I can't not do something, sir.'

'Get this man some shaving water.'

Everything Major Graham did was done quickly. By ten o'clock, Ian found himself on a train bound for Berwick-on-Tweed and two days later he was learning to drive an ambulance. Three weeks later he was remembering the sergeant as he hung on to the sides of a ship as it heaved and tossed across the Channel. If his night in a prison cell had seemed endless, this journey across a stormy sea was eternity.

'Nothing can be worse than this,' was his only coherent thought throughout the entire voyage.

*   *   *

Mairi and Colin heard from him two weeks after the awful morning when Mairi had found his room empty and the letter on his table.

'He says he's learning tae drive. What aboot that, Mairi? Oor Ian, driving like one of the toffs.'

'Thank God he's safe,' said Mairi and burst into tears.

Colin had no idea how safe driving an ambulance in a war zone might be but he said nothing. He was so relieved to know, at last, where his son was. When Mairi had brought him the letter his first impulse had been to go into Dundee and demand that Ian return to the farm. He was needed. The war was good for farmers. They could sell as much as they could grow or raise and that was necessary war work. But he had read the letter again and again and the words had affected him.

'I'll never understand him, my own flesh and blood. Where did he get these daft ideas from? War's not legal murder . . . it's, it's . . . war and that's not murder.'

Now he looked helplessly at Mairi and had no idea how to calm her tears. 'Ach, lassie, he aye wanted to go abroad,' he said but that only made Mairi cry more than ever.

'Oh, I hate Robin Morrison,' she said and ran into the kitchen. Colin stayed in the front room and heard what sounded like his daughter throwing pots around.

'Women,' he sighed in exasperation. Why she had chosen to mention the Dominie's son, he could not imagine. He did not understand that Mairi was comparing her brother's first overseas trip with that of Robin. He did not know that she had kissed Robin and slapped him on the same night. He

141

could not know that she prayed daily for a message from him. He did not realize that her love for Robin and her fear for his safety were now bound up again with her love and fear for Ian. He decided, wisely, to stay out of the kitchen.

Mairi stopped banging the pots around and began to peel potatoes, a mindless task that allowed her to think. She would write to Ian. She would write as often as she could and she would tell him everything that happened. She would describe every leaf unfurling on every tree; she would note where the swallows built their nests and she would tell him of the antics of the babies as they leaned precariously out of the nests. She would tell him when a salmon was caught in the burn and she would describe the antics of lambs and calves as they played by their mothers in the flower-strewn fields. She would start immediately after supper.

First she told him of her unimaginable pride in her big brother.

Dad's not saying much except a man's got to do what he believes to be right, but he's very proud of you. He spent the whole of teatime telling me about every test you had ever taken at school.

'The Dominie always said our Ian was a brain.' If he said that once he said it a thousand times, and then he talked about the picnic and how you won the shooting and Sir Humphrey's respect. Sir Humphrey rode over a few days ago and Dad told him you'd joined the Army.

'I thought the lad would see sense,' said Sir Humphrey.

'He's aye seen sense, Sir Humphrey,' said

Dad. 'It's me that couldnae see.'

I sent Miss Huntingdon a note and told her what you said. Dad doesn't want to know about that. 'He's got mair than enough problems,' was all he said.

Miss Huntingdon answered Mairi's note in person. One afternoon when Mairi was wringing blankets before hanging them out to dry, Arabella, accompanied by a groom, rode into the steading. Mairi looked at the beautifully attired girl on her superb blood-horse and glanced down at her own dress, soaked in spite of her huge apron, and she could have wept. Instead she wiped her soapy hands on a dry corner of the apron and went forward to meet her visitor.

'Miss Huntingdon,' she said.

Arabella turned to the groom. 'Walk the horses, Ewan,' and when he had complied she turned back to Mairi. 'I'm sorry to disturb you at a busy time . . .'

'It's always a busy time on a working farm.' Mairi was angry and she did not know why. Somehow she felt that Arabella had to see what Ian's life was like. He was a farmer, not a poetic dreamer.

'Ian,' said Arabella. 'Mr McGloughlin . . . he has gone into battle, your note said. He has joined the Army then?'

'No,' said Mairi. 'He has been sent to a non-combatant corps. He's going to France to drive ambulances.'

Arabella's face grew pink with excitement and she clasped her gloved hands together. 'Oh, how wonderful, true to himself. You must be so proud of him.'

143

'He didn't need to go; he wasn't conscripted,' said Mairi mulishly.

'I know, I mean I know that farmers are still exempt. Please, Miss McGloughlin, will you tell him that . . .'

She stopped as if she was unable to continue and looked at Mairi.

Mairi smiled. 'Why don't you tell him yourself, Miss Huntingdon?'

Arabella seemed to be considering many questions. 'Yes,' she said after a while. 'We must all help our brave . . . men. It would be a kindness to send a letter, a simple message of encouragement, wouldn't it?'

'I have the address in the house.' Again Mairi compared her plain homespun dress with the tailored clothes of the other girl. She might as well see everything, she thought.

'Would you like to step inside out of the wind, Miss Huntingdon, and I'll write the address for you.'

Arabella followed her into the house, stepping straight from the farm yard into the front room. Mairi looked at her home for a moment through the other girl's eyes and she was ashamed and then she was even more ashamed when Arabella said delightedly, 'Why, how comfortable this room is, and how your furniture shines.'

'I use vinegar and water; my mother put store by the old ways.'

'And no wonder.' Arabella looked up at the ceiling which was astonishingly close even to her own head. 'Mr McGloughlin must find some difficulty in standing erect.'

'No, oh, you mean Ian. Yes, he stoops. I don't

144

suppose he even thinks of it any more.'

'And how useful to be able to change a gas mantle without standing on a stool as the people at home do,' said Arabella and blushed furiously. 'If I may trouble you . . .'

Mairi hurried to the desk where Colin kept his accounts and copied the address that Ian had given them on to a piece of notepaper. Arabella took it, folded it neatly and tucked it into a pocket of her dashing little jacket. 'Thank you,' she said. 'And do forgive me for disturbing you.'

She hurried over to her groom who was waiting by the horses, stepped into his hands and was pushed up into her saddle. She did not look round as they trotted away.

Mairi went back to her mangle and finished wringing out the blankets which she then pegged out on the drying green. She stood watching the wind whipping them up into a wild dance but she was seeing the delicate and lovely figure of Arabella Huntingdon standing in the front room of the house.

'She's seen where you live, Ian, and she's seen *how* we live. Maybe she'll be too fine a lady to write to one of her uncle's tenants. And if she is, Ian, then she's not worth your interest in her.'

CHAPTER FOURTEEN

It wasn't mud; it was slurpy, sucking clay. It reminded him of the sound the pigs made as they sucked up their scraps: slurp, slurp, slurp.

He stood in it, some places three to five feet

145

deep, and listened to the high explosives dropping all around him.

There were about twenty of them in the dug-out, packed tight like fish in a tin. The water came up to his knees. He looked at it lapping there like the sea on the beach at Carnoustie. Oh, just to slip down under the water. There would be cold, wet sand and shells; there would be shells and it would be salty and the seaweed would drift in front of his tired eyes until he closed them and then he would sleep, sleep, sleep, away from this madness.

His ambulance was a pile of charred metal somewhere near a place called Arras. The wounded who had been in it were charred embers too. He had to get back to them, he had to. Maybe someone had survived. Please, even just one. The soldier who had pulled him out of the blazing van, and had held him in an iron grip while the ambulance became a funeral pyre, had insisted that no one could possibly have survived the direct hit, let alone the fire. But he had to see for himself. He would wait for nightfall and then he would climb out and go back. He was an ambulance driver. He had to stay with his ambulance.

No one saw him go. He crept out of the dug-out like some primeval creature emerging out of the mud and onto dry land and he slithered back in the direction from which he thought the men had brought him. Eventually, when he was too tired to crawl any farther and too distraught to care whether or not he would be shot, he stood up and began haltingly to limp along the road.

By morning he was miles from the battlefield and he lay down in the shelter of a hedge and fell asleep.

He woke, cold, stiff, and hungry, but he was used to these sensations. He could hardly remember when he had not been cold or stiff or hungry. He stood up, slapped his arms, jumped feebly up and down and began to walk.

The joy to be away from the mud! But these were fields where men like his father had toiled for hundreds of years, coaxing a living from the reluctant soil. Now there was nothing. Not a blade of grass, not an insect. He walked on. Once or twice that first day a shadow passed overhead. It was a hawk floating, floating on the wind as he hunted carrion. There were bodies. Dear God: he would not let those birds have the bodies, dead boys who sat there for days, for weeks, with their dead eyes staring out to see if someone would come to bury them, to give them some dignity. He straightened the bodies as best he could, so that there was only the obscenity of death, no lewd gestures, no naked limbs grotesquely offered.

The sun came out and the smell rising from the fields made him sick. He fell asleep in his own vomit, not a decent healthy sleep but the exhausted state of a mind and body that is at the end of its tether. When he started awake he heard himself mumbling, 'As before,' and knew that was his prayer for the dead, and for the living dead in this war, for he had no words of prayer left. Now he expected God, if there was still a God, to know that he meant those same prayers that he had said a lifetime ago when he was young and sensitive, when he had been able to think and to feel.

He had absolutely no idea where he was but he did know that he was dying of hunger. When had he last eaten? Yesterday or was it the day before that? He passed a burned-out farmhouse and searched desperately for something, anything, that he could eat, but there was nothing.

He was unconscious when the patrol found him and he did not wake when they laid him in the back of a wagon and carried him back to their post.

He was aware of sounds, of voices that he could not understand. The smell of mown hay drifted in through the open windows on the wings of heat. Hay? Heat? How could it be? It was April, no it was May or perhaps June. Yes, he must have been in France a month or two. He had had a letter, two letters from Mairi and . . . he groped wildly at his chest . . . one from Bella.

'Bella,' he cried and woke up.

'*Bien*,' said a voice and then he felt a cool cloth on his forehead and strong arms lifting him up. A cup of water was held to his mouth and he gulped it feverishly.

'Thank you,' he said and he looked around.

He was in a hospital ward and a nurse was standing beside him. He heard her speak to someone he could not see and then she lowered him against the pillows.

The doctor came then and examined him and he spoke but Ian did not understand.

'British?' asked the doctor when he had finished poking and prying and Ian gasped, 'Yes.'

'*Bien*,' said the doctor and left him.

Later a man came who told him that to be a deserter was 'ver' bad theeng, not nice', and Ian wondered what on earth he was talking about.

But he forgot it when an orderly brought him a meal, soup, hot and thick, not like the watery rubbish he had been eating with his unit. He did

148

not recognize the flavour but he believed that it was the most wonderful taste he had ever experienced.

The man who spoke some English came back and asked him questions but his English was so poor and Ian was so weak that he did not think he was making a good job of his answers. The man seemed to think he was a deserter.

'I was looking for my ambulance,' he said over and over again.

'Regiment?' the man asked.

'Non-combatant corps,' Ian said but the face peering into his looked blank.

'Conscientious objector,' he tried. 'Pacifist.'

That was understood. The man stood up abruptly. 'We shoot *canaille* in France,' he said and stalked away.

Ian never saw him again but two days later the first nurse helped him to dress in trousers and a shirt that did not belong to him and leaning on her arm he went out and was assisted into a car. There were three French soldiers in the car and they said nothing to Ian, possibly because they spoke no English and he spoke no French, and he was driven off.

They drove for hours and, to Ian's surprise, it was autumn. They had passed one or two fields where crops had been allowed to grow or, more likely, had narrowly missed being laid waste, as had much of France. He put his hand in his pocket and the nervous soldier beside him pushed a rifle butt into his stomach. Ian removed his hand and with it the personal effects the nurse had given him, the letters from Mairi and Arabella.

'Ah,' laughed the soldier, *'votr' amante,'* and he

149

laughed knowingly and Ian, who had no idea what he had said, smiled since that seemed the best thing to do in the circumstances.

At last they came to a small town that showed few signs of having been devastated by approaching or retreating armies. They stopped at a large building in the centre and Ian was hustled inside. He was, once more, in prison.

Again he found himself in a narrow cell with a board to lie on, a piece of wood that was supposed to act as a pillow and a thin blanket which he did not think he would need, the day had been so hot and dry.

It was two days before he was allowed out of the cell and that was the day he was brought before an officer who spoke good English.

He answered the questions which were hurled at his head by a dry voice.

'Ian McGloughlin, Non-Combatant Corps, Ambulance Driver.'

'You were without uniform, identification, had been wounded, and were certainly without ambulance.'

He did wait while Ian tried to explain.

'I am an ambulance driver. My vehicle was hit by enemy fire. I was pulled out by some men of the Gordon Highlanders. The vehicle was burned with my patients inside. The Highlanders took me with them, patched me up, but I worried about my ambulance. Maybe it didn't burn completely; I had to get back to see. I just left the unit and started walking back, I think in the right direction. The last name I remember is Ypres.'

The officer looked at him from under thick black eyebrows. His eyes too were dark in his suntanned face. 'You walked a long way, *mon brave*, and you say to find a burned-out ambulance?'

'I had to see for myself. I was responsible for those men. They were all hit, every one.'

'You know what happens to deserters?'

'I did not desert.'

The officer shrugged. 'You have heard that conscientious objectors have been executed here in France? British C.O.s. You are, how they say, in between the devil and a very hard rock. The world wishes to shoot you.'

Ian said nothing.

'I believe your crazy story, *Monsieur* Ambulance Driver. We will keep you here, maybe a little more comfortable, until we can get some of your own people to take you off my hand. There are enough already here to feed.'

He stood up and walked out and Ian was left standing by the table. He remained there for some time and after a while was conscious that his legs were having some difficulty in supporting him. Should he sit in the officer's chair or wait to fall down? He compromised by leaning against the wooden table. And that was where he was when the orderly came back to take him to his cell.

The next few days were not too unpleasant. At six in the morning he was roused and given coffee. He had never had coffee before and he thought he would be unlikely to want to drink it again but at least it was hot and wet. From seven until nine thirty he went into the yard to exercise with the other prisoners and at ten he was given some soup. *Champignon*, the mushroom, became his first French word. He smiled to think how surprised Mairi would be to hear that the most delicious and

151

nourishing soup could be made from something that grew wild all over the farm. From ten thirty to almost four o'clock he was back in the yard and once one of the guards allowed the prisoners to play football. Language barriers dissolved as they ran madly about the dusty square. Ian limped or hobbled as best he could up and down; sometime in the past few months, possibly when the ambulance was hit, he had injured his leg but he was unable to remember much about the time he had been in France. Some memories were very clear and other things were a haze.

Still, he would remember these dusty, sunny days, especially the football day when everyone seemed to forget that they were prisoners, and gave themselves up to keeping a deflated ball from anyone else.

The game ended, and the exercise period, and they went in, as usual, for more soup, this time thicker and with more vegetables, mainly potatoes. After this meal they went out into the yard again and this time Ian was able to read as he walked up and down or sat in the shade. There were few books in the prison and only one in English, a tattered copy of *Pilgrim s Progress*, and since no one else wanted it, he was able to have it every day. At seven o'clock he was locked once more in his cell where there was nothing to do but stare at the walls until the light went out at nine. He would spend the time reading and re-reading Arabella's stilted, formal little note that wished him well and he would compose answers in his head. He refined them and refined them and laughed to realize that, even without paper or pencil, he was once more writing poetry.

'Well, it's certain naebody'll ever see these poems, since they cannae get written.'

His French hiatus came to a rude end one morning when he was taken out of his cell, not to the exercise yard, but to the interrogating office and saw, to his horror, that the British officer they had found to interview him was his old adversary, Captain McNeil.

'Should I save the Government the cost of a Court Martial and shoot you here and now, McGloughlin, you lily-livered bag of scum?' he said, pointing a service revolver at Ian's chest.

'I have done nothing wrong, sir,' said Ian stoically, although his heart was beating uncomfortably hard in his chest.

'First you're too scared to fight, to do your duty to your King and country, and then you desert your post. You'll be shot, McGloughlin, and I hope I'm there to see justice carried out.'

CHAPTER FIFTEEN

They had lived through this scenario before. Jack was on his horse beside the theekit pump in the yard and she was on the barrel, but it was a different horse and she was not looking for a kitten, she was cleaning out a rone. She had to work all day, every day, anything to keep her mind from worrying, worrying.

'You shouldn't be doing jobs like that, Mairi. What's yer dad thinking on?'

'He's thinking on the fact that his son is missing in action, if you must know, Jack, and he has no

153

idea that I am cleaning the rones.'

Jack dismounted and held up his hands to her. 'Come down, Mairi, and let me do that for you; it's no a lassie's job.'

Mairi looked down at him and saw how he had changed in the past two years. The eyes no longer danced with devilment. Jack Black had grown up. She allowed him to help her down from the barrel.

'Any job that needs doing is a lassie's job these days, Jack. There's a war on, in case you haven't noticed.'

He turned white beneath his ruddy complexion and she could have bitten her tongue. She had meant to be flippant, not to hurt.

'I went up against the Board, Mairi. All legal. I'm needed on the farm.'

'Oh, Jack, I'm sorry. I didn't mean anything. I wouldn't wish going to war on my worst enemy and you were never that.'

To her surprise he seized her hands. 'Then you'll start walking out with me again, Mairi?'

She pulled her hands away and started to walk towards the house. 'We've been through this . . .'

He interrupted her. 'Who are you waiting for, lass? Some daft prince tae come riding by on a white stallion? Could you no accept a man on an auld bay?'

Who was she waiting for? A picture of Robin Morrison came, unbidden, into her head. He must get leave soon. He had returned once to Britain but only to a hospital in England to recover from dysentery. His father had said that Robin was ashamed that, while his friends were dying around him, he had succumbed to a disease of the bowels. He had left the hospital as soon as he was able to

154

stand upright and was once more 'somewhere over there'. Robin, Robin's father, Ian, so many people to worry about and now Jack standing here gripping her hands again and looking at her with sad cowlike eyes. It was easier to give in than to fight.

'We can go to the pictures now and again if you like, Jack, but only as friends.'

'Och, Mairi, that'll be great. In the paper it says that we get plays and even opera in the toon these days. Whatever you'd like. I'll get the best tickets.'

'Opera? Italians screaming at one another in Italian? I wouldn't understand a word of anything like that, Jack. A good murder story or a tragedy— no, maybe not. There's enough tragedy to go around just now, isn't there?'

Immediately he was calm, concerned. 'No further word then?'

'He's disappeared into thin air. His ambulance was hit and all the wounded in it were burned to death. They say he was pulled out, but by whom?'

'Maybe the Gerries got him and he's in a camp somewhere.'

She looked at him and he saw brave far-seeing eyes. 'He's not dead, Jack. I would know. He's been the closest person to me in the world since I was six years old. I would know,' she stated again.

'It's a mess over there,' he said. 'Letters take months to get out and he was maybe hurt a wee bit when his ambulance got hit.' He thought of his old school mate actually driving an ambulance. 'I wish I could drive a car. A doctor in Dundee's got one. Everybody'll have one in a year or two.'

Mairi dismissed such nonsense. 'Aye, and in two shakes of a ram's tail, we'll all be using these

155

tractors they had at the Highland Show. Farming without horses, I ask you.'

'I'm surprised at you, Mairi. If there was ever a woman that was running helter skelter into the twentieth century it was you. I thought you'd welcome change.'

Mairi sat down on the old iron set at the farmhouse door and Jack sat beside her, his bonnet in his hands.

'Things have changed too much in the last few years, Jack. I can't keep up. So many gone, too many dead, too many missing like Ian and Sinclair, lads who should be marrying and settling down here. I want the old days back.' She stopped and let her mind remember the old days, school days when every new day was a miracle, the only concern being whether or not Robin Morrison would beat Ian to the Dux's medal, and he had, he had. And now Ian was missing somewhere in France and Robin was so far away, not only in distance but in experience. She could never meet either of them on the same terms again. She heard Robin's voice—*when are you going to stop fighting your brother's battles?*—and she began to cry.

Jack jumped up from the seat. 'Crivvens, Mairi, don't greet. Here's your father coming. He'll think I've said something.'

But Colin was too excited to notice his daughter's quickly dried tears. He was walking, almost running up the path, dogs gambolling like puppies at his heels, so infected were they by their master's good spirits.

'I met the Postie and saved his auld legs a walk,' he shouted. 'A letter, Mairi, a letter from Ian. He's alive.' For the first time he noticed Jack. 'Hello,

156

lad. Your father sent you for something? Come on in and Mairi'll make us some tea while I read this again. I didnae take it all in the first time.'

He hurried into the house but Mairi still sat. Ian alive? Her knees felt very weak as if they could not possibly support her if she were to stand up now. They had had one telegram from the War Office to tell them that Ian was missing and that had arrived weeks after their last letter from Ian himself. What if this letter had been written before the telegram was sent? What if Colin's joy were to be dashed to pieces again? She could not bear that.

'Mairi. Are you all right?' It was Jack. Jack being gentle and sympathetic; goodness, how much more was to change? That at least was a change for the better and Mairi looked up at him and smiled. He was all right, Jack, not nearly so bad as most people said; a little spoiled, nothing more.

'Thanks, Jack, it was just a shock, that's all. Thinking about Ian and talking about him and there was Dad with a letter. Didn't seem real for a moment. Let's go in and see what Ian has to say.'

Colin was sitting at the table and the light had indeed gone out of his eyes again. Even his shoulders sagged as if his great back could no longer hold up their weight.

'They're saying he's a deserter, Mairi. They're going to shoot my boy.' He held up Ian's letter and Mairi took it in trembling fingers and began to read.

Try not to worry because I know it will be all right. The truth will come out; it always does. Isn't that what you always said, Dad? The French Colonel believes me and he is speaking for me.

In the meantime, I'm in jail, but it's not too bad. Some of the jailors are decent men and some are right buggers, but isn't that what life is like everywhere. If the worst happens, believe that I was only trying to find my way back to my unit, which seems to have been wiped out in the raid that hit my ambulance. I had to see them for myself, my patients. You do understand that. I was responsible for them, and the Colonel thinks that I was probably concussed; it wasn't treated because it was a bit difficult there for a while, and so, when I left the boys who picked me up, I didn't really know what I was doing. They're letting another officer come in to question me. It will probably depend on whether or not he believes me. Mairi, if anyone asks about me, tell them I carry the letter everywhere.

Your loving son and brother,
Ian C. McGloughlin

'What's he talking about, Mairi, if anyone asks for him?'

'Later, Dad.' She could not tell him about Arabella Huntingdon while Jack was in the room.

'This sounds a bit scary, Colin,' said Jack. 'Him being in a French jail. They shoot . . .' Too late he realized what he was saying,

'My son never ran away from anything in his life, Jack Black. He volunteered for this bluidy war he doesnae believe in and he wantit tae do his job properly. Gin he was injured when his ambulance got hit, he should hae had medical attention.'

'But who will speak for him, Dad? Who will tell this officer that he's a good brave man?'

158

Colin leaned forward at the table and put his head in his hands. He was scared stiff. His laddie was in a French prison and they wanted to shoot him. For the first time in his life he had absolutely no idea what to do.

Mairi put her hand on his broad shoulders and picked up the letter. 'This French Colonel is going to speak for him.'

'Whit good's a Frenchman tae my boy?' Colin would not be consoled.

'I'd better away home,' said Jack. 'It's not a good time to stop.'

Colin did not even acknowledge him as Mairi walked with Jack to the door.

'I'm sorry, Mairi. If there's anything I can do . . . ?'

Mairi smiled bravely up at him. 'Thanks, Jack, but I've had an idea.'

'And you'll not change your mind about going to the pictures with me?'

'Maybe you'll change your mind about wanting to be seen with the sister of a deserter?'

'Oh, I'd never do that, Mairi,' said Jack as he turned his horse round and prepared to mount.

'Wrong answer,' said Mairi as she watched him ride away. 'You should have said: *Ian's no deserter.*'

She returned to the farmhouse where Colin was still sitting, head in hands. 'Dad, it's a bit early for your tea. I'd like to go out for a bit. I won't be long.'

He said nothing and Mairi looked at him sadly, her big strong father who had handled everything always, and hurried upstairs where she washed her face quickly, brushed her hair into some order and put on her Sunday dress. She was going to the Big

House.

'Sir Humphrey,' said the very superior person who answered the clanging bell on the front door, 'is not at home,' and he went to shut the door in her face.

'Please,' begged Mairi, 'I suppose I should have gone to the servants' entrance; I wasn't thinking. I *have* to see the Laird. It's really important.'

Inexorably the door was closing on her. 'Please,' begged Mairi.

'Good heavens, Beaton. There's no need to manhandle callers.' Rupert Grey-Watson in a dinner jacket and bow tie had come into the hall.

Mairi had never seen a man in evening dress before. He looked, he looked ... so ... so right. She smiled at the young man and he smiled back.

'You should really have gone to the other door. The housekeeper would have answered that one, but come along in and Beaton will show you down to her room.'

Mairi stepped into the hall but refused to go with the butler. 'I came hoping to see the Laird,' she said and was grateful that her voice did not squeak nearly so much as she had thought it would. 'He did say if he could do anything ...'

'I thought you were looking for employment, Miss, Miss ...' He abandoned the effort to remember the insignificant daughter of one of his father's poorer tenants. 'M'father's in Town, I'm afraid ...'

He broke off as they heard a door farther down the great hall open, and he turned. Arabella Huntingdon in a lovely dark blue satin dinner gown stood in the doorway.

'It's nothing, Bella, just one of the tenants with a

problem. I suppose it is a problem?'

He looked down at Mairi again. 'I say, you're the sister of, what was his name, terrific shot?'

'Ian McGloughlin.'

'Miss McGloughlin.' Arabella had hurried forward. She had a lace handkerchief in her hands and she lifted it in a graceful gesture to her lips. 'Miss McGloughlin,' she said again. 'Is anything wrong?'

'Come into the library,' said Rupert. 'The entire household is going to hear your business if we stand out here wittering at one another.'

He propelled Mairi into the room that Arabella had just left and even in her distress, Mairi could see how beautiful it was, with its high ornate ceilings, its huge windows draped with dark blue velvet curtains that were held back by gold cords, its dark shiny bookcases with shelf after shelf of dark leather-bound books.

'I'm sorry to disturb you,' Mairi said. Somehow the room calmed her. She was no longer afraid. 'We have had a distressing letter from my brother and I hoped to ask Sir Humphrey to . . . intervene, use his influence, I don't know.'

'Sit down, Miss McGloughlin,' said Arabella gently. 'Rupert, be an angel and pour us some wine.'

As he turned to do her bidding she whispered agitatedly to Mairi, 'Don't mention my letter, please. Ah, Rupert, how nice. Here, Miss McGloughlin, sip this slowly. It's one of my uncle's best clarets.'

'Claret doesn't travel,' said Rupert. 'Just as well, or he'd have taken it with him. Now, let's have the problem, Miss McGloughlin.'

161

Mairi put the glass down carefully on a little table by her seat and clenched her hands on her lap. She had to say the right thing, she had to. Arabella was on her side, she knew, but she could tell nothing from Rupert's demeanour. And he was the one who could help, if he chose.

'Ian volunteered in the spring. He became an ambulance driver and he was sent to France. So many battles, he said, and no rest between. They have to try to get the wounded out. He wrote about how content he was. He hates the war but he felt he was doing something useful, something that wasn't against his principles. Then he disappeared and we heard that his entire unit was hit by aircraft fire; Ian was missing, presumed dead. But now he's sent a letter. He's in prison and they say he's a deserter.'

Arabella gasped and again the useless little scrap of lace went to her lips. Rupert gave her a strange look but turned to Mairi.

'Explain, Miss McGloughlin.'

'He was pulled out of his burning ambulance by some men of the Gordon Highlanders but they wouldn't let him go back; he wanted to check his passengers. He *needed* to check them. They were his responsibility. He thinks he was injured because he's lost a few months, can't understand where July and August went, but he tried to go back, in case, just . . . I know it sounds strange but he needed to see for himself. A French patrol found him and he's in jail. The French Colonel knows he's not a deserter but it depends on . . .' She could say no more.

Rupert's face was cold. 'And what do you expect my father to do, Miss McGloughlin?'

'He said, if there was ever anything he could do.'

'He has no military rank, no influence.'

Arabella almost sprang up from her chair. 'But you do, Rupert. You're a lawyer and a soldier. You know Ian would never desert. I think he's so wonderful to try to find his men.'

'Your feelings are embarrassingly obvious, Bella, and would do nothing in a court of law. Evidence is what's needed, not hysterical outpourings from silly little girls.'

White-faced, Mairi stood up. She had failed. She would leave before she humiliated herself further. 'Thank you for your patience,' she said quietly. 'I'm sorry to have disturbed you.'

'Do sit down, Miss McGloughlin,' said Rupert. 'My father would at least expect me to find out as much as I can about your brother. He had him in mind as gamekeeper here one day and, Lord knows but good servants are getting harder and harder to find.'

CHAPTER SIXTEEN

In March 1917 the German Army retreated to the Hindenburg Line and on 6 April the United States of America entered the conflict by declaring war on Germany. In May American destroyers arrived in Britain, which had been suffering from the unrestricted German submarine warfare.

Mairi helped her furious father deliver two sets of twin calves, male and female. Colin was angry because he knew that for some reason the males would be useless. Male twins always were. Thank

163

God most of the sheep were dropping twins or even triplets in some cases; no problems with male lambs. Another good year. The war was good for farmers, good enough that Colin could send a donation to the Scottish Rural Workers' Friendly Society which had told members that there were now fifteen thousand members on active service and so even more money was needed to help the Society make small sickness and disability payments. Everyone was looking for money. Churches wanted funds to help with Sunday morning refreshments to soldiers. A Parcel Fund for Prisoners of War had started.

Colin worked as he had never worked before and he had always been tireless. Only by exhausting his mind and his body could he hope to fall asleep when he reached the haven of the old double bed he had slept in alone for over twenty years.

'When's somebody going to ask for a donation for people like me, Mairi?' he asked in despair as he watched his daughter work beside him. He had never wanted her to soil her hands with farm work. Useless for her to tell him that she was happy. How could she be happy?

But Mairi was happy, as happy as she could be. She loved tying herself into a pair of Ian's old trousers and working outside, day in, day out. She loved watching the sky in all its moods; she enjoyed seeing lambs making up games to play with one another. If only, if only . . . but she would not think, she would not allow herself to think.

'Mairi.'

The voice from behind her was a voice she dreamed about but had not heard for too long. She forgot that she was wearing her brother's clothes;

164

she forgot that her nails were broken and her hands were dirty. She turned round and joy shone out of her eyes.

'Robin,' she said and threw herself into his arms and then, rigid with embarrassment, she pulled herself back. 'Sorry,' she stumbled. 'It's just so lovely to have someone come back alive.'

She sensed him pull away too. She looked up at him. There were grey wings of hair above his ears. Robin? Grey? He was only twenty-eight. I'm twenty-six. We forgot to celebrate my birthday. She laughed ruefully and Robin smiled, relaxed again.

'Do I look so funny?'

'No, you look . . . distinguished. As you should, a decorated soldier.'

'I've only just heard about Ian. Can you tell me what happened? I didn't write because I didn't know, Mairi, not because I didn't care.'

'It's so wrong, so very wrong.' She looked up at him again and this time she saw the lines of pain etched into his face. 'Come in and sit down, Robin. I have some soup on.'

He went with her and she saw that his left leg was stiff. 'You didn't get that skiting down the Schoolhouse steps, did you?' she said, and was delighted to hear his shout of joyous boyish laughter.

'I could have wrung your neck, Mairi McGloughlin. That hurt like Hell. Small consolation to note that you did look back to make sure I hadn't broken my neck.'

He went to the table and she noted that he was glad to sit. He saw her looking at him and sat up straight. 'I'm almost fit,' he said. 'One more check up by the medics and it's back to work.'

'Work? Is that what you call it?'

'Calling it work keeps me sane, Mairi. *Back to killing Germans* doesn't fill me with enthusiasm.' He grabbed her hand and looked at the dirt engrained in her fingers. 'Who first said war is Hell?'

'Probably one of your silly old Romans,' she said but she did not pull her hand away. 'I'll get the soup, Robin,' she said gently, 'and then we'll talk.'

He released her and she went into the kitchen and tried to scrub her hands clean and then she filled two bowls with her vegetable soup and carried them back into the front room.

'I've coddled a couple of eggs in the soup, Robin. We're allowed to keep any that are cracked and one of our hens has an awful habit of pushing one or two eggs out of the nest every now and again.'

'Long may she continue to be so clumsy,' he said as he almost inhaled the soup. 'We're having an awful lot of oatmeal brose at home just now.'

'Isn't Jessie Turnbull doing for your father? I thought she was a good housekeeper.'

'Oh, the place is immaculate and Dad says she kept good fires going last winter. She's doing the best with what she can get.'

'No flair,' Mairi pronounced complacently. 'I'll give you some of my oatmeal cakes to take home with you. Oatmeal, potatoes, a cracked egg . . .' She stopped talking. She was deliberately chattering to avoid talking about Ian.

'He did not desert his post,' she said.

'No one who knows Ian would ever think he did, Mairi.'

She smiled at him gratefully. 'I'll never be able

166

to thank Captain Grey-Watson enough. I'm sure that his intervention prevented Ian from being shot. The officer who was sent in to question him was the one who had spoken to him when he went into Dundee to join up. He called him a Conchie, said he had never wanted to fight, but Rupert, Captain Grey-Watson, explained that Ian had enlisted before he was conscripted, and he was heading back for the battlefield when the French patrol found him. That was in his favour and the Highlanders sent a statement about kitting him out with bits and pieces because his uniform had to be destroyed. He had no identity tags or papers, nothing but a letter from me and . . . one from a friend.'

'Why is he in prison?'

'I don't know. It's not fair but Ian says nothing is fair and to remember that they could have shot him. He's in a prison camp, hard labour. They said it was a warning for others that they won't be treated so leniently. He had what was called a hearing, not a full court martial, and I think they didn't really know what to do with him.'

'Can I write to him?'

She looked at him steadily and saw Ian's best friend, Ian's oldest friend. They had gone travelling after all, but not together. For a moment she saw them, backs against an old tree, books of poetry in their hands. Where were those innocent boys now? Did they still live in the grown men?

'I'll get the address.' She went to the desk where Colin kept Ian's letters. 'There will always be this stigma, Robin,' she said, her back to him so that he could not see her face. 'He's in prison, doing hard labour, and so obviously he did something wrong;

167

that's what people will think.'

He was behind her. She had heard him scrape the chair back from the table, listened to the uneven footsteps as he dragged his bad leg across the floor. He put his hands on her bowed shoulders and turned her round to face him. How easily she fitted into the circle of his arms.

'What people think doesn't matter, Mairi. It's what we *know* that matters.'

'Fine words, Robin.' She could not meet his eyes.

He lifted her chin with his right hand and bent slowly until his lips touched hers, gently, sweetly, the kiss of a child and then his arms went around her and he pulled her to him as if he could not get her close enough and his kiss became powerful, demanding, the kiss of a man. She could not move even had she wanted to move and she did not; she wanted to stay there for ever, with Robin's body blocking out the light, the pain, the worry.

He let her go. 'You'll notice I was careful to hold your hands down, Miss McGloughlin. My jaw has a long memory and I'm a wee bit frail at the moment.'

'I didn't hit you that hard,' she said and they were bickering again and then Robin stopped it by kissing her again and this time her hands were, of their own accord, around his neck and she was kissing him back as heartily as he was kissing her.

'And I look such a fright,' she said breathlessly as he released her rather abruptly.

He limped back to the table. 'I didn't notice,' he said and she wanted to hit him but she couldn't. She knew that she would never hit him again; she doubted that she would ever want to squabble with

168

him again either. She wanted him to kiss her again. That had been very satisfactory. She had forgotten her old trousers, her broken finger nails, her untidy hair. She went to the table and sat down beside him and they looked at one another.

'What a lot of time I wasted thinking you were a wee nuisance.'

'I was.'

'I would like to kiss you again.'

'Me too.'

'I can't. You are having the most extraordinary effect on me.'

'I know. I used to have that effect on Jack too, but I liked it with you.'

He smiled. 'It won't be long now, Mairi. I think Russia and perhaps some of the smaller Eastern countries, places like Romania, will sue for peace soon. Everybody has had enough. Almost a whole generation has gone. Not just us but the French, the Germans, the Italians, the Russians. So much waste. You should have seen Italy before the war. Unbelievable beauty and history and art and music all tumbled together, and the smell of Italy, like nowhere else; lemons and garlic and olive oil and heat. Heat smells, Mairi, and it carries the smell of ripening fruit. I'm afraid to go again. La Belle France? Very little *belle* about it now.' He stood up. 'I have to go. When do you expect your father? I would like to have waited to see him but . . . oh Hell, Mairi, kiss me again and tell me that wasn't a dream.'

She was only too happy to comply and the next few minutes were among the loveliest the young couple had ever lived through. 'I must go,' he whispered against her mouth as he kissed her.

'I know,' she whispered back but she made no attempt to loosen herself from his strong arms. 'We have wasted so much time, Robin.'

'You never wrote to me once, not even when I was wounded.'

'I thought Edith . . .'

'Who's Edith?'

'Jack's sister.'

'Who's Jack?'

'I don't remember.'

This time Mairi broke free first. She had to while she could still think. 'He'll be in any minute, my father.'

'I won't wait,' said Robin from the door. 'My father will think I'm in a ditch somewhere.'

'Wait, wait, the oatmeal puddings.'

'Tomorrow, bring them tomorrow, in daylight when the whole village can see you walking into our bachelor paradise and my father in school with his snotty-nosed bairns.'

Snotty-nosed. Billy Soutar. 'Oh, Robin, he's dead, Billy Soutar.'

'I know, but we're alive, Mairi, and from now on it's roses all the way.'

*   *   *

There were few roses growing for them. Robin went to see the medical board and was declared fit to return to his unit and soon she heard that he was somewhere in France and, as she read the papers, she prayed that he was nowhere near a place called Passchendaele or somewhere named Cambrai. She wrote to him every day and she wrote to Ian at his oddly named 'Home Office Work Centre' where he

170

was building a road with several other ill-assorted prisoners.

> Thank God they have sent a few skilled Irish navvies to show us what to do with the dynamite or we'd blow the whole place up and ourselves with it.

Ian did not mention Arabella and so Mairi felt that she could not mention the young aristocrat either. At least there seemed to be no ill treatment of prisoners in this work camp. Ian had been beaten up several times in his first prison and had spent a great deal of time in solitary confinement. Unlike too many others, he had not gone insane, possibly because he had continued to write his poetry in his head. Colin had been furiously angry when Ian had admitted to being bullied but the father's anger was directed, not against the bullies, but against his son.

'Why doesn't he lay a few of them out, Mairi? He's strong as an ox and a bully needs to be put in his place.'

'It's because he's stronger that he doesn't fight, Dad, and forbye, maybe there's one holding him while another one thumps him,' Mairi had said and had gone off to make Robin smile when he read her next letter by telling him all about the hopelessly inept Ian being let loose with dynamite.

It had been a great relief when Ian had been transferred to the work camp where some of the guards were soldiers too badly wounded to return to their units. If the powers that be had thought these men would make life miserable for the pacifists, they had miscalculated hopelessly. The war had taught the soldiers cruel lessons. They rejected the idea of war as wholeheartedly as did their prisoners.

Now Mairi sat at the table in the front room and watched rain streaming down the windows as she waited for Colin. She had not started their supper, for a tinker family camping in the nearby woods had brought her a trout and it would not be cooked until Colin was already seated at the table.

He was late. He had walked into Arbroath to pay some bills and to talk to the bank manager, but he should have been back by now. No doubt he had met another farmer at the bank and they were deep in the accounts of the prices of winter feed.

Mairi went back to her letter to Robin. She had just written: *and Jessie came over and I showed her how to make the puddings,* when the door opened and she looked up to see her father standing there staring at her. Something had happened; she just knew it but she would stay very calm.

'Ach, Dad, you're soaked. I'll fetch the bath and you can have a nice wash here in front of the fire while I cook the fish.' She was prattling. She did not want him to tell her.

He could feel her fear. He had to get it over with. 'I've joined up, lass,' he said wearily and stopped dejectedly in front of her, water soaking into the rag rug on which he stood.

They looked at one another steadily, giving and receiving messages in some wordless communication.

'Then you'll need your tea,' she said at last. 'I'll fill the bath and let you steep for a while.'

He waited until she had gone into the kitchen and then he sat down on a wooden chair—he would not soak her cushions—and began to

172

struggle with the knots on his boots. Mairi came in but she did not look at him as she put the tin bath in front of the hearth and began to fill it from the kettle bubbling away at the back of the fire. She took the empty kettle with her and he heard her going out to the yard to the theekit pump. He'd better lag it well in the morning. God knows when it would get done again.

She came back with some clean underclothes, his other shirt and trousers, a pail of hot water from her range and the cold water from the pump; this she put on the large hook that hung from the chimney. The hot water she emptied into the bath.

'I've another pail,' she said, 'and that should give you a nice hot bath. Don't take too long. Fish cooks before you have time to turn your back on it.'

'Mairi, please, lassie, I have to explain.'

'That you're so ashamed of your son that you'll go in his stead? Ian's not a coward, Dad; he's a braver man than you'll ever understand.'

'Ach, don't hate me, Mairi. It's just something I feel I have to do.'

'For the neighbours? And what about the farm, Dad?'

He looked stunned. 'I didnae even think on it,' he said after a pause. 'You'll manage, lassie. You've always been a better farmer than Ian.'

She did not smile. 'You'd best get your bath before the water gets cold.'

When he was undressed he lowered himself gingerly into the hot water, lay back enjoying the euphoric feeling that unaccustomed hot water always gave him, and then splashed loudly for fear that Mairi should come in and see him in his nakedness.

173

When he was finished he stepped out cautiously and pulled himself, half wet, into the dry clothes. Then he took the bath outside and emptied the dirty water into the drain. Mairi had his fish on the table when he returned.

'Sit down with me, lass. I'm leaving in the morning and there's a lot we have to talk about.'

She perched on the edge of her chair. She was not comfortable. She did not want to stay. He knew that if he said the wrong thing she would explode from the chair like a pheasant scared up by a dog.

'Can you understand that I'm scared and excited at the same time? I'm no an old man, Mairi, though I've behaved like one often enough since I lost your mam. My youth went with her and is buried in the Kirk yard but I've got a second chance now. This war is wrong but Ian sees the wrong wrongs. There are wrongs that decent men have to make better and the world is full of them the noo. Evil and wickedness is marching all over Europe and it has tae be stopped and I think I can help. I'm no an auld man, Mairi,' he said again, 'and too many laddies that don't ken what they're doing are being killt. Maybe if same mair aulder ones that ken the front end of a gun frae the back end were tae join me, we could lick the Hun in a month or two and be back tae help with the spring sowing and my boy would be out of that damned work camp and home where he should be.' He stopped talking and looked at her steadily. 'Will you care for our land here for me while I care for it over there?'

She nodded wordlessly.

'The Blacks'll help—gin ye need any help,' he added quickly, 'and just maybe they'll let Ian oot tae work the farm. I've heard of that being done. Even some fighting men have been released for a while tae help with the harvest.'

She looked up at him fearfully.

'No that that's why I did it but, you never ken, lass, it micht help my laddie, his auld man marching tae the front. I'm getting a kilt the morn. Your dad's in the Black Watch, Mairi McGloughlin, the finest regiment in the world, bar none.' He stood up. 'Private Colin McGloughlin of the Fifth Battalion at your service, Madame.'

For the first time in over twenty years he enfolded his daughter in his arms and let her cry till she was exhausted. His face too was wet but men don't cry, do they?

Mairi went with him to the station the next morning. 'If you see Robin . . . ?'

'I'll no kiss him for you, lassie.' Colin hugged her. 'Noo that I'm in, it's just a matter of time, lass, and then I'll be back and I'll bring your Robin with me and we'll have a wedding Angus will talk about for years. You'll write tae me? Is there enough paper in Angus for all the letters you write?'

'More than enough,' Mairi said. She felt old this morning, old, old, old. Much older than her father who was babbling like a nervous schoolboy. 'I'll write as often as I can. The farm's lost its best worker . . .'

'Talk tae Jack. He's got broad shoulders. The neighbours will help if they can and maybe you'll get some of these land girls that wifie Macgregor is teaching. I have tae say the ones I've heard aboot are doing a grand job. Watch oot for the tinkers when they find oot I'm not in the house. You'll need to lock the door at night now and keep at least one dog in with you. Bluidy hell, the things I didn't think on when I was feeling that patriotic.'

'I'll be fine, Dad. I'll maybe get some woman in to live while you're away. I'll be fine.'

With that Colin had to be content and he stood at the window and watched his daughter until the train rounded a corner and she was gone.

*   *   *

Mairi squared her shoulders and went back to the farm. This was what she had always wanted, wasn't it, to run a farm? She would never ask Jack or his father for help and so she looked for help for herself and found it in the strangest place. There was a news item about a soldier's wife who was going to be put out of her council home because, out of the twenty-three shillings a week she had to live on, she could not afford rent. The woman had three children, two boys and a little girl. Mairi wrote to the paper offering them a home with part-time work for the mother and the two boys.

She wrote to her father.

The boys are a bit rough but the Dominie will soon straighten them out and they are both fascinated by the farm and are pleased to be away from the town. The wee girl's nice and I've given her all my old frocks. Do we ever throw anything away? Mrs Baxter, Milly, is clean and capable and she is going to take over the house while I work full time on the farm. She wants to try with the hens too and now that Angus and Bert have stopped chasing them, I'm sure everything will be fine. Can you imagine the

176

bairns were scared witless by the dogs? The only ones they'd ever seen were fierce brutes. Imagine how awful to live all your life up a stair in a big tenement. They find it too quiet here but once they learn to listen they'll hear the night noises.

Milly and wee Jean are in your room and Milly is so grateful to have a home that I'm sure everything will work out well.

She did not tell him that Bert, the younger of the boys, had drawn pictures all over Ian's precious books, and she certainly did not tell either her father or her brother about the subject of his precocious artistic endeavours.

She told Colin instead how pretty the winter skyline was and he stood in a trench ankle-deep in water and tried desperately to picture his fields.

Later she told him that bread had gone up to an impossible 8d for a small loaf and admitted that she had been allowed to send some to Ian in his prison camp where the food was barely enough for survival. Colin saw boys his son's age and younger die horribly every day, with nothing gained, and he began to think with his reason and not with his heart and he wondered how his boy was coping in a prison camp, he who had been happiest sitting under a tree. And he worried about the responsibility he had thrust on his daughter who had now accepted even more. How could she cope with the farm, and the house, and now a complete stranger and three children?

'It's 1917. It's got to end this year and I'll go home to my fields and Ian will come home, and Robin. He and Mairi will marry and this soldier will

177

return and he'll take his wife and bairns back to their closie, and everything will be the way it was before this madness came over us all.'

CHAPTER SEVENTEEN

Cleaning out the cattle shed was one of Mairi's least favourite jobs but it was one that had to be done. Colin had prided himself on the fact that his inbye cattle were always kept as fresh as possible and so Mairi was standing up to her knees in urine-soaked straw shovelling it into a pile as quickly as possible. Her back hurt and her arms hurt but at least she could no longer smell the warm sickly smell of the soiled straw. The human body, she often felt, was incredibly able to adapt itself. After a while the nose became so used to stink that it no longer noticed it.

She noticed the smell of the clean straw though. That first forkful conjured up visions of summer fields full of waving, dancing cereal crops and the feel of the warm sun as it turned the fields golden.

'Mairi, there's a mannie wants tae see you.' Jean Baxter, in one of Mairi's own outgrown frocks, was standing in the doorway. Jean should have been at school but, as a result of the recent bad weather, she had had a bad cold and her mother had kept her at home for a few days. Mairi had enjoyed helping the child with the work the Dominie had sent home but the experience had reminded her of how long it had been since she had picked up a book other than her father's account books. Now she smiled at Jean. Who could it be disturbing her

178

in the middle of a busy day? Someone from the estate office? No, the lease was in order. 'Who is it, Jean? If it's a travelling salesman, tell him to talk to your mum.'

'It's yon mannie on the horse. Will you ask him to let me up while you two are talking?'

Jack? In the middle of a working day? Who was cleaning out his byres? She threw down her fork, pushed her hair back from her face with rather dirty hands and stomped in her wellington boots out into the steading. Jack was standing seemingly deep in contemplation of a large puddle which a kitten was patting tentatively. He smiled when he saw her.

'I know you said you didnae fancy this, Mairi, but it's never been sung in Arbroath afore and they say it's got some nice tunes in it.' He handed her an advertisement cut from the local paper and while she read it, he lifted Jean on to the old horse's back. 'Don't fret. He'll no move unless I tell him.'

Mairi looked up from her reading. 'Friedrich Von Flotow? What kind of name is that? It's not Italian.'

'Well, the name of the man that wrote it isn't important. "Martha" is a good lassie's name and so it should be something to take our minds off the war for an hour or two. I cannae say I really fancy it myself, no having heard opera afore, but the main singer's Welsh, Mr Ewen Jones. The paper cries him, *the brilliant Welsh tenor*. If you don't fancy that they're doing one cried "Rigoletto" but that's bound to be Italians.'

Mairi looked at him. She did not want to get involved again but it would be nice to put on a dress and stockings and go out, leaving the house and the farm and all the problems that the last few years had brought, just for a few hours. 'Jack, you know I'm writing to Robin Morrison.'

He looked straight into her eyes. 'I heard. I'm asking you to go to the opera, not to get married, Mairi.'

'Well, thank you, Jack. This "Martha" would be nice.'

He grinned. 'Good. I'll get tickets.' He took her arm and led her away from the horse with its perfectly content passenger. 'How's your lodgers getting on? My mother met Mrs Baxter on the school road. She seems a nice enough body.'

'They're not lodgers, Jack, not strictly speaking. Milly is working for me and the boys work after school and on Saturday and they both worked full time during the tattie holidays. Anyone over twelve can work. Wee Jean there was furious that she's too young but I've said I'll find something for her to do to earn a few pennies.'

He looked at Jean who was leaning on the horse's neck whispering into his twitching ear. 'Seems a nice enough wee lassie. What are you going to do when your dad comes back?'

'Corporal Baxter will probably get back at the same time, so it will all work out.'

Jack shrugged. 'I hope so. You could end up with permanent lodgers.'

Mairi had worried about that self-same problem herself many many times. What if anything happened to Milly's husband? She could hardly throw the poor woman and her children out on the streets again when their presence became a nuisance.

'Jack, I'm in the middle of mucking out . . .' she

180

began.

'I know,' he said with a smile. 'I could smell you from the gate.' He turned away. 'Tomorrow night then. It starts at quarter past eight so I'll fetch you about half past seven. Don't wear your wellies.'

She laughed and watched him as he walked back to the horse. He did not lift the girl down immediately but, instead, led the old horse around the steading a few times talking to Jean all the while. Where had Jack Black learned to get along so well with children? A new side. Mairi liked it and was smiling as she returned to her work.

She wrote to tell Robin that she was going to the opera. He had been several times when he lived in Rome and had enjoyed himself.

'Damn, should I wait to let Robin take me? Should this be something I experience first with him?'

Too late to think of that and Mairi allowed excitement to build up as she prepared for her evening out. The boys were banished to the barn as she and Milly heated up kettles of water so that she could take a bath and wash her hair in front of the kitchen fire. Milly professed to be 'good with hair' and after Mairi had towel-dried her hair by the fire, Milly twisted the long auburn curls up into an elegant roll on top of her head.

'You're losing weight, lassie,' said Milly as she helped Mairi into her best costume, the one she had bought for the picnic, and had rarely worn since. 'You'll need tae dae something about that. A man likes a nice armful in his bed and your Robin with his Latin and Greek is nae different frae any other man.'

Bed? Mairi was shocked by the coarseness of

Milly's speech but then she realized that Milly was, by her own lights, merely being practical.

'I'll put more butter on my bread in the morning,' she said lightly and Milly was scandalized.

'At three shillings and sixpence the pound when it should only be just over the two shillings? You will not! You'll jist have to stop running around madly daing the work of three men.'

'When the war's over, Milly.'

'Aye, we'll baith stay in bed all morning eating cakes.'

This picture was so funny that they both started to laugh.

'Goodness, is a belly laugh no fell good for you. There, lassie, you're a picture.'

Mairi had to agree. It was so long since she had made an effort that she was pleased with how she looked.

So was Jack. 'You look good enough to eat,' he said.

'Anything looks good after war rations, Jack,' said Mairi lightly. She did not like the sudden gleam in Jack's eyes.

'Can you no take a compliment, lassie? Oor Edith's like that an all. You say, *My that's a bonny blouse* and she says, *What are you after?*'

'Sorry, Jack. I'm out of practice.'

'And whose fault is that? Come on, we'll away and see what this Grand Opera is all about.'

They went to the Palace Theatre and found that they were not alone in seeking a respite from the cares of the day. Almost every seat was taken. Mairi sat beside Jack and enjoyed looking around at the rather care-worn opulence of the old theatre.

Without exception, the audience had made an effort and she even saw a lady in a purple evening gown and a diamond necklace. At least she thought it was diamonds.

At last the gas lights were turned down and the music started. Oh, how different from dances at the Kirk Hall. This was Music with a capital M. Mairi sat and let it flow over her. At first she was distressed that she had no idea what the cast was singing about but she read the synopsis in the programme at the interval and then sat back just to enjoy the rest of the performance. John Ridding's English Opera and his Welsh tenor were an unqualified success.

'Pity they didn't say their words between their big songs,' was Jack's comment as they drank a cup of strong sweet tea before setting off on the dark road home.

'Oh, I loved it,' said Mairi thoughtlessly. 'I kept wondering whether Robin had heard this when he was in Italy . . .' Too late she realized what she was saying.

'That's nice,' said Jack. 'Thank you very much.'

'I didn't mean to hurt you, Jack. I told you about Robin.'

'You told me you were writing letters to him, not that you swoon about him every minute.'

'I don't and I'm sorry I hurt you. I'm very grateful that you took me to the opera, Jack.'

'All right.' He drained his cup and stood up. 'We'd best get on the road.'

Chastened, Mairi stood up. How stupid. She had never intended to hurt him and she was grateful that he had taken her out for the evening. She wanted to go home and write to Robin, telling him

183

that she had loved the music and the singing and that she would love to go again. For two hours she had been lifted right out of herself, aware of nothing but the sound and the knowledge that even remotely she was in touch with the man she loved. One more thing, one more thing that they could share. She chattered inanely to Jack, trying to make amends, going over the costumes and the scenery and the cleverness of the lighting effects but he said nothing and eventually she gave up and they made the rest of their way in silence.

Mairi thought the journey would never end. She could hardly wait to see the lamplight shining out of the darkness. Milly would be there, and the children. Their homework would be done and the boys, no doubt, would be arguing about bedtime.

She was wrong. Angus and Bert had been so well behaved that, had their mother not had a great deal to think about, she might well have wondered why they had gone off so uncomplainingly after their sleepy sister.

Angus and Bert did not like Jack. They did not know why and would have argued fiercely if it had been pointed out to them that they were jealous. They knew only that Mairi belonged to them: her father, her brother, even her love were far away. She had given them a home and their mother dignity and they were her champions.

'He pits one finger on her and I'll hae his heid aff,' whispered Angus as they crept from the house.

'But what if she likes it,' argued Bert. He had seen a film and he knew that girls liked to be kissed.

'Likes it? Likes Jack Black when there's . . .' He realized in growing maturity that he had been

184

about to say: 'there's me', and he shied away from such an admission '...when there's Robin Morrison.'

Bert said nothing but nodded his head in the dark. Yes, there was Robin Morrison. He crept along behind his big brother until they were well clear of the steading and then he walked boldly beside him towards the town.

Unaware of his reception committee Jack stopped the buggy when they were almost within sight of the farmhouse.

'So you're grateful, Mairi. Show me how much,' he said and putting his arms around her pulled her to him and began to kiss her.

At first Mairi was too shocked to move and when he thought that she was acquiescing Jack began to kiss her more brutally and to her horror she felt his tongue thrusting into her mouth.

She gasped and pulled back, struggling, but he paid no attention. He held her with one hand as his free hand sought for the buttons on her coat and she began to struggle even more wildly.

'Oh, I like a bit of a fight, Mairi,' he said. 'Come on.' Now his hands were inside her coat and she could feel him fondling her breasts through the thin wool of her best dress.

He took his mouth off hers for a moment. 'Christ, Mairi, it's months since I've had a woman.'

He pushed her down on to the floor of the buggy and his hand was lifting her dress. She would die. She knew she would. She tried to cry out but his mouth, his horrible tongue choked her and then suddenly Jack stopped and she heard a voice.

'Get aff her right noo, you bluidy bastard or I'll blow your head off.'

185

The Baxter boys, such unprepossessing figures of legendary knights in shining armour, were standing beside the buggy and in the strong hands of thirteen-year-old Angus was Colin's favourite shotgun. It was pointing at Jack's stomach. No doubt Angus felt that 'blow your head off' sounded better than 'blow your stomach off'.

Mairi started to laugh hysterically and then to cry.

'Come on, Mairi,' said Bert. 'Gees your hand and come doon aff there. Mam's waiting up for you and we thought we'd come and meet you. She disnae ken that, mind, so dinnae tell her.'

Mairi found her hand held in the warm soft grasp of a twelve-year-old but there was strength there for he helped her down from the buggy and as she wavered his grip strengthened. Little boy Galahads. She loved them.

She stumbled away from Jack with the boys and then she was at the house and before the boys could hide the door was open and Milly was there.

'Mercy. What happened to you?' she asked, taking one look at Mairi's face and then another at those of her sons. She did not fail to notice the gun in her eldest child's young hands. 'You put that back right now afore I leather your backside. Just wait till your father gets home.'

'We saved Mairi, Mam,' explained Bert as Angus, too dignified to explain himself to his mother, stalked off to shut the shotgun in its cupboard. 'Thon mannie was trying you know what and we thought Mairi was liking it and then Angus saw she was trying to fight so he stuck the gun in his ribs. He got a real fleg, I'll tell you.'

'I'll bet he did,' said Milly and began to laugh

186

and Mairi began to cry and found herself wrapped in a woman's arms and comforted.

'Away and tell your brother I think he's a wee treasure and I'll no tell your dad, and then put the kettle on and we'll all have some cocoa.'

'I was so lonely, Milly,' sobbed Mairi, 'and I wanted to put up my hair and go to the theatre and feel like a woman, not a farmer, and to forget Dad and Ian and even Robin just for a while.'

'I know, lassie, but listen tae me. If you was a millionaire what would you rether have, a bit steak or a quarter of mince?'

'Steak,' sniffed Mairi.

'Well then, men are like steak and mince, lass, and once you've found the one for you he's the steak and so you dinnae bother with mince. You wait fer yer steak, even if you have tae wait an affie time. Look at me. I met my Jim when I was in the Mills at fifteen and he joined up tae get a regular job. Twenty year we've been marrit and he's been away maist of that time but dae I go the dancin' with other soldiers' wives and maybe pick up a wee mannie for a night or two, I do not. I wait for Jim and it's mair than worth the days and nights of loneliness. He's my top steak.'

'And Robin's mine.'

'Then we'll wait thegither.'

'We will.'

'Good, now go and wash yer face and I'll make some cocoa and then we'll away tae bed for there's work waiting.'

Mairi thought of Jack and the unexpected or unwanted end to a pleasant evening for only a few minutes and then her healthy young body demanded sleep.

187

She woke early as always and washed and dressed in the dark before opening her curtains to look out at the farm and the sea way, way beyond. There were still some stars in the sky and a glimmer of moonlight stroked the water. As Mairi watched, the blue-grey of the sky became tinged with pink as the sun struggled to oust his sister moon from his place in the sky.

'Sun, moon, and stars in the sky together. Maybe I should wake the bairns to let them see.'

She decided to leave the young Baxters, deciding that the moon and the stars would have quite disappeared before the children's tousled heads could be forced from their pillows. It was pleasant to sit alone watching the play of light in the sky. The pink turned red, great huge burning banners stretching across the sky just where it met the grey-blue of the sea.

'Shepherd's warning? No, that's only when the red is in the sky late in the morning, not now at the birth of the day.'

The remembrance that the world was at war cut across Mairi's day-dreaming. She thought of her father, her brother, and Robin. How beautiful was the sky under which they were waking to another day? She prayed that it was as lovely as this one. Colin and Ian were aware of the sky and the games the sun and the moon played at four-thirty on a winter morning. Was Robin? Had he ever seen the birth of a day? Or were all the soldiers from all the armies awake and alert as they waited for the sun to rise to show them how best to attack and kill their enemies?

'Oh, let them all see beauty,' Mairi thought sadly as she turned from the window and went downstairs and outside to the barns to the softly lowing cattle who pushed up their heads and blew softly at her as she walked across the steading.

Later that morning Mairi intercepted the postman on his bicycle. There were no letters for Mairi but two for Milly from friends in Dundee.

'She'll need them,' said the postie as he told Mairi grimly that among the list of names in the post office window was that of Corporal James Baxter—killed in action.

This time it was Mairi's arms that did the comforting.

CHAPTER EIGHTEEN

Would the misery never end? Fourteen-year-old Angus Baxter ran away to join the Army. He was going to kill the German who had, according to the distraught boy, murdered his father.

It was the Dominie who went to Edinburgh to bring him home.

'He's a bright lad, Mairi,' he said when they had Angus upstairs and in bed, his mother sitting by his side. 'Another Ian. No poetic talent but a very good mathematical mind. I hoped to encourage Mrs Baxter to keep him at the school.' He looked at Mairi. 'Things are going to be very difficult now.'

Mairi sighed. 'They're all right here for now, Mr Morrison, and by the time the war is over we'll have thought of something.'

Things are going to be very difficult now. She supposed he meant that when Colin came home there would be no room for Milly and her children;

189

one more problem. For herself Mairi could hardly see that things could get any worse than they were already. Both Colin and Robin had been wounded and were recuperating in the same hospital in France. Ian was somewhere in Italy—she could hardly bear it that war had taken him to the land he had dreamed of as a boy—and now, just as it seemed that Milly was able to walk around as if she no longer saw an unbridgeable chasm opening at her feet, Angus had frightened her like this. He was a big strapping lad and had fooled several people before one overworked recruiting officer had taken a second look and sent him home to grow up.

'And I can't even write Robin a loving letter,' thought Mairi as she sat staring into the fire after the Dominie had left. How nice it would be to explain the difference between steak and mince but Robin had no real idea of how Mairi felt about him. His letters were the letters of a friend, as if he was somewhat embarrassed by his behaviour on his last leave. And she had taken her lead from him, as she had done all through their childhood. Robin and Ian led and Mairi followed along behind.

It would soon be the holidays. The school was closing for ten days, and, despite war shortages, there was going to be a party for the children in the Kirk Hall. Rumours abounded to the effect that Sir Humphrey was coming home for the holidays and that he intended to give every child in the school an orange. Mairi had been asked to help with the party; Edith Black, whose fiancé was a prisoner of war in Germany, was going to play the piano for games and even Violet, Mairi's first friend at school, was going to be there since she had four children who each spent some time at the school.

'Bert, you must try, for your mother's sake, to enjoy this party,' she told Milly's younger son, who was showing every sign of defying them both by not attending.

'It's a bairns' perty. I'm no gan near the place.'

'Yes, you are,' said Angus. 'Because I tellt the Dominie we'd baith come to keep the bairns in order.'

Mairi, who was sure she was going to hate the party as much as Bert did, watched anxiously to see how he would deal with being ordered around by his brother. Bert looked at Angus and saw how big and strong he was.

'You and me, the baith of us?'

'Oh, aye. The Dominie thocht you'd come for the orange but I said you couldnae be bought,' said Angus blandly as he tied his laces round and round his legs.

'Have I ever had an orange?'

'Aye, hundreds of them,' lied Angus, 'but no since this bluidy war stertit.'

Mairi was so glad that they were going to do what their poor mother wanted them to do that she turned a deaf ear to Angus's language. It would be good for Milly to get out of the house, which she had not left since the telegram had arrived. It was fitting that Christmas should be the time for her to start her painful journey back to a life without the hope of her husband returning.

'Get a lantern, Angus, and we'll be on our way,' she said and then turned as Milly came down the stairs with Jean.

Poor wee Jean. What agonies she must have endured to achieve those tortured plaits. She smiled tearfully at Mairi and got her coat from the

191

pegs by the door.

Milly walked over to the fireplace and put the guard protectively in front of the damped-down coals. 'A wee poke when we get hame and we'll hae a nice wee blaze.'

'A Christmas party should be fun, Milly. Everybody will be there.'

'Everybody that's left, lassie.'

'Oh, Milly.' Mairi had thought that Milly's willingness to go to the party had signalled a new start. Perhaps it did.

'It'll get better.'

Milly looked at her and in her eyes Mairi saw the empty years stretching ahead. 'I'll endure it—for my bairns' sake. Och, dinnae fret, lassie. I'm tough, I'll survive, but it'll never get better. How can it?'

Mairi could say nothing. There were no words of comfort. She reached for her coat and followed the children out into the darkness.

They heard the sounds of revelry long before they reached the village. The piano, which even to Mairi's untrained ear sounded badly out of tune, was being played as if loudness might make up for accuracy but the children did not seem to mind. They were running from one side of the hall to the other, from the top to the bottom, bumping into one another, into angry and overworked mothers who thumped, without discrimination, whichever child they could reach, and they were having a wonderful time.

The hall had been decorated with holly but there were no candles. Some of the smallest children could have no memory of socials and parties when the hall had been ablaze with red candles. They did not mind. It was decorated. A piano was being

192

played and they did not have to go to school for a whole week. Could life get better?

It could. For one magic night the war was forgotten, at least by the children, and at nine thirty, just as the Minister and the Dominie were beginning to whisper together about the lateness of the hour and the dangers involved in long walks home in the dark, someone heard the sound of a car and there was Sir Humphrey with his oranges— and his niece Arabella Huntingdon.

She was wearing silver grey furs and looked exotic and wonderful. Small children pressed close to her just to drink in her perfume or to touch the stuff of her coat. Jewels sparkled in her ears and on her soft white hands and Mairi, more than ever, was aware of her own reddened skin, her broken nails, her ugly, ugly, too large dress. And then Arabella smiled and Mairi, together with everyone else, was captivated again.

Bella left her uncle deep in conversation with the Minister and came over to Mairi who was watching the Dominie, flanked by his henchmen Angus and Bert, give out the precious oranges.

'Miss McGloughlin,' said Bella, 'how very lovely to see you again.'

Ian loves her and she is a fairytale creature who has forgotten him.

'It's nice to see you, Miss Huntingdon,' she said stiffly. She had to be polite, had to be. Arabella, after all, had persuaded Rupert to exert his influence on Ian's behalf. 'You have been away a long time.'

'One has to do what one has to do,' said Arabella. 'My uncle and aunt want me to have the life they think a girl from my family ought to have.

193

I have tried to play their game.' Suddenly she looked directly at Mairi and her face was no longer smiling. 'Have you heard from him lately? I'm so worried; there was such a ghastly battle at a place called Caporetto.'

'Caporetto?' Mairi's mind seemed sluggish.

'Italy. It went on for weeks and weeks and I tell myself that he was probably in quite a different part of Italy, probably sitting under an olive tree writing a poem . . . that's how I make myself see him, to keep myself sane.'

'You know where he is?' Mairi could hardly believe what she was hearing. Ian had never mentioned Bella and Mairi had hardly dared remind him of the Laird's niece.

Bella laughed. What a lovely musical sound. Several of the children who were stroking her coat looked up at her lovely face to hear the laughter better. 'He hasn't told you,' she said. 'What a wicked boy. Is he ashamed of me, do you think?'

'Perhaps you're the only lovely thing in his life, Miss Huntingdon, and he wants nothing to touch you.'

'Goodness, how lovely. You're a poet too. And do call me Bella. If we are to be sisters in the eyes of the law . . .'

'Goodness, Miss . . . Bella. No, I'm sorry, I can't. I can't take this in. I didn't think you and Ian . . .'

'I haven't seen him since the picnic. Those picnics were, well, you won't believe me if I say they were the highlights of my year. I saw Ian first when I was fourteen. He's so beautiful, isn't he?'

'Would you like a cup of tea, Miss . . . Bella? I need to sit down.'

'Me too. Let some of these little acolytes fetch

194

tea for us. We can sit over here.'

She walked across the hall, children trailing in her wake like seagulls after a trawler, and sat down against the wall and Mairi had no choice but to follow her. Milly brought them tea and slices of the latest attempts at eggless cake. Arabella smiled up at her. 'You must be Mrs Baxter. We were so sorry to hear about your loss.'

Milly smiled but said nothing and Mairi drank some of her tea and wondered what on earth to say. Ian beautiful? Ian was a farmer's son who had almost been shot for desertion. What would Sir Humphrey have to say about that?

'It won't be easy, Mairi, but what is easy? My aunt will have a fit and Ian isn't terribly easy to convince either. He spouts all this stuff and nonsense about my being too good for him and miles above me and all that rot.'

'It isn't rot at all, Miss Huntingdon.'

Bella turned in her chair to look at Mairi. 'But I thought you would have been on my side.'

'I'm on my brother's side. Has he asked you to marry him?'

'Good gracious no. I have to do all the running. He has such fearfully outmoded ideas. I keep telling him that the war has changed everything. I was going to try with "love changes everything" but Ian would give me up out of love. Now I'm working on, "when you're acknowledged as an absolutely brilliant war poet, everyone will say you're marrying beneath you" but he hasn't replied to that one and so I'm frightened.'

Mairi was having trouble in taking in all that she was hearing. Ian and Sir Humphrey's niece, a debutante, a girl who had been presented to their

195

Majesties at Court: they were writing to one another, had been for some time. 'I haven't heard in weeks,' she said at last. 'I've been so involved with poor Milly Baxter and her children, but quite often there's a huge gap and then three letters arrive at once . . .'

Arabella stood up. 'That's what I'm hoping. Uncle's leaving. I must go. When you hear from Ian, you may tell him that I've told you of my feelings. Perhaps then he'll write to you about his. Funny, isn't it, but he's actually more of a snob than Rupert and that's saying something.'

She walked to the door chatting to all the little acolytes who followed her and when the door closed behind her the room seemed cold and empty and dark.

A few days later another visitor, Mr Sutherland the Minister, brought Mairi more bad news. Ian was missing, assumed captured by enemy soldiers.

She could not bear it; she could not. It was too much. Robin in hospital, Dad out but sent back to his unit, and now this.

'Do you know what day it is, Milly?' she asked as they sat side by side before the fire that Angus kept stoked for them. 'It's the first day of 1918. We should have the whisky out and black bun and a fiddler playing all the old tunes.'

'It'll get better, lassie.'

Who had said that last?

'He's been in prison, Milly. It nearly drove him insane. He'd rather be dead. Oh, God, I have to tell Bella.'

Milly lifted a spoon of the hot broth she was trying to make Mairi drink. 'Come on, lass.'

Mairi took the spoon from her and tried to

196

smile. 'You think you're dealing with Jean, Milly.'

'Ach, we're all children when we're in pain. Who's Bella?'

And Mairi looked at her honest face and told her everything. 'But how can I tell her on New Year's Day? They're bound to be having a wonderful party.'

'It won't hurt to keep it till tomorrow. Let her have her fancy party.'

'He's a prisoner of war. He's alive and he'll come home. Right?'

'Right. And then your dad'll be back and your Robin because this war has to end, Mairi. They won't go on until there's no one left to fire the guns.'

Mairi stood up. 'We'd best away to bed. There's more than enough work for the two of us tomorrow.'

'Give Angus some chores. He'll need to do some of your work or you'll no have time tae visit the lassie.'

'I wonder if I should just send her a note—I went to the front door there once—I'll not make that mistake again. I don't know what excuse I'd make for wanting to see her.'

'It's still better than letting her read it, lass.'

Milly was right, of course, but Mairi did not relish the embarrassment of being asked by a servant to state her business and she knew that would happen. She lay awake for most of the night worrying about Ian and trying to think of a reason for a farm girl to call on the daughter of the 'Big House' before eventually falling into an uneasy doze.

Milly was already awake and the porridge was

197

plopping softly over the heat when she went downstairs the next morning.

'I'll do what has to be done here and then I'll walk over, Milly. Will you have a look at the logs, Angus? Maybe Bert could give you a wee hand and, Jean, you'll do the hens this morning for me, won't you?'

By one thirty she had no excuses left. She combed her hair, tied it back neatly, put on her coat and her boots and set off for Sir Humphrey's home. She rehearsed what she would say when a maid came to the back door to see who was knocking.

Arabella was walking in the garden, throwing sticks for her spaniel to retrieve. She saw Mairi on the driveway and, abandoning her puppy, hurried to meet her.

The cold air had made Arabella's cheeks pink and her eyes bright and she looked ethereally lovely. As usual she made Mairi feel plain and dowdy but she could not care about that today because she was going to extinguish the light in Bella's sparkling eyes.

'A prisoner? But he'll hate that.'

'He's alive . . . Bella.'

Arabella smiled. 'He hated prison. It wasn't so awful when they sent him up to the highlands to build roads but the prison cells were terrible, frightening. He couldn't write; they wouldn't give him paper and so he kept sane by memorizing his poetry. He's a genius, but you know that.'

Mairi hung her head. They had never taken Ian's poetry seriously. 'Men like Rupert wrote poetry.' She was startled to realize that she had spoken.

'Then what about Burns, Mairi? Men like Ian

198

write poetry. You have no more news?'

'No, I'm sorry. The telegram came yesterday . . .'

'And while I was dancing in the ballroom, getting squiffy on champagne and toasting the end of the war that is bound to come, you were alone.'

Mairi felt exasperation rising. How melodramatic. Two poets together. Ian and Bella were perfect for one another. 'With Milly, Angus, Bert, and Jean, and a farm to run so that Ian will have a home to come back to. I'd best get back.'

'Yes, of course, and you'll let me know when you hear something. Oh, blast, I'm going to Town later this week. You must ring me on Auntie's new telephone; I'll give you her number.'

'I've never seen a telephone machine, Miss Huntingdon. There isn't one in the village.'

Bella looked at her and impulsively grasped Mairi's hand. 'You're angry, calling me Miss Huntingdon. I'm sorry, You will write to me though, just as soon as you hear something definite?'

'I'll write.'

Bella called the spaniel who was having a wonderful time rolling in the soft snow and Mairi stood and watched them make their way back to the luxury of the Big House. Ian would not be at ease there. There could be no future for him and Arabella Huntingdon, no matter how romantically they looked at their situation. And it was obvious that the young aristocrat was keeping her letter writing from her family or perhaps she tossed off her interest in Ian with a . . . *writing to one of the tenants, you know. One's got to do one's bit for our fighting men.*

Mairi remembered how Rupert had reminded
199

Arabella pointedly that the young farmer was one of her uncle's tenants. And he was not even that. Colin was the tenant; Ian no more than a hired hand. A match between the two young people would never be allowed and, even if it were, how could Ian support a girl who wore furs and diamonds to a school party?

The only thing to do now was to write to Ian with love and support. And after that letter was written there was one to Colin who also needed support and then Robin . . . How wonderful to be able to pour her heart out to Robin but she would have to write him a friendly letter, telling him about the children's party and the oranges and Arabella Huntingdon's beautiful clothes, and then she would tell him that Ian was a prisoner of war and she would be so positive that everything was going to be well.

She did not have to write the letter, for when she got home Angus rushed out to tell her that the Dominie had walked to the farm to tell them that the war was over for Robin, who was being invalided out to recover at home.

CHAPTER NINETEEN

'Hey, fermer, can ye no see ma sheets?'

The cheery cry rang out from the drying green and Mairi straightened up from the fire she was lighting to wave to her housekeeper.

'The wind will change, Milly, honestly.'

'I'll believe you,' shouted Milly, leaving the end of the quotation, *thousands wouldn't,* left unsaid.

Mairi laughed and went on with burning the stubble. She was months behind with the work on the farm; things just did not work so smoothly with Colin and Ian away. This had to be done and it was a shame that Milly had chosen to change the beds on the day she had elected to light fires so near the farmhouse. The wind would change—eventually.

Just as the war would end—eventually, and Ian and Colin would come home. And Robin? Mairi sighed. Robin would talk to her—eventually.

Oh, he did talk. He was painfully polite when a meeting could not be avoided but it was obvious that communicating with anyone at all was an almost unbearable burden.

'He's no the man he was, lassie,' said Milly. 'Your Robin is still there somewhere, but there's layers of experiences on that laddie and he has to learn to live with them afore he can think on living with anyone else.'

'But I don't want him to marry me—I mean, of course I do, but I know he's not ready. I'm terrified that he doesn't love me any more, that maybe he never loved me at all. He kissed me, Milly; he never said he loved me. Oh, damn, why is being an adult so difficult? Can't he see that I want to help him. If he'd talk to me, really talk, not just mutter things about it being a good spring for planting, I know I could help him.'

'Give him time. Give him space. My Jim used to jump up in the bed at night screaming bluidy murder; used to frighten the life out of me—and the bairns. It's whit they've seen, whit they've had to do.'

'I seem to have wasted so much time, Milly. I took years to realize how I felt about him and now, just when I thought that perhaps he cared for me too . . .' Suddenly Mairi looked up and saw Milly's kind, sympathetic face and she remembered that Milly had lost her husband and here was she, blubbering like a school girl.

'I'm sorry, Milly. I feel so ashamed.'

Milly wiped Mairi's face with her dishcloth, just as she did with Jean and occasionally Bert. 'Come on, let's have a cup of tea and a scone. There is nothing to be ashamed about, lass. Jim's dead, and I'll carry that grief for the rest of my life but surely that should make me better able to comfort. You helped me when Jim got killt, I help you when Robin gets hurt. Women always pick up the bits after their men, lass. The way of the world.'

Mairi looked at the older woman and again felt ashamed. Milly had loved her husband dearly, yet after allowing herself hardly any time to grieve, she was back at work, looking after the house, caring for her children and their grief, keeping a worried eye on her elder son who, of course, felt the loss of his father so much more than the younger children who had hardly known him, and being constantly, unfailingly cheerful.

'Milly, did you never think of joining any of the clubs . . . I don't know, knitting socks for servicemen or something like that?'

'My God, lassie, have you ever seen my knitting? Jim didnae marry me for my knitting skills. I'm perfectly content here with you and the bairns.'

They both looked quickly out of the window as they heard a furious cry from Bert but it was no more than high spirits. It was good to see the three children running around happily, as if they had not a care in the world.

'This is a lovely place you've given us,' said Milly. 'Jim died knowing his family were safe. I'll never be able to thank you enough for that.'

Mairi followed her into the kitchen. One more worry that would not go away. What would become of Milly and the children when the war ended and the men came home?

*   *   *

Robin knew that he was hurting Mairi but he had no idea what to do about it. The wounds on his body were healing and the doctor at the hospital had assured him that the scars on his mind would heal too, given time.

But days passed and he felt worse, not better. He was home, alive. A girl was waiting for him to make some move; he just knew it. She was so tense when they met and he was taking every chance to ensure that they did not meet. He refused to accompany his father to church and he refused to stay in the room when the Minister came preaching forgiveness. He could never forgive. But the person he could not forgive was himself. He was alive and his friends were dead. But worse than that—other men were dead at his hand.

Every night he dreamed of the men he had killed. He saw their faces as they knelt before him, their hands together in supplication; he heard them begging him not to kill. He ignored their cries. Useless to tell himself that he had killed only once in arm-to-arm combat and his victim had been too busy trying to kill him to beg for anything. But still he saw them. He could smell them in the dream too. He smelled rotting putrefaction, the sickly

203

sweet smell of warm blood. He gagged in his sleep.

Now he had begun to dream again about Mairi and they were not the dreams that had kept him sane—he laughed aloud at the thought of sanity—during those terrible days and months and years. In these dreams he was killing Mairi, not making love to her, and he woke trembling and sweating, resolved to stay away from her as much as possible. For maybe the killer in the dreams was the real Robin Morrison and if he found himself alone with her, maybe that horror would become a reality.

His father, so gentle so kind . . . could he tell him of the nightmares that plagued him? No, never. The Dominie was so happy to have his son home safe and well. Well. Robin sobbed again at the thought of being well. Dear God, how easy it was to fool everyone. Was there anyone in the world who knew him so well that he could confess his worries and feel relief and not guilt that he had added a burden to the loved one?

Ian. Ian, who had been his friend since their first day at school, he would listen and he would understand, even about Mairi he would understand.

Dear Ian,
    I think I'm going mad. There, I've said it. I fooled the poor overworked medic who wanted me to go to Craiglockhart. (There's someone there who specializes in people who've gone off their rocker a bit.) He said I would recover in time, but I'm getting worse, and what in the name of God will it do to my father if they lock me up in a loonie bin somewhere. Oh, Ian, why am I writing to you? You're a P.O.W. I should be

204

writing letters to cheer you but, in spite of your poetry, you've always been the most stable person I know.

Does this letter sound fairly sane? See how clever I am but if I tell you about my dreams, night after night, that make me cry like a baby for my mother ... I think I'm capable of killing someone I care for deeply ... there, there it's out, but I won't. I stay away from everyone. My father believes the Minister can help me but I can't bear to be in the same room with him. I think, if he spouts one more damn cliché about forgiveness and turning the other cheek, I'll strangle him with my bare hands. Father worries, I know he does, but he can't find answers to me in any of his books and so he's at a loss and the weight of guilt I feel is crushing me. He deserved a son who really was a hero, who deserved these bloody medals. Do you know, when I wore them, I felt them burning through my uniform into my flesh, but there are no marks. I can't see the marks ...

He was crying. Bloody hell, he was crying and it would ruin his letter. He couldn't send it anyway, couldn't send such drivel to Ian in a prison camp, so it didn't matter about tear stains. He had to get out. Such a beautiful day. Was it a beautiful day in France too, in Germany, in Russia? No, Russia was too far away. There, he was thinking rationally. He was not mad. He would walk to the sea, away from Mairi; he could not meet Mairi because he might try to kiss her. Oh, sweet, sweet Mairi. How often had he dreamed of kissing her, of loving her, so strongly that he could feel her in his arms? Now, if

205

he kissed her, maybe the dream would come back and he would find himself killing her. No, he would walk to the sea. He must stay as far away from her as possible.

His father saw his headlong flight down the road towards the coast as he stood at the window of the schoolroom listening to the primary four pupils reciting the six times table. As soon as he could he rang the bell for an afternoon break.

'You have all worked so hard on this fine afternoon,' he told the surprised children, 'that I have decided to award you a fifteen-minute playtime. Now, Maggie Stewart, you keep an eye on the wee ones while I go into the house for a book I need.'

He hurried across the playground and into the house. It was empty and quiet. His heart was pounding. What had distressed Robin so much that he had been running, for it was not the run of an active young man out for exercise. It was terrified flight. He looked into all the rooms on the ground floor. Nothing. Everything was neat and tidy. Using the banister like an old man, he climbed the stairs and went into the room Robin had occupied since they had come to the village.

The letter was lying where Robin had left it and, at first, the Dominie ignored it. Letters were intensely private and not to be read by anyone but the intended recipient. The bed was neat, the window was open and the spring breeze was ruffling the letter so that it coquetted on the surface of the old school desk.

'His legs are too long for that desk,' thought the father practically.

The Dominie went to the window and looked

out at the children running madly around the yard. What a pleasure an unexpected playtime was. Oh, to be so young and innocent and so easily made happy.

The letter. He looked at it. He had been writing a letter. Why would that upset him? Surely he might be upset by a letter he had received, not by one he was writing—unless, of course, he had to convey bad news.

He snatched up the paper and read the words and they struck at him so fiercely that he had to sit down on the edge of the iron bedstead. 'Oh, my baby, my boy,' his heart cried. 'What a burden of guilt and grief and fear. You couldn't hurt Mairi, my wee laddie, just as you can't disappoint me.'

The last words came back to haunt him. *When I wore them, I felt them burning into my flesh, but there are no marks.*

'Oh, Robin, my lamb, the marks are burned into your soul.'

He sat for some minutes. He had to get back to the children. He had made up his mind. He folded the letter, put it into an envelope and addressed it to Ian. Then he slipped it into the pocket of his gown and returned to the school.

None of the children dared to tell him that he had forgotten the book he had gone to the house to collect and the afternoon plodded on. He left as soon as he decently could that afternoon and walked into Arbroath where he posted the letter. He thought of Ian in prison receiving and reading such an outpouring of grief.

'Robin comes first. He's right. Ian has always been stable. If anyone can handle it, he can. Ian, Ian, help my lad,' he cried across the miles and

207

then turned, dry eyed, and made the long walk back.

As he had hoped Robin had calmed down and had returned home before him.

'You're late, Father,' he said and his voice was normal although he was paler even than usual.

'I had to go to a meeting,' the Dominie lied. 'What did you do with yourself this afternoon?' He hoped he sounded casually interested.

'I went to the beach, had a grand walk. Clears the head no end.' He stopped and looked puzzled and somewhat unsure. He looked at his father. 'You know, sounds silly, but I thought I had been writing but there's no paper on my desk.'

'Gracious, Robin, you're beginning to sound just like me. I was quite sure I'd done the primary seven essays this morning and there they all were on my desk, untouched by human hand.'

Obligingly, Robin smiled. 'Some of that lot . . . perhaps yours was the first human hand that touched them.' He shook his head as if clearing away a fog. 'I was so sure . . .'

'Come and help me burn the Shepherd's pie we've been left for tea.' He walked quickly into the kitchen and was relieved to hear Robin following along behind him.

CHAPTER TWENTY

Colin was delighted to read that his local football team was strenuously recruiting juvenile players. He was not so happy to read that it was because many of the adult players had enlisted and too many of them were never coming back.

'Here, Chay.' He handed the boy in the dug-out beside him the three-month-old copy of the *Herald* that Mairi had sent out. 'Were you no telling us you were a great goalie? Arbroath's looking for you, laddie. You're aboot the age they want, seventeen and never been kissed.'

The boy soldier laughed and took the paper and Colin watched him painstakingly spell out the words, his young soft mouth forming every consonant, every vowel, as he tried to decipher the article.

Eventually he finished the task. 'I'm free the morn, Sergeant. I'll drop in and let them hae a look at us.'

'Fine. I'll make sure naebody takes yer space.'

He sighed at his own pitiful attempt at humour. The boy beside him might well never have been kissed, but he had survived a bayonet wound, shrapnel in the shoulder, constant shelling, disease, hunger—and these all before his eighteenth birthday. Dear God in Heaven, this was all wrong. He remembered other articles in the papers his wee girl made such an effort to send to him. Pals' Battalions: boys who had grown up together, enlisted together and fought and died together. There were the Bantam Battalions, later known as the Demon Dwarves, who were first deemed too small to fight, and later were anxiously conscripted into the Army where they fought and died like tigers.

He would have to write to Ian and tell him that he had been right all the time and that his father had been too thick-headed to see it. This wee laddie should be at hame trying out for his team,

209

no dodging bullets, and my wee lassie should be married tae some nice lad, Robin Morrison maybe, and having healthy babies. Instead she's working like an Irish navvy. I promised her mam Mairi'd have it better than she did and what have I done to her? And her Ian, her son, her pride and joy—and mine too? Oor laddie with his scribble scribble aboot sunsets and sun on the water and the beauty of spider webs. Spider webs, for God's sake. I never took the time tae let him show me beauty in a spider's web. But I'll watch them with him yet. I'll listen tae him, and I'll try looking at things with his eyes. Dear God, does he even know I love him? Did I ever show him, tell him? I'll put it in the letter and he'll cringe with embarrassment, or maybe he'll no.

He sorted through his pockets but there was nothing and he called across to the boy who was still making heavy weather of the newspaper.

'Chay, you dinnae hae a bit paper?'

The boy looked through his pockets. 'No really, Sarge, but you can have my mam's envelope. I dinnae need that.'

He handed it over and Colin tore it open with his capable farmer's hands and smoothed it out gently. 'I need tae write tae my son,' he said as if an explanation was expected. 'There's such a lot I never told him.'

The boy looked at him. Sergeant McGloughlin with a son? He had thought that the man had been born an iron sergeant in the Fifth Battalion the Black Watch. Impossible to think of him out of uniform, out of mud and sweat, fathering a baby.

'Whit's his name, Sarge?' he dared.

'Ian. Grandest son any father could ask for.'

'Is he in the Regiment?'

Colin looked at the thin, undernourished, tired little face in front of him and saw instead Ian's handsome, sensitive face. 'No, he's a Conscientious Objector,' and he said it loudly and proudly. 'He fought two wars, Chay, the enemy and his own side and he won. He's in a prison camp in Germany now. I write tae him when I can but I just realized'—and here he was talking to himself and not to the young private—'that I never write about anything important, like how much I love him, and admire him, about how proud I am that he can make beautiful images wi words, that, when this is all over, I'll be the first one tae tell him it was all wrong.'

He turned back to his envelope and did not see the boy soldier squirm with embarrassment at the use of a word like *love* and neither did he see the embarrassment replaced by a look of envy on the boy's face. He was trying to find the words. He knew that men on all sides were disillusioned with the war and were calling for peace talks. Colin no longer believed in what he was doing and he could see no way that the war could end in honour. For a while this year he had even believed that Britain would be defeated.

The Germans had mounted a terrible offensive in the west and had come close to Paris. They had lost 800,000 men but the Allies had lost more than a million troops.

'Sweet Jesus, a million men no returning to their mammies, their wives, their bairns. The world cannae recover. There cannae be many men left at all ... if there are any. There's my Ian ... in prison.'

211

He licked the tip of the pencil and bent again to his letter, but his ears, attuned to the soft bleating of a lost lamb, heard the whistle of the grenade as it flew over the rim of the trench. He saw it as if in slow motion. He felt himself unfold from the ground; he saw the startled look on young Chay's face as he became aware that death was seeking him.

'No,' screamed Colin. 'Not him, you bastard,' and he threw his body over the boy and his back took the full impact of the explosion.

'Jesus Christ,' said Corporal Russell some time later as he helped the injured soldier out from under. 'What a mess.'

'The sergeant, Corporal, the sergeant,' screamed the boy. 'Where is he? I felt him pushing me out of the way.'

The corporal turned away for a second to school his heaving stomach. Then he turned back to Chay. 'You're wearing him, laddie,' was all he said.

*   *   *

Thirty-six hours later, on 11 November 1918, the last shot was fired in France.

Mairi received the notification of her father's death several days after what soon became known as Armistice Day; his name, with too many others, was posted up in the local post office and the Minister cycled out with the news. At first Mairi refused to accept it. Death was impossible. The war was over. They had seen it in the paper. They had participated in modest celebrations at the Kirk Hall. The war was over and prisoners of war would be released and soldiers would soon be returning to

212

the bosom of their families.

'It's a mistake, Milly,' she said, pushing away the shot of Colin's whisky that Milly had unearthed from under the sink. 'The war's over. But you mustn't worry about you and the children; we'll work something out. That's what Dad will want. He was . . . he is so grateful that you're here. And Ian too. You'll like Ian. It will take a while for him to get home, I suppose. They'll have to go to Germany and find the prisoners, won't they? They'll hardly just open the doors and let them walk home. If they do,' and she started to laugh, 'we'll never find our Ian because he'll find a view somewhere and he'll sit down to write a poem. Did I tell you he was a poet?'

And Milly, with her age-old common sense, let her talk and talk. Eventually she slept and the young girl who had been Mairi McGloughlin died in that sleep, and the woman, Mairi, was born. There had been too much sadness: Ian, Robin, and now Colin.

*   *   *

The Dominie had read the name Sergeant Colin McGloughlin and walked wearily home to tell his son. This would surely move him, show that somewhere under the remote stranger, Robin Morrison was still there.

But Robin looked horrified at the thought of offering Mairi his condolences—or anything else. 'You'll do the right thing, Dad. You'll tell her what we feel.' Robin, taller and thinner than ever, was hanging on to the mantelpiece for fear that his knees might buckle and he would fall forward into

213

the flames. He swayed and his father made as if to support him.

'Don't touch me,' Robin snapped. 'I'm perfectly all right.'

Euan Morrison looked at his son. He was not all right. His body was healing but what about the wounds that he could not see?

'You'll come with me to pay our respects?'

Robin turned away almost violently. 'You go,' he said. 'I don't know what to say, how to say it.'

'Maybe it will be enough for you just to be there, Robin.'

'I can't.' He moved towards the door, to escape.

'Robin, I don't know what happened between you and Mairi but her father is dead and her brother is in a camp in Germany and God alone knows if he is still alive or when he'll come home if he is. She needs her friends.'

Defeated by a lifetime of habit Robin stopped but he did not turn to look at his father. 'You won't leave me . . .' He was the child Robin again, afraid in the dark.

'I won't leave you. Come on, get another woolly jumper and your coat; it's tipping it down out there.'

Robin did as he was told, climbed upstairs to his room where the bed for some years had been too short and he took a woollen pullover out of the chest of drawers, pulled it over his head and went back down to where his father was standing, Robin's coat in one hand and an old farm lantern in the other.

Robin allowed his father to help him on with his coat and then he took the lantern and walked first out of the Schoolhouse. He stood at the top of the

214

steps waiting for the Dominie and remembered the time—a lifetime ago—when he had kissed Mairi, been slapped hard for his pains, and had then fallen ignominiously down the steps.

His father's hand was on his shoulder but instead of calming him, the touch seemed to fill him with panic.

'I can't,' he said. 'I can't,' and he sank down at his father's feet in the rain and began to sob.

The Dominie dropped to his knees and put his arms around his child. 'It's all right, Robin lad. It's all right.'

He helped the young man to his feet and into the house. Then he half carried him up the stairs, undressed him as if he was indeed just a little boy, and tucked him in.

'You have a rest, Robin. I'm going out for a wee while and when I come back I'll make some tea.'

Robin said nothing but his sobs had almost subsided and his father sat for a few minutes until all the shuddering had stopped and then he left.

But he did not turn right and head towards the McGloughlin farm. He turned left to the village and the doctor's house and was admitted to the front room where the doctor was sitting toasting his socks at a roaring fire.

'I hope you've come for a game of chess, Euan.'

'No.'

Dr Muirhead folded away his newspaper. 'Sit down, man, and have a dram.'

When he had poured the drinks he sat down in his chair facing his uninvited guest and said, 'Drink that first, and then tell me the problem. It's your laddie, I suppose.'

When Euan had finished telling him everything

that Robin had said or done since he had been invalided out, he sighed deeply and lay back in his chair, his hands round the crystal tumbler, and his eyes watching the fire.

'I can't help with mental problems, Euan. I'm way out of my depth here.'

Euan started up. 'I have to get back to him. I put him to bed. I never did that in my life before and here he is nearly thirty years of age.'

'Sit down and finish your dram. He'll sleep. I said I couldn't help but there are doctors who're specializing in psychiatry, There's a professor in Edinburgh, Rivers, an anthropologist, would you believe, but he's done wonders with some of our wounded lads. I could write to him for you.'

Euan sat up and his face was immediately happier and George Muirhead felt the weight of his calling heavier than he had ever felt it before. This trust: it frightened him sometimes. He couldn't possibly measure up all the time. He sighed. 'It'll take a few weeks, Euan. Finish up your dram and I'll come back with you and have a look at the boy.' He heard what he had just said. *The boy.* Robin Morrison had not been a boy for a long time.

'Damn, but I'm getting too old for this job,' he thought but he kept his thoughts to himself.

'Robin was an officer, wasn't he? That makes it easier. Rivers is in a hospital for officers in Edinburgh. Pity they released Robin from the hospital without letting a psychiatrist have a look at him. Still, doesn't sound as if he's a danger to himself or anyone else.'

Euan decided not to mention the contents of the letter.

CHAPTER TWENTY-ONE

Thank God for the land. As the winter of 1918 passed, Mairi took refuge in making plans for the spring sowing. Sir Humphrey Grey-Watson's solicitor had assured her that Ian would have no trouble in taking over the tenancy.

Ian was coming home. She had had a letter dated November 1918.

Mairi wondered sadly if the letter might have been written on the very day that Colin had been killed but she tried to put that thought out of her head. What did it matter when it had been written? In late November, Ian was still alive, and so he would be coming home with all the thousands of other prisoners. It would take time. But Mairi and the land had time. Sometimes she felt that she had nothing else.

Ian's letter had hinted at changes in his life that he wanted to discuss with his father. She sighed and Milly who was sewing patches on her sons' trousers looked up.

'It was nice of the Laird to send that wee note, Mairi,' she said in hopes that remembering Sir Humphrey's kindness might cheer Mairi. 'And the Dominie, and the Blacks, and the Minister. Jings, everybody that's onybody has been in this house these past weeks.'

But not Robin, thought Mairi, not the only person who mattered. 'People are like that in the country,' was all she said.

'Och, had I been up a stair in Dundee when my man was killt, the neighbours would hae been at my door tae.'

Milly held the strong thread between her teeth and bit at it until it broke and Mairi got up and went to her sewing box for her scissors.

'You'll break your teeth, Milly.'

'We had teeth afore we had scissors, lassie, but since you've got them, I'll use them.'

They heard the rattling of the old windows as the wind freshened and changed direction.

'Damn,' said Mairi as the room filled with smoke blown back down the old chimney piece. 'I forgot to get the sweep in.'

That had been one of the many jobs attended to by Colin.

The women coughed furiously for a few minutes and then Mairi went to the door and opened it a little. Smoke went out and snow blew in.

'The smell of wood smoke's braw though, Mairi,' laughed Milly as she joined her shivering landlady at the door. 'Better nor some of the stuff we used tae burn. Mind you, if the bairns are cauld you'll burn what you have.' She pulled her old cardigan round her shoulders. 'Come on, lassie. It's freezing with that door open.'

Obligingly Mairi closed the door. 'The world is so pretty with snow on it.'

'It's prettier and warmer without it,' said the practical Milly as she sat down again beside the fire.

She sewed steadily for a few minutes and then put down her mending. 'Mairi, can you sew?'

Startled, Mairi looked up. 'Sew? I'm sorry, Milly, do you need some help? Of course I can sew.'

'No, it's no that. I like my hands busy. I was jist thinking that your Ian'll have lost weight in a prison

218

camp. Maybe we should be making him some new shirts, a wee welcome home present.'

'I haven't told him . . .' She still could not say the words *our father is dead.*

'Might as well keep the bad news till he gets home. It'd be different if he was going to be years yet. One day soon he'll jist be here.' She looked at her employer. 'Are you hearing what I'm trying tae tell you, lassie? I've brought this up afore.'

Mairi looked up and there was such an expression of pain on her face that Milly's heart was touched. 'There won't be room for us, lass. He's the tenant. Even if he didn't want his dad's room, he'll need his own.'

Mairi saw the justice of this. In all probability Ian would prefer not to use the bigger room, unless he brought a bride to the farm. She saw the beautiful Arabella Huntingdon but could not picture the young aristocrat in this farmhouse. Poor Ian.

'You haven't started to look for somewhere, Milly? The children are happy here at the school, in the village. Ian won't want you to leave. We'll think of something. I can't bear for you to go. I would even miss Bert.'

They laughed. Bert was what was commonly known as a holy terror.

'He misses Jim but the Dominie's got the measure of him,' said Milly and then, more quietly, 'I'll have to go, Mairi. I can maybe get a job in the Mills.'

Mairi stood up. 'But not yet, not yet. Have the winter here at least.'

And so they left it although Mairi stayed awake for some time worrying. If she worried about Milly and her children it left less room to worry about Mairi McGloughlin. When she worried about herself and her future, her heart bled for Robin, Robin who had kissed her so sweetly and had talked of a future full of roses, but who had come back from the war and avoided her at every turn, who had not even come to say he was sorry that her father had been killed.

What had happened to him? What had happened to his love for her? For she knew that he did not love lightly. He had meant what he had said. What had she done to make him change his mind, because she must have done something.

A few days later Milly went to fetch the children from the school and Mairi found herself alone in the house. It was pleasant to sit and listen to the sounds that she had not heard since those three delightful but noisy children had come to stay: the tick-tock of the old clock on the mantel, the spitting of wet wood in the fire, the snores of the dogs as they lay at her feet.

'This is nice,' thought Mairi. 'I'd forgotten how comforting clocks and dogs are.'

She heard the sounds of someone approaching the door and looked up at the clock, surprised that Milly was home so quickly. She had thought she might walk in to the town, small as it was. Milly liked the country but she missed the bustle of Dundee.

Mairi got up and opened the door and Robin's father stood there. 'Twice I've tried to come and tell you, lass,' he said.

Her heart almost stopped beating. Tell her what? Robin. Something dreadful had happened to Robin. That was it; of course that was it. He had

220

not come to see her because, because . . . No, no, hold on, Mairi, hold on. You would have known, had he been dead.

'Come in and sit down by the fire,' she said when she could speak. 'Tell me what, Dominie? Is something wrong with Robin?'

He looked at her and away again and it was shame and embarrassment that were in his face as well as grief. Then he faced her again.

'I won't dress the miserable truth in pretty clothes, Mairi. My boy is in a lunatic asylum. He's had another breakdown, a complete one this time. Thank God I spoke to Dr Muirhead.'

Mairi wasn't really taking in the words *lunatic* and *asylum*. She had expected to hear that final word, *dead*, and so her heart was slowing down and she was even conscious of relief.

'A lunatic asylum? Where?'

'He's been admitted to a hospital in Edinburgh.'

Edinburgh. It could have been a million miles away. How could she get to Edinburgh? No matter. She would get there. A lunatic asylum. What was that? A hiding place for the mad. Robin was mad. No, not Robin. But what was madness?

'Can I see him?' Desperately she prayed that she could deal with madness, with insanity. What was it? Perhaps if Robin had asked to see her . . . She remembered once falling in the mill pool. Her frock had bloomed like a giant flower up over her head and she had fought kicking to reach the surface, to breathe. She felt the same now. Then Ian and Robin, yes, Robin had pulled her from the pond, swept the weeds from her dress and begged her not to tell her father. Robin needed her.

'May I see him?' she asked again.

The Dominie looked surprised. 'You wouldn't want to see him where he is. I hated leaving him there.'

And Mairi began to hear what he was saying. 'Robin is mentally ill. That's what you're saying, Dominie.'

His face crumpled as if he was going to cry. 'Such a fine mind, a fine mind.'

Mairi McGloughlin had never been ill a day in her life. She had no experience of illness, having been so young when her mother had died and she knew nothing whatsoever about illnesses of the mind. But illness was illness. Some you could see and bandage up and some you could not. It was as simple as that and if it was not, then wishing and praying should make it so.

'He'll get better,' she said fiercely and the Dominie looked at her, startled by the note of determination in her voice. 'Of course, he'll get better. When may I see him?'

He sighed and handed his burden over to younger, stronger shoulders. 'Not yet, my dear. It's too early. He's . . . well, they give him something to keep him quiet.' He leaned over and gripped her hand and it was the first time that he had ever touched her. 'I think he's afraid.'

The Dominie was an old man. Not in years; surely he could only be a few years older than Colin. But he looked old, old and frail.

Afraid? Robin afraid? Never, ever. Ian sometimes, but never Robin. His father was afraid too but this fear could be handled.

'Stay and have some soup with me, Mr Morrison, with me and Milly when she gets back. You remember Mrs Baxter?'

222

'Of course, my dear. I'll be glad to stay a while, Mairi.'

Mairi did not go to the kitchen to see to her soup. Instead she sat down beside Robin's father. This conversation was vitally important. She had to understand everything.

'Dominie, Robin's fear. Is he afraid of me? Afraid that I might hold him to promises? I won't. I thought I had made that clear when he first came home. I'm here to be his friend, if he wants that.'

The Dominie thought of the letter that he had sent, so rashly to Ian, and he thanked God that it had never arrived. Robin was afraid that he would kill someone very dear to him. He had been alone for months with his father and had shown no violence whatsoever, so the *someone dear* had to be someone else. He had always known that Mairi was very special to his son and he knew too that Robin had been desperately afraid ever to be alone with her.

'We don't know much about the way the mind works, Mairi, why one man's mind can take all the blows it's dealt and another man is destroyed by the same blows. I think every soldier has been changed by the war and even a few for the better but the change in Robin . . .' The father sat back and stared at the ceiling. 'He can't cope. He tried to do it all on his own, refusing to believe he was ill, then he did ask for help but he never got it, and now, now he is in the only place where they have some idea of what to do to help him. I don't know if he will ever get better. He wouldn't expect you to wait, Mairi.'

Mince or steak? Steak or mince? There was no choice.

'If he loves me, Mr Morrison, it would never occur to me not to wait. I've waited so long already.'

'Do you understand what I am telling you? We know so little about mental illness.'

He slumped in the chair and she saw how hard that admission had been for him. Robin had been wounded twice in the war and his father had told of his injuries proudly. Honourable scars. But wounds to the mind, to the soul, wounds that could not be bandaged, were these not also honourable?

'He'll get better, Dominie,' she said again. 'You and I have to believe that and then Robin will believe too.'

'Mairi, you are still so young, so pretty . . .'

He was letting her go. He was casting her off. She could forget the gentle moments, the hope of a lifetime full of roses. Only one thing mattered. If Robin had asked him to set her free . . . She steeled herself to ask the question that would change the whole course of her life. 'Did Robin ask you to tell me that?'

He shook his head. 'He says nothing at all, nothing. He sits in a chair and looks at the wall or out of a window if the nurse has the chair turned that way.'

'He'll get better,' Mairi said again and she smiled at Robin's father. 'I'll fetch us some soup.'

Milly and the children came in from the village just as Mairi was ladling the soup into the bowls.

'Good,' Mairi called. 'You're just in time for supper. Wash your hands, Bert, and bring the scullery chairs to the table.'

'We cannae eat with the Dominie, Mairi,' hissed Milly. 'The bairns'll die of fright.'

'In here he's just a man with a son in hospital, Milly. The children will be good for him. You can talk to him about Angus staying on at the school.'

But instead Milly talked about returning to Dundee and Mr Morrison bravely set his own problem aside and applied himself to worrying about hers.

'I would suggest waiting until Ian comes home, Mrs Baxter. Come along, wee Jean, drink up your good soup while it's hot.' He waited to see that the girl was being obedient and turned back to her mother. 'You certainly don't want to start looking for a job and a home in the middle of winter. And have you thought of getting a cottage near here? Surely there are empty cottages on the Estate, Mairi?'

'It's the rent, Dominie. Mairi'll no need me when her brother comes home.'

Mairi took the big knife and started slicing some of her own bread. 'Ian said he has things to discuss with . . . Dad. Maybe he'll talk them over with me, but I don't think you should do anything, Milly, until we see what happens.'

'Are we going to stay here then?' asked Bert and Jean, and Mairi looked at Angus and saw that the answer meant a great deal to him.

'Yes,' said Mairi. 'We'll work something out.'

And only Mr Morrison knew that she was thinking about Robin.

*   *   *

She wrote to him that night when Mr Morrison had walked home and Milly and her children were all in bed. She did not refer to his illness, told him only

225

about her work on the farm and then she added something about the antics of Bert. Robin, too, had been a schoolmaster. He would have met boys like Bert.

Mairi did not know that, in his camp in Germany, Ian was writing to his friend. Mr Morrison's desperate appeal for help had just reached him and Ian had set aside the daily letter he was writing to Arabella to communicate with his old friend. He did not mention that Robin had been unable to finish the letter; he did not say that he assumed that it was Robin's desperate father who had sent it. He told him how his company of conscientious objectors had been captured by a German patrol. He did not tell Robin of the inhuman brutality meted out by men who should have known better but he did tell him of the humanity of others. And he told Robin what he had told no one else. He wrote of his love for Arabella.

Her love has kept me sane, Robin. No matter what happened, I would conjure up a picture of Bella, and I would challenge fate to throw at me whatever it would. I managed, somehow, to keep the scarf she gave me. It would have been so difficult to believe that she and her love were real had I had nothing. Letters go missing and sometimes they were so late that I would convince myself that she had stopped loving me. Why would a girl like that love a wreck like me? But she does, Robin, she does. Why, I don't know, but I will treasure her love and her faith in me every day of my life.

In battle, Robin, my dear friend, you did what you had to do and the girl you love—and I know it's my wee sister—will help you live with what you have had to do. You couldn't hurt her, Robin, not physically; it's not in you. And I think you're afraid that you are killing her love, not her, Robin, her love. But she's strong, Robin, and she's faithful, and she guards those she loves. Remember how we used to laugh at her, the cocky wee bantam, standing up for me that could lift her up with one hand. She'll lift you, Robin, as Bella lifts me. What did we do to deserve such women? Don't question, old friend, accept, and be grateful. You, as you are, as you were, as you will be, are the man to whom she has given her heart. Take it and treat it gently.

Robin received that letter on a warm summer's day in 1919. His father, looking better than he had looked for some time, Robin noted, had brought him the letter with a pot of Mairi's strawberry jam.

The Dominie was nervous. He prayed the letter was not an answer to the one Robin had written, but Robin took the letter and the jam and he read the letter without speaking.

'Ian's got a girl,' he said, when he had finished reading. 'Someone called Bella. I don't remember a Bella anywhere in the village.'

'Perhaps it's someone he met in one of the camps, a nurse or such like.'

Robin looked at the pot of jam. 'Strawberries. I remember the smell of growing strawberries, Dad, and the warmth of the sun through my shirt as I picked them.'

'That'll be in the jam, laddie.'

Robin smiled. 'You're as much of a poet as Ian. This is Mairi's way of writing poetry. She and Ian are so alike; I never realized it before.' He was quiet for a moment. 'I wish I could see her smile.'

'She'll come to see you, Robin, if she thinks she's welcome. She would not want to intrude.'

Mairi intrude? Robin saw her small sturdy figure as it followed him and his friend all over the farm. She had intruded on him all her life. He tried to laugh and although it sounded more like a snort, his father took hope from it and courage.

'It's nice out here in the garden, lad. I could bring her some Sunday and you could walk around the garden. She always liked flowers.'

'I could show her the flowers I'm helping to grow. I've tried to remember. Is it the spring flowers she likes, or is it the roses?'

'There were some white briars in a jam jar on the kitchen table.'

Robin smiled. 'White briar roses,' he said.

CHAPTER TWENTY-TWO

Ian arrived in England on 4 October 1919 and went first to Godalming in the pretty county of Surrey. When he had completed his business there he took the train to Scotland.

He walked from Arbroath and the weather matched his mood. It was a perfect autumn day. The sky was blue, the sun was shining, and the wind, a southwest wind, was not too strong but just strong enough to tumble the leaves that had already fallen along the grass verges. He whistled and he kicked them with the polished toe of his new shoes.

New shoes. Leather. For nearly two years he had worn strips of dirty cloth wrapped around his feet in a vain attempt to keep them warm. Arabella had wanted him to have shoes especially made by a London shoemaker but he had refused. What he could afford, he would have. He had allowed her to buy him one pair of cashmere socks, *but only this once, Bella, and just, if you must, as a welcome home gift.*

He thought of Bella now . . . no, when was she ever absent from his thoughts? He had been afraid that the girl of his dreams, the girl of the letters, would not be the girl who met him at Guildford. But she was and although they had met before only a few times, they knew as they walked towards one another down that station platform that they had been heading towards one another all their lives and that once they met and Ian held out his strong arms and enfolded the delicate girl to his heart, they would never again be apart. She was with him now, although she was still in her beautiful Surrey home. An elderly, and very disapproving, aunt had chaperoned the young couple because Lady Grey-Watson refused to have anything to do with either of them.

'I can't expect you to go through this for me, Bella,' he had cried, his lips against her golden hair.

And she had laughed and raised her face so that her lips met his. 'It's nothing to what you have gone through for me. And they'll come round because they love me and if they don't, I'll manage if you love me half as much as I love you.'

And he laughed now as, swinging his bag, he walked jauntily along, remembering the precious minutes they had spent trying to decide who loved the other more.

'Are you the daftie?' A broad Scottish voice broke through his romantic glow.

Ian looked down at the boy and an anger so fierce swept through him, that he, who had never raised his hand in anger during five years of Hell, felt that he might strike the child.

'The daftie?' he asked, although he already knew the answer.

'Aye, the daftie. The Dominie's son that was that clever, went tae Oxford and a'thing. Daft as a brush but he's coming home. You don't look daft. My mam says we'll no sleep safe in oor beds wi a daftie runnin loose.'

Ian looked in horror at the child for whom he and Robin had fought and nearly died.

What had Shakespeare said?

> I hate ingratitude more in a man
> Than lying, vainness, babbling, drunkenness,
> Or any taint of vice . . .

'Ask your mammie to pray that you'll ever be half the man he is,' he said and cursing himself for letting himself get angry, his mood soured, he walked the rest of the way home in silence.

He saw another boy, slightly older than the first ragamuffin, as he turned off the main road onto the one leading to the farm, and, at sight of him, the boy took to his heels and ran.

Ian laughed. 'That must be Mrs Baxter's Bert, the terror of the entire county, off to tell Mairi.'

Sure enough, when he breasted the brow of the hill and looked down towards the sea to where the farmhouse nestled comfortably among its fields, he saw his sister, it had to be his sister although this running creature was a woman, a woman with Mairi's wild red-gold hair. He too began to run and he caught her up in his arms and swung her around as he had done so often when they were children, before setting her on her feet. She looked up at him, her eyes shining with tears and her hair glinting gold where the sun hit it and, to his surprise, she burst into tears, and he held her like a baby and let her cry.

He was amazed. Mairi had never been the kind of little girl who took refuge in tears. She had been much tougher than he was and here she was, and he felt how slight she was, soaking his new, department shop shirt.

'It's all better now, Mairi,' he said softly. 'The war's over and I'm home and Robin will get better, I know he will . . .'

She sniffed loudly, made a tremendous effort and looked up at him through her tears. His appearance shocked her. He was so thin that he looked even taller than his six foot. He was a living walking scarecrow. Bella's hairdresser had tried to do something with the hair that had been kept tidy with the use of a kitchen knife but it would be some months before it grew properly and—it was not gold but silver. A boy had gone to war and an old man had come back. What had happened to his young strong manhood? She would not let him sense her horror. 'You know about Robin?'

As she spoke to her brother she thought of that first day when she had gone to the hospital in Edinburgh. She had been so nervous that she had been sick twice on the train. She had pictured the asylum, a huge grey sprawling building with iron bars on the windows. She had heard the screams of insane patients and she had smelled the nauseating carbolic smells of cleanliness and lack of hope. How could someone as fastidious and sensitive as the Dominie spend every free moment there? So simple, so simple. He loved his son.

And then she had arrived and she had walked up a tree-lined lane to a large sandstone building which stood benignly among its paved walks and abundant flower beds. A nurse in a starched white uniform had opened the door to her and she had smelled lavender and had seen the sun shining on old polished furniture and books. She had breathed a deep sigh of relief.

The nurse had obviously seen the reaction before. 'This is the twentieth century, my dear. There is illness here, and sadness, but there is hope and joy. Captain Morrison is in the garden with his father.'

Mairi looked up now at the gaunt face of her brother.

'He wrote to me,' he said simply and then he looked over her head towards the farmhouse. 'But Dad?' he asked. 'I thought he'd come out to welcome the prodigal . . .' He felt her tense in his arms and draw away from him. 'Mairi?'

There was no way to soften the blow, nothing that could be said that would make the pain go away. 'He's dead, Ian. He was killed almost a year ago, just a few hours before the Armistice.'

The pain hit him like a knife between the ribs: his father, the provider, the arbiter, the meter out of justice, the solid bulk of security, the teacher, and later the friend, dead. How had he not known that the world no longer contained Colin

232

McGloughlin? He looked at the fields his father had loved, the dry-stone dykes he had helped him build or at least repair, the trees where they had sheltered with their pieces. They were the same. They had no right to be untouched.

'He was awarded the Victoria Cross, Ian. I wish you'd been there to receive it.'

He pushed down his pain to deal with later. Another blow that Mairi had coped with on her own. He looked down at her, saw that the round softness of the girl's face had been replaced by more mature womanly, but not matronly, lines. It was a too-thin face, but beautiful. Whoever would have thought Mairi McGloughlin would grow up beautiful?

'So much you've had to thole on your own, wee Mairi,' he said and wondered how he could do what he wanted if it meant leaving her alone again. Nothing was easy. She must go with him. Bella would insist.

She dimpled. 'Not on my own,' she said. 'I've had Milly and Angus who is wonderful and Jean who's a smaller Milly . . .'

'And don't forget Bert,' he said. 'It was Bert who told you.'

She laughed and they turned towards their home and began to walk to it.

' "There's a golden giant walking along the school road." That's how he announced you. "Has to be your brother and he's no getting my bed." '

He laughed. 'I'll sleep in the kitchen if it makes him feel better. It won't be for long.'

She took a quick look at his face but saw that he was not ready to talk. 'You'll be hungry,' she said.

'What would you do with yourself if you didn't

have men to feed, Mairi? A good meal cures all the ills of a troubled world.' But he said that bitterly.

'It goes a good way,' she said simply. 'Bert and Angus will sleep at the Schoolhouse for a while. Mr Morrison is trying to cram Angus for his highers.'

'How is he?' And he knew that she knew he meant Mr Morrison and not Angus.

'Better now that Robin is improving. It was slow, slow progress, but definitely progress and then, after your letter came, he seemed to accelerate. I visit him once a fortnight and now his father leaves us alone for a while. I think he expects, well, I'm not sure what he expects, but Robin is the same whether he's there or not.' She sighed and he looked down at her sadly.

'But he's not afraid to be alone with you?'

She looked at him in surprise. 'No. We walk in the gardens. Growing flowers is part of his therapy. He loves it and he's good at it. I don't know what we'll do in the winter. He seems nervous if I'm too close to him but at least we talk now, about books and music, the newspapers. We used to walk and stop to look at a flower and sometimes he'd pull one and thrust it at me. Now he tells me about them. Of course, it's Michaelmas daisies and chrysanthemums now.' She sighed and then looked up at Ian and smiled. 'He'll be glad that you're home.'

They were at the house and the next few minutes were taken up with introductions. Ian met Milly and recognized her, as he would have recognized her had he met her first in the street, from the descriptions in Mairi's letters, and then Angus, a quiet muscular boy who looked so much like an amalgam of the boys Robin and Ian that the adult

Ian almost wept. Next he met Jean who was so tongue-tied that she could say not a word but constituted herself his slave and set herself to wait upon him, hand and foot, until he feared that he might step on her, and Bert, the pirate, whose wicked black eyes told him he would have to fight for his right to sleep in his own bed if he had not already abdicated that right.

'My father is dead and yours is too and I hope there was nothing left unsaid between you two,' he said, speaking to the boy who surprised his mother by dropping his pugnacious appearance and hanging on the back of Ian's chair in case he missed a word that the returning hero had to say.

He was disappointed. Ian had never been a loquacious man and, especially when there was so much to be said, he found the process very difficult, if not impossible.

He answered the children's questions as truthfully as he could and Angus soon learned when he would not be drawn but young Bert worried at him like a dog at a bone until his mother, seeing Ian's exhaustion, sent him off, with his brother, to the Schoolhouse.

'I'm no sleepin there. Bad enough Mairi made us eat with the Dominie.'

Milly insisted and, after seeing Jean into bed, went off with her sons to ensure that Bert did not turn round and run back to the farm.

Mairi and Ian were alone.

'Funny not to see him sitting there with his paper and the dogs. He went to make up for me, didn't he?'

He was looking straight at her with those eyes that had always seen so much and she could not lie.

'Not exactly, Ian. He wanted it to be over and he was tired of boys being killed; he was always such a good shot. I think he thought if experienced men went it would help the laddies. He did help the laddies, Ian. Dad threw himself in the way of a grenade to save the life of a boy from Arbroath. He knew what he was doing. Such incredible bravery makes it bearable, I think.'

'Not for me. I never, all my life, did anything properly that he wanted me to do, and now, to know that he felt that he had to go and possibly die in my place . . .'

She threw herself down on the rag rug at his feet and held on to his hands as if he or she or both were drowning. 'It wasn't like that, Ian. It *wasn't*.'

'Oh, please, Mairi, spare me that. I have so much I need to talk over with you; plans that need to be made. First I have to know if you and Robin have come to some kind of arrangement.'

'It's not possible to "come to an arrangement", as you put it, with someone who is like a piece of glass, like the wee piece he brought me from Venice, so fragile that the least puff of wind will blow it over and smash it.'

He put his hand on her hair. 'You said he was improving.'

'He is. He is, but he's holding himself away from me. He's so polite to me. We were always so at ease with one another; he was just like you. I could scold him and argue with him and fight him. Now, I'm on my best behaviour. I don't want to scare him into thinking he has to marry me because he kissed me once or twice and said there'd be roses.' She shook her head and looked up at him and in the mischief in her eyes he saw his wee sister. 'Now, you, Ian

McGloughlin, have you no news for me?'

He laughed. 'I've met a rare wee bully too. Just like you, doing what's good for me whether I like it or not.'

'And don't you like it?'

'I love it.'

They sat quietly for a moment, listening to the logs complaining in the flames.

'So all is well, Ian?'

'I sometimes can't believe it, Mairi, but Arabella Huntingdon loves your brother, and I love her. She wrote hundreds of letters to me. Sometimes I got none for weeks and then I'd get twenty on the one day and she'd numbered them so I know that some never turned up. She could have been dining and dancing with all her posh friends but she stayed at home writing to me.'

He went quiet and from the smile hovering around his lips Mairi knew that he was recalling some of Arabella's letters.

'And when are you going to see her? You *are* going to see her?'

He looked guilty and the first pangs of jealousy hit her and she tried to push them away. A sister was not nearly so important as a lover.

'I went there first, Mairi. I had to know . . . if she was real, the girl who wrote the letters. We met in Edinburgh once, when I left the work camp, and she was so shy and so sweet and called me Mr McGloughlin and asked if she might write still when I was in France. I loved her then, I think. I hadn't before. What is love, Mairi, that chooses one against another and says, this is she? I'd been a wee bit embarrassed, you know, at the shooting, the Laird's niece, and then she smiled at me and gave me her scarf and I knew it was more than the scarf she was giving, but I was afraid that I didn't want her gift, that I couldn't appreciate it.' He looked up from the fire. 'You think I should have come to you first?'

She noticed that he did not say, *I should have come home first*, and so she lied. 'No, Ian, it was right for you to go there first.'

'I don't know what we're going to do. Her aunt and uncle are furious. Her parents are dead, poor wee lamb. Sitting here in the kitchen, I think I'm crazy to think I can marry her.'

'The tenancy, Ian?'

'I doubt they'd give it to me anyway and they won't give it to a woman, lass. If I leave here, you're homeless, and if I stay, who knows? Maybe Sir Humphrey will hound us out.'

'The agent says the lease is yours.'

'That's before Arabella told them. She kept it secret, Mairi, dated men in her own set, as they say.'

'Devious wee madam,' thought Mairi, and wondered when, if ever, he would realize that *she* had written her letters while working day and night to keep his home together, and apart from her one and only night at the opera with Jack, had dated no one *in her own set*.

'She won't want to live here.'

'Can you see her as a farmer's wife?' asked Ian and he laughed tenderly. 'But, Mairi, I have to tell you, I don't want to farm. I want to write. Thanks to Bella, I wrote all during the war, and . . .' He looked away from her as if embarrassed. 'I've sent some stuff to a journal. I won't let Bella help. I want to stay here and I'll work the farm, Mairi, I'll do the best job I can and when and if I start to

238

make some money then I'll leave and marry Bella. She's rich, you see, in her own right, but I couldn't live on a woman.'

She had forgotten that Bella had known about his poetry. Bella had told her, her face alight with enthusiasm, that Ian was a genius, that he had memorized the poetry he was writing in his head because, in prison, he had had no paper.

She stood up. 'I'm tired, Ian, and I have to be up early.'

He stood up too and walked with her to the stair and at the bottom step she stopped and looked up at him. 'Please, Ian, you mustn't worry about me. I couldn't bear that. You stay here only as long as it takes to get yourself established. Bella thinks you're a genius.' She grinned up at him, the old, teasing Mairi. 'Mind you, women in love have nae judgement, or so I'm told, but I'd like to see your poems too, maybe, if you'd like me to see them.'

'I'd be honoured to have you read them, Miss McGloughlin. There's even one called "Mairi". It's about this horrible wee girl who plagued the life out of her long-suffering brother.' He stopped laughing and was suddenly serious. 'And there's one called "Friend". We'll take it with us when we go to see him.'

It was too much. She could bear no more. She moved quickly away up the stairs and when she had gone a few steps she turned and saw that he had not moved. He was so tall that she was eye to eye with him. 'I was so afraid there was no God, Ian, but there is. You brought Him back with you.' And she turned and ran lightly up the rest of the staircase.

CHAPTER TWENTY-THREE

The village postman cycled out to the farm more times in the last two months of 1919 than he had done in the whole of his career. Arabella wrote to Ian almost every day and Mairi soon learned to recognize her writing and her distinctive, expensive stationery. But other envelopes began to arrive too and Ian grinned or groaned each time he saw one, depending on its thickness.

These were letters from publishers interested in his poetry.

Just before Christmas Ian told Mairi that an extremely reputable publishing house had offered to bring out a limited edition of his poetry in the spring and, possibly more importantly to the lover, if not to the poet, Arabella was spending Christmas with her uncle at his Scottish estate.

'Now that I'm going to publish, Bella thinks Sir Humphrey will take me more seriously.'

Mairi looked up from the shirt she was sewing. 'And if he doesn't?'

'She's of age. I would prefer that she not be at outs with her family but . . . if it has to be . . .'

'You'll still marry her?'

'I don't expect you to understand, Mairi,' he said and she could hear the embarrassment in his voice, 'but I ache for her.'

Dear God in Heaven, how self-absorbed the nicest of men were. Women didn't ache, didn't lie awake night after night, longing, longing. Mairi sighed.

'Robin's father walked up with Bert this

afternoon after school.'

Immediately Ian looked contrite. 'How is Robin? We'll visit again before the New Year if you like. Bella arrives on the twentieth. Perhaps just before that. What do you think?'

'He didn't come to talk about Robin, not mainly. It's Milly. He wants her to keep house for him. His daily is getting married at Ne'erday and since Milly will be looking for a job and a home'—she looked at him as if hoping that he would either confirm or deny this—'and he already has the boys most of the time . . .'

'Sounds good, Mairi. An ideal solution.'

Mairi cut off the thread and folded up the shirt. It was a Christmas present for Ian but she assumed that he would not know that most of it had been sewn right under his very nose. 'An ideal solution to what, Ian?'

He had got up to put some coal on the fire but he recognized the iciness in her voice. 'Mairi, I'm sorry. Have I not been listening? My mind is so full of thoughts of seeing my work in print, in a book, Mairi, with covers and my name on the spine, and Bella, sitting where you're sitting, reading my new poems in her lovely voice. Ach, I'm selfish. I was thinking that if the Dominie needs Milly and has room for all of them in that cold barn they call a Schoolhouse, it would be an ideal solution.'

Arabella Huntingdon sitting in the front room reading poetry? He had left his brains as well as his naivety in that prison camp. 'Ian, we have to talk about the future. If you marry . . . when you marry Arabella, you don't expect her to live here?'

He laughed and it was his nice real Ian laugh. 'Can you see Bella living here?' He looked at his sister's white, set face. 'Gosh, Mairi, I didn't mean that it isn't a perfectly comfortable, probably the most comfortable of the small farms, but Arabella is a lady, oh, God, I didn't mean that either. What I mean is, she has her own home. I told you that. But I won't live with her there until I can support her.'

'And what about me?' She had not meant to say that; she had been absolutely determined that she would never say it but it was out now. Her fear was Ian's now.

'You can live with us,' he said easily, 'you know that. You're my wee sister. Bella wants to treat you like a sister.'

'But your Bella is a *lady*. I'm a farmer, Ian. That's all I've ever wanted to be, and if you leave I will have to leave too. They won't give a woman the lease, not a single woman my age.'

Obviously he had never thought the whole thing through. He was in love and his beloved loved him in return. Mundane, practical matters like leases had never crossed his mind.

'But you won't need it, Mairi. I've spoken to Bella. Where I go, you go.'

She was angry again. 'And if I don't want to go where you go? If I was old or married, then it would be different, I could run the farm with everyone's blessing, but since I'm still quite young and have no husband, they'll conveniently forget that I ran this farm for years with the help of a woman and two wee boys. The first man back from the war that has experience and wants a lease will get my home.'

'Robin?'

'Is going to Italy.'

There, she had said it and now the tears that she

242

had kept dammed burst out of their prison. 'His father told me a week or so ago. Robin will leave the Sanatorium but he won't come home. He didn't want to be released back here, not yet, not until he's convinced himself that he's well.'

Ian remembered the urchin who had asked him if he was the daftie. Oh, yes, Robin would have to be quite sure of his mental health before he ran the gauntlet of the village.

'But then he'll come home and you'll marry?'

She managed to stop sobbing. Ian could not cope with tears and he had suffered so much; she did not want him to have to deal with them—not hers, Bella's maybe. If rich, beautiful women in love ever cried . . . ?

'We never once talked of marriage. We never said the words . . . marriage or love, never once.'

Ian wondered if he should tell her about the letter. *Robin is afraid that he might kill you.* No, he could not tell her. He took her in his arms, awkwardly. She was his sister. They were not used to embracing one another. 'Mairi, Robin loves you; I know he does. He's not a farmer. He's a teacher. And he won't teach here in the village. Where is the nearest town that needs a Classics master? Maybe Dundee, maybe Edinburgh. Who knows? When you marry Robin, you'll have to leave the farm. This way it's just a little earlier. I wish I could stay and be a farmer for you but I never wanted to farm. I will stay until I can afford to leave. If there hadn't been Bella, I would probably have stayed for ever and written my poems to keep me sane. But I love her and I need to be with her and I can't ask her to live here. You do see that?'

'Of course I do.' She blew her nose loudly and

243

dried her eyes. 'I'm sorry and I never meant to cry and upset you. Goodness knows, if Robin asked me to go with him, I'd leave without even closing the door behind me, wouldn't I? And I don't expect you to stay here for me but, Ian, I couldn't live with you and Bella in a big mansion house. I'm a farmer. I don't know how to talk to her. I don't know how to dress. I'd embarrass you and I couldn't bear that.'

It was obvious that such a thought had never crossed his mind. 'Och, Mairi, you're havering. You and Bella always look so nice. But let's leave this for now, please. We'll talk to Bella and her aunt and uncle at Christmas.' He stood up because he was so excited that sitting down he could not contain his excitement. 'What a Ne'erday we'll have and then, because of Bella, we'll have to start celebrating Christmas in the English fashion. I've an idea, Mairi, for Bella and for Milly's bairns. We'll get a Christmas tree and put candles on it and presents under it for Bert and wee Jean, and maybe even Angus too, although he thinks he's grown up. What do you say?'

She could not bear to disappoint him and so she tried to sound enthusiastic. Was love enough to smooth all the bumpy paths that he was preparing to walk along? And what would Miss Arabella Huntingdon really think when she saw, daily, the conditions in which her love had grown up? There's nothing romantic about an outside privy, even in the height of summer.

*   *   *

Arabella came the first time when the house

smelled of wood smoke and baking bread and Christmas cake. Mairi thought that she looked like a fairy lost from her Christmas tree in her silver white fur coat and tight little hat. She had gifts for under the tree and Milly and the children exclaimed over the beauty of the wrappings, paper and ribbons so expensive that Mairi blushed at the waste. She could not bring herself to thank Bella for the packages or exult at their beauty. All she could think of was that they made her home-made efforts look so provincial and she hated herself for her jealousy.

'Will you take some tea, Miss Huntingdon?' she asked stiffly and Bella looked at her in surprise.

She slipped off her fur coat and threw it over a chair and Jean and Bert, together, rushed to pick up the glorious creation. Jean fetched her mother's best padded coat hanger from the old wardrobe and they hung the coat up neatly on a nail at the door.

'Thank you, darlings,' said Bella but she was laughing and Mairi found herself hating her for her easy laughter.

'Mairi, please, we are to be sisters. You must call me Bella.'

'Bella,' said Mairi and tried to say it naturally. 'You'll take some tea?'

And all the while Ian stood loving them both and wondering why on earth everything was going wrong. Bella tried and Mairi tried but the visit was a trial for everyone and, too soon, before they had really talked, Bella stood up and Ian almost ran to get her lovely coat.

'I'll walk you back,' he whispered.

'Silly, I didn't walk all that way in these,' she said

pointing to her soft leather boots. 'Uncle's motor is waiting. Let's take Bert and Jean. Come on, you two, if your mamma agrees you may have a ride in the motor.'

They ran in to the scullery shouting for Milly and Arabella looked at Mairi.

She seemed to sense that she should not offer such a treat to her and instead thanked her for the delicious baking. 'You must teach me, Mairi; if I am to be a farmer's wife, I must learn about the food that a farmer likes.'

'Ian's a poet, Bella, and has little idea about what he's eating. I'm sure your cook will manage.'

Oh, how she hated herself for that mean twisted voice that spat out these remarks. What was wrong? Was it that Arabella was so beautiful and elegant, and more importantly, nice, and did not deserve her animosity? Was it because she, Mairi, was jealous of the way that Bella and Ian looked at one another, at the way they let their hands touch over the homely tea table? How can I live in the same house and watch them love and know that Robin does not want me? Will I become the mean, twisted maiden aunt that their children will mock? She ran out after them into the beginnings of the first snow of the winter.

'Bella,' she called, 'come back soon. This house is brighter with you in it.' And then she ran back inside because she was so embarrassed by her own spontaneity.

'Bonny lassie, that,' said Milly as she boiled the kettle for water for the dishes. 'She's no really seeing hersel as the wife of a working fermer, though, is she?'

'I don't think so, Milly. More like Marie

246

Antoinette playing at being a shepherdess with her specially built perfect wee farm. Ian will give up the lease as soon as he's making a living from his writing and then they'll go to England and live in her big house.'

'I aye thought you had tae be dead tae make a living as a writer, if you ken what I mean.'

'The world wants to hear from the poets of the war; to make sure we don't get into such a mess again.'

'Well, amen to that, but what about you, lass? If I leave with the weans next week, you'll be on your own when Ian gets wed.'

'I'll manage, Milly. There'll be plenty of men needing work.' She would not worry Milly by telling her that it was highly unlikely that the Estate would give an unmarried woman a lease on the farm. If Ian and Bella were married before September, Mairi would be out of, not only her occupation, her life, but her home too.

*   *   *

Ian was not too sanguine about the prospects of an early wedding. 'I can hardly bear to be so close to her and know that we have to wait so long,' he told Mairi next morning as he poured fresh cream on his porridge. 'The Grey-Watsons won't even see me. Bella says she'll leave before Christmas if her uncle remains so obdurate . . .' He flushed as he saw her look of surprise at his vocabulary.

'Nothing else to do in prison but read what's there, Mairi. In Germany it was a German-English dictionary.'

Mairi smiled stiffly. He's beginning to sound like

247

them, she thought. Even Robin, a Greek and Latin scholar, did not use such words around her.

'Obdurate? I suppose that means he's a thrawn old bugger.' She tried to smile.

He beamed warmly. 'Aye, but he'll come round. He loves Bella. He's been her guardian since she was three years old. He'll come round.'

Sir Humphrey agreed to meet Ian early on the morning of 24 December. It could only be a short meeting. There were so many social engagements that had to be fulfilled. Ian, of course, had nothing to do but look after his stock; for working-class labouring farmers there were no social engagements.

Mairi pressed his suit and washed and ironed his best shirt. Then when he was dressing, she took her Christmas present from the little pile under the tree and took it up to him.

'Does it spoil Christmas if you open your present before midnight?'

He took the parcel. 'Not if it's that lovely shirt a wee lassie has been working on for weeks.'

She smiled happily and went downstairs to wait. He had noticed. She would be more careful in . . . no, there was no future. His future was with Bella. He would never again sit by the fire in this farmhouse and pretend not to see his sister make his gift.

'But that's right,' Mairi told herself. 'That is the way it should be and it's what I want for him.'

When he had left for the Big House, she sat quietly reading by the fire. Since Ian had come back she had found renewed delight in the written word and in the few minutes each day when her hands were not busy she took one of Ian's books and made a new acquaintance or renewed an old one. She felt she might read a great deal more in the years ahead. It would be something to do, she thought, thoroughly sorry for herself.

*   *   *

Ian meanwhile had every right to feel sorry for himself. The interview with Sir Humphrey, his landlord, was not pleasant. He was shown into the magnificent panelled library where a fire was consuming, at one go, more wood than he would use all day, and where exotic hot-house flowers pretended that it was not mid-winter.

Sir Humphrey was seated behind his desk. He did not get up when Ian was announced and he did not ask him to sit. Ian stood in front of the desk and remembered how he had felt when the officers had tried to break his spirit. He had managed to resist then. He would not allow his spirit to be broken now.

'I have to say I'm surprised at your effrontery, McGloughlin. Can't say I expected it from your father's son.'

'I never expected to fall in love with your niece, Sir Humphrey, if that is the situation that insults you.'

'You're the uneducated son of a tenant farmer, man. You're not fit to clean her boots.'

If he had expected Ian to blush with shame at such an insult he was disappointed.

'I couldn't agree with you more, Sir Humphrey.' He would not say that it was Arabella who had done all the running. 'But I have fallen in love with her and, she with me.'

'She's a very wealthy young woman . . .' Ah, he had scored a hit. Ian pulled himself up and stood, if possible, taller and straighter, and a muscle worked in his jaw.

Sir Humphrey looked at him. 'Unworthy,' he said. 'I think I know that it's not her money, but, Ian,' and here he stood up, 'you must see that it wouldn't work. I know you are going to publish some poetry but, dear God in Heaven, do you seriously think being the author of some maudlin verses makes you the equal of a Huntingdon? You have nothing in common, lad. Bella thought it was romantic to champion you; you and she against the world. But when her world turns against her, and it will, then what? How long will the great Romance last?'

'If Bella's family and friends spurn her for marrying a decent hardworking man who will love and cherish her all her days, then she's maybe better off without them, Sir Humphrey.'

This time it was Ian who had scored the hit. Sir Humphrey went an alarming shade of red. 'How dare you! When did you leave school? When you were twelve, thirteen? How can you even converse with our kind of people?'

Ian laughed. 'Sir Humphrey, even for an aristocrat, Bella is appallingly ignorant, but I'm remedying that. I came to ask, not for your permission, but for your blessing. If you can give us neither, then I will tell you that I will offer to let Bella go. I love her and would not harm her. But if she will not leave me, then as soon as I can afford it, I will marry Arabella Huntingdon.'

'We'll see about that. I own the house you live in, remember?'

250

Ian had not expected this. He would not get angry, he would not. He leaned forward and held on to the edge of the heavy oak desk. 'Then you would punish my sister too. I had not thought it of you, Sir Humphrey.'

The Laird slumped back down in his chair. 'If I throw you out to sleep under a hedge I play into your hands. Bella will merely insist that you move to Surrey with her. She is of age.' He picked up a pen, thrust it into a solid silver inkwell and then began to draw circles on the blotter in front of him. He looked up at Ian who still stood ramrod straight. 'Damn you, boy. Can't you see it's for you as well as Bella? She'll make you miserable in six months. She's used to balls and parties. Damn it all, she's welcome at Court.'

'And I'll take her away from all that? You do Bella an injustice, Sir Humphrey. She is a finer woman than you realize. If we think we can make a marriage work . . .'

Sir Humphrey stood up and went to the door and Ian had no choice but to follow him.

'Marriage between equals is difficult enough. You are just released from the prison camp, Ian. Is it love or pity? Give her a chance to really get to know you. Until October you'd met fewer than five times. Give yourself time.'

'I won't hurt her, Sir Humphrey. Try to convince her that she's making a mistake if you like. She must be sure in her own mind and heart.'

The sound Sir Humphrey made was almost a snort. 'Basic psychology. I tell her no. She'll dig her heels in. Damn it, I wash my hands of the pair of you. Invite her to your cottage. Let the difference in your lifestyles speak for me. And you'd best

251

emulate Kipling and win the Nobel prize with your writing. Even that might not be enough. I won't wish you the joys of the season. Good day to you.'

Ian walked out, head high, and managed to get to a bend in the driveway before being violently sick in the shrubbery. When he had recovered he turned and looked back at the great house. Was Sir Humphrey right? Was there too great a difference between them? Maybe Bella was living a fairy tale but this frog would never turn into a prince.

And then he saw her, running towards him down the driveway and he forgot all his good intentions and ran to meet her.

'My darling, my darling, we'll make it work. Ask Mairi if I may dine with you tomorrow?'

He kissed her cold little nose and then her cheeks and then her mouth.

'I don't know about dining, Arabella Huntingdon, but you're welcome to take your dinner with us.'

And in full view of the disapproving windows he kissed her again.

CHAPTER TWENTY-FOUR

The Estate was being sold. Mairi could not believe it. It had been in the hands of the Grey and then the Grey-Watson families for nearly three hundred years. It was rumoured that an Insurance Company was prepared to make a sizeable offer as was one of the Ammunitions barons who had found himself, on the cessation of hostilities, with both a fortune and a title.

252

'Well, let's hope we don't have to work for him,' was Ian's comment when he read this item in the local news.

'Didn't Bella say *anything*?' Bella's letters, since she had returned to London in late January, were if anything more frequent than before.

'She hasn't seen too much of her family, Mairi. It only leads to argument and distress for everyone.'

Mairi sighed but said nothing. Ian had returned from the Big House on Christmas Eve, a little shaken, but he had said nothing except that Bella would be coming for Christmas dinner. That news, as he had expected, had thrown both Mairi and Milly into a panic and they had swept and dusted the already swept and dusted house and threatened the children with all manner of horrible penalties, should they drop a crumb anywhere. Ian wisely stayed away until Mairi herself decided that 'Bella can lump it or like it.' Still, when the children were in bed, she returned to the scullery to make one more baking of shortbread to add to the already heavily overburdened table.

Bella arrived wearing her silver fur coat. She had not considered not wearing it. If Mairi was to be her sister-in-law she would have to take her as she was, fur coat and all. And if Ian was to be her husband, and she was determined that he was, then it would, in all probability, be her last fur coat.

She ate a hearty dinner, insisted on helping Mairi clear the table and so Ian felt that he too had to offer to help. In the end everyone helped and each got in the other's way and they had a delightful time.

Then, delicately, Arabella asked about hygiene arrangements and so Mairi took her to the outside privy which she had made as comfortable as she could, although nothing could prevent it from being cold. Bella judged it 'lovely fun' whilst silently vowing never again to enter the door, no matter how desperate she found herself.

She helped Jean and Milly dry the dishes and only dropped one cup. Bert and Angus fell madly in love with her and fought desperately to sit close to her by the fire. She foiled them by sitting the wool-clad Jean on her satin lap and Mairi watched and tried not to feel jealous of the beautiful girl's ability to win over everyone. But at last Christmas Day was over and Sir Humphrey's motor arrived to convey the silver princess back to her palace. Ian went with her and returned two hours later to tell the waiting Mairi that Rupert Grey-Watson had asked him in to take a glass of brandy with him.

'He was as nice as ninepence, Mairi, and very civil, but he thinks it won't work.'

'Perhaps he wants Bella for himself?'

'I must admit I thought that might be it. The Grey-Watsons lost money during the war while Bella's fortune seemed to multiply, but to Rupert she is merely a young cousin. He's fond of her, as you are of wee Jean, no more.'

For several days Bella seemed to be in the farmhouse more often than she was at her uncle's home and, on one auspicious day, Ian went into Dundee to hire an evening suit, shirt, tie and shoes. He had been bidden to dinner.

Mairi thought he looked magnificent. So too did Milly.

They watched him enter the Grey-Watson motor which had been sent for him and then drive off to the manor house.

'He'll easy be the best-looking laddie there,' said Milly proudly. 'That Rupert seems like a nice enough young man but he's no a patch on oor Ian. Well, I mean tae say, he's cried Rupert.'

'I think Rupert is very handsome,' teased Mairi as she shepherded Milly back indoors for their very last evening together, 'and I think Rupert is a lovely name.'

'Ach, you're Ian's sister right enough when you say daft things like that. Men should be cried Jim, or Angus, or Bert. You know where you are with a Jim.'

'Steak,' said Mairi softly.

'Aye, lassie, steak. Now come on and help me with my case. Noo that the Dominie's away tae see off Robin, I'll need tae get in there and take care of the dirt. I'll hae it readied up for him when he gets back.'

Mairi helped Milly with the family's accumulated belongings and tried to keep her mind off Ian's visit to the Big House and Robin's retreat to Italy. She would not allow herself to think about Robin, she would not. She would not remember that night before he went back, for the last time, to a war zone. She would not permit herself to think of the sweetness of being held against him while she listened to his heart.

Our hearts are beating together, Mairi. Can you hear them? Lub dub, lub dub. What can lub dub, lub dub mean?

But she had not been able to answer or to hear him tell her because the Dominie had come out and although he had pretended not to see and had hurried back into the Schoolhouse, the spell of the moment had been broken. They had laughed, a little shamefacedly, a little resentfully—they had had so little time together—and they had gone back into the house so that Robin could share his last moments of leave with his father.

His last moments of leave. Were they, had they been, his last moments of sanity? But he was well, well enough to be released from the asylum. And instead of coming to her, he was running to Italy, the country where some of his best and his worst memories were buried. No, she would not think of it. She would think only of folding Jean's little nightdresses, her Sunday smock.

'Goodness, would you look at the size my laddies have grown here in the country, Mairi. If their daddy could just see them. Good country air, good country food.'

Mairi put the jumper Milly handed her into the box labelled 'Salvation Army'. 'The country is no paradise, Milly. There's some here as stunted as bairns in the towns. Look at that wee lassie Jean plays with.'

And they chattered on because neither could bear to talk about the future or the past. At last the cases were packed and they had no excuses left.

'How did I manage to gather all these things, Mairi, and still fill a box for the Sally Army? How can I ever thank you?'

'Please, Milly. If you talk like that it will feel as if you are going away for ever instead of just down the road.'

'Aye, and we've you to thank for that and all. The Dominie says my Angus has a brain.'

Mairi blew out the lamp and led the way downstairs to the kitchen. 'Your troubles will really start when he tells you Jean has a brain.'

Milly snorted with laughter. 'A lassie that's in love with Jack Black's old horse, a brain?'

They laughed together as they made a last pot of tea.

'Och, I'll miss having you to laugh with, Mairi. You've kept me sane these last few years.' Milly stopped, aware of what she had just said. 'Och, lassie. He'll come home to you, safe and well.'

Mairi stood up. 'We'd best go to bed, Milly. I don't want Ian to think we're waiting up for him as if he was a bairn.'

Milly moved as if to touch her and she shied away from the gesture. 'Don't say any more, Milly dear; we've been good for one another. I shall miss you so much but you'll only be in the village. Heavens, you could be going sixteen miles away to Dundee. Then I really would have something to be miserable about. Come on, off to bed, and we won't say goodbye the morn's morn, just cheerio.'

Milly said goodnight and went quietly off upstairs and Mairi fussed with the fire and the fire guard for a few minutes.

'Robin gone, now Milly and the children, and, if this dinner party has gone well, and how could it not, when they see Ian properly, Ian will be going soon too. If I have the farm I'll manage. Let them leave me the farm.'

She put out the light and followed Milly upstairs but she did not sleep. She lay wide awake, long after she heard Ian come back and climb the wooden stairs. She could tell nothing from his step. It sounded just as it always did.

*   *   *

257

She was, as usual, the first one up in the morning, and only someone who looked very closely at her face could tell that she had not slept at all.

Jean was excited about going to a new home but she was unhappy too and only the promise that Ian was going to walk with them to the Schoolhouse carrying their cases calmed her down.

'And you can come back as often as you like, wee Jean,' he said. 'Especially since Mairi only makes crumble when you're there to eat it.'

'And why not, since Jean's always willing to go out and pull rhubarb, unlike some I could mention.'

That remark, of course, set Milly off. 'Mairi McGloughlin, you cannae expect a man that's working all the hours God gives him to come hame and dig up his dinner afore he eats it.'

'And why not? There's maybe cause for saying a man should learn to cook. Mind you,' she added, as she noted joyfully the appalled expression on Milly's honest face, 'if anybody at the Schoolhouse had learned to boil an egg, there's you would be out of a job.'

Milly looked at her. 'Well, I'm off then. I have every afternoon off. Give me a few days to clean the place properly and I'll come back tae see you.'

'Fine,' said Mairi lightly. She did not want Milly and the children to go. They had known each other such a short time but, so much grief and happiness had been woven into their time together, it was as if they had always been friends. She hugged Jean and went back into the farmhouse as if this morning was just one of many mornings and she did not watch them walk off over the hill and down the school road.

Another step. Another stage. When Ian returned perhaps he would share his memories of the evening with her. Right now she had work to do. She would take the bedding from the big bed and soak it; too cold today for washing it and hanging it out to dry. She would have to wait for a dry day with a bit of wind.

Ian came back when she was turning the big mattress. 'Here, I'll give you a hand,' he laughed. 'And then I'll tell you about my grand dinner afore you burst.'

'Milly and I didn't give you a thought, Ian McGloughlin. We had far too many other things to discuss last night.'

'That's better, more your feisty wee self. Come on. The world won't end if you sit down before the sun sets. Now what do you want to know? Not the ladies' frocks, I hope, because apart from Arabella who was wearing a sort of blue thing, I haven't the smallest notion. I near died of fright when I went into the dining room. First I had to take in, that's what they say, take in some old auntie who put her hand on my arm so gingerly for fear she would catch something, and I was seated miles away from Bella. The table would have filled the big barn and come out the other end and never in my life have I imagined so many dishes and glasses and bits of silver. Bella had shown me place settings—that's what it's called, a place setting, the right number of spoons and forks and knives for this, that and the next and a glass for this wine and another for that wine and a special one for water—but everything she had told me went right out of my head and up the chimney.

' "Not to your taste, young man?" asked this old

259

lady on my right but she was smiling and holding her fork almost in front of my nose so I smiled back at her and picked up my matching fork and then ate what she ate and used the same fork or spoon she was using. And don't ask me about the food although there was chicken, I think, but I couldn't see it for sauce, and there was fish before the chicken, and they take a kind of frozen icecream between courses and different wine with fish and even a wine with the pudding, but not a dish a patch on your game pie . . .'

'And I suppose you told them so,' said Mairi, since he appeared to have run out of breath.

'I was too scared, Mairi,' he confessed. 'There were so many people and it was so hot and then the wine . . . I'm not used to drink. Sir Humphrey kept introducing me as "Bella's protégé, you know: damn good young war poet". But I let him talk. It was his house, after all, and I listened and tried to answer questions. At these affairs, it's like people are on strings. You talk to the person on one side and then everybody's string gets tweaked and you turn and talk to the person on the other. I got to talk to Bella after dinner in this huge room with two fire places and more wood burning than we've used all winter and she said it was going well.'

'And what did you think, Ian?'

He got up and put another log defiantly on the fire. 'I don't know. Rupert's a decent bloke and he thinks it would be wrong for me to marry Bella.' Ian laughed, but it was not a pleasant sound. 'It's me he's thinking of; he thinks Bella will make me miserable, even if I let her keep me, which I will not do. His mother is a different story. No matter how much she smiles and seems polite, I can tell that Lady Grey-Watson can't stomach the thought of me at her table. One or two of the other elderly ones seemed all right, interested in the war and in my poetry, but at least one of the old ladies thought I was a shirker and therefore ought to have been shot. They let Bella come back with me in the motor. She wanted to come in with me, force them, if you know what I mean, and it nearly killed me to send her away but everything has got to be right, above board, honourable, if you want to use such a word. She leaves today and I must get this book out and it has to do well, give me some kind of reputation.' He fell silent and they sat for several minutes looking into the fire.

'Will she come to say goodbye?' asked Mairi after a while.

'No. I don't think I could let her go again, Mairi. It's easy to be noble when she's not in my arms. Ach, damn it.' He jumped up. 'I shouldn't be talking like this to you.'

'I understand, Ian, of course I do. Goodness, war has an awful lot to answer for, doesn't it, or at least the people that cause the wars. Can you remember when we were wee, running to the school, scared to be late? If anyone had asked we would have said that by this time we'd be married with families of our own, and here's Dad dead and not even enough bits of him to bury, you, with your experiences, and Robin, my gentle Robin with his silly old Romans, marked so badly and cruelly that no one can even see the marks. Write your poems, Ian, and maybe even a book about the nature of pacificism, and write them so well that people will read and understand and vow that nothing like this will ever happen again.' She stopped, embarrassed,

261

and, as usual, took refuge in mock anger. 'Now, will you get your great feet out of my kitchen and let me get on with my work. There's a farm to run, in case you had forgotten, and only you to run it.'

He went to the door, put on his coat and cap, and went out without a word, but she knew he was not hurt or angry. He would do his work and when he came in, his dinner, piping hot, nourishing, and recognizable, would be on the table, and things would be back to how they were before the war, except for the empty seat by the fire and the empty spaces in their hearts.

CHAPTER TWENTY-FIVE

The postman, Davie Wishart, who had had a fairly good break from cycling all the way to Windydykes farm, was back on his rounds by February.

'Could you no consider gettin one of thay fancy telephone machines in, Ian, tae save my auld legs?'

Ian brought him in to the warmth of the fire. 'I would but we won't be here that long. I doubt the next farmer of Windydykes will have use for a telephone.'

'Unless I'm the next farmer,' said Mairi lightly as she handed the postman a steaming mug of strong sweet tea. 'I've decided to apply, Ian. They can only say no.'

Ian looked at her in astonishment but he would say nothing in front of old Davie.

He was eloquent enough when the man had gone, free-wheeling down the hill and then struggling up the other side.

'Talk to me, Mairi.'

'What would you like to talk about?'

Ian looked at her bowed head in exasperation. 'Mairi, was that a joke, a female emancipation thing, now that you're nearly eligible to vote?'

All men over twenty-one and all women over thirty had become eligible to vote in 1918. Ian had happily availed himself of the opportunity to participate in the government of his country but Mairi, of course, had still over a year to wait.

She looked up from her mending. 'Possibly, but I hadn't meant to say it until it popped out.'

'You are going to apply for the tenancy?'

'Ian, I don't want to live with you and Bella, if you ever swallow your pride and marry her, and frankly I want to be here if Robin comes home. The new owners of the Estate will put a tenant in the Big House and so you and Bella won't come back.'

'Yes, we will ... I mean we would if it was necessary.'

'Ian, you can hardly wait to leave this farm, and I don't mind, really I don't. I think you and Bella should start somewhere else, probably not in her house either, but that's up to you.'

Mairi had done a great deal of thinking since Christmas. A marriage between Ian and Arabella would not be welcomed by the Grey-Watson family but it would happen and Arabella Huntingdon-McGloughlin would not fit in at Windydykes farm. Neither would Mairi McGloughlin fit her sister-in-law's life style. Ian would. He would adapt. He had never liked the farm; a cuckoo, perhaps, in another bird's nest.

'We will marry this year, but nothing will be done

263

before I see how this first book is received.'

Mairi looked at him shrewdly. He was so strong when his beloved Bella was hundreds of miles away. His love and desire for her shone from his eyes when she was with him. Which would be stronger, his principles or his longing?

She smiled. 'Ian, does it really matter who is paying the rent? Don't waste your life or Bella's. Marry her and don't think about me. Maybe the new owners will be enlightened men and will allow me to take on the tenancy.'

Ian stood up. It was winter and there was nothing growing in his fields but there was still work to be done. 'If I could see you settled, Mairi. You're my sister and it's my duty . . .'

Mairi rounded on him and her eyes were full of anger. 'Duty? You owe me nothing, Ian. You have more than done your duty. If the Estate throws me out then of course I will stay with you and Bella until . . . until some other arrangement can be made, but for God's sake, put Bella and her happiness first. Don't have her growing old and wrinkled and frustrated too.'

Ian laughed and got slapped for his sense of humour. 'Och, Mairi,' he said, still laughing, 'if you could see yourself. Anything less old and wrinkled I have yet to see.'

She went to slap him again and then started to laugh too. 'Well, give me frustrated at least. Away and tend to your beasts and I'll take my frustrations out on a batch of dough. And when are you going to look at the post after old Davie cycling out here and him two minutes from retirement?'

He had forgotten the letters and she watched him flip through them, smiling as he saw the usual

264

thick missive from Bella. She turned away. No, once again there was nothing, not even a picture card from Robin. She was wrong to keep hoping. To leave the farm and follow Ian south was probably the most dignified way to handle the situation. He had known that he was going to leave her, that last day when she had visited him, and she had known but neither had had the courage to speak of what was really in their hearts.

*   *   *

She had met him in the greenhouse, a greenhouse bigger even than the one belonging to the Big House.

Robin had smiled shyly when she had come in.

'It's snowing, Mairi,' he had said.

'Yes, but it was exciting watching the snow from the train, Robin. And the train was warm.'

She had moved closer to him and immediately he had picked up two of his little pots. 'Seedlings. I shall give you one, Mairi.'

She moved back towards the bench on the other side of the room and he had relaxed again. 'Is Dad with you?' He had looked round as if expecting his father to materialize before him.

'He's talking to the doctor. He'll join us for tea.'

'You're good to come here, Mairi, but it's such a long way and . . .' He stopped and very carefully, as if it were the most important thing he would ever do, he measured soil into a pot. 'There must be other things to do, I mean, other . . . friends . . .'

'No one more important than you, Robin.'

At that he had turned and taken a quick step towards her and then he had stopped again and turned back to his bench. He had put his pots down and his hands gripped the edge of the bench so that she could see his knuckles standing out against the dirt on his skin. She ached to run and hold him, to turn him against her breast, to show him that he was safe, but she dared not. He was too fragile.

'I've brought my last pot of raspberry jam,' she said instead.

His voice was low. 'I love your jam, Mairi.'

'April! April,' yelled Ian behind her and she was propelled back into the present. She turned to see his face suffused by joy. 'April,' he yelled again. It seemed to be all he was capable of saying.

'April what?'

'Publication, Mairi. My poems are to be published in April.'

Immediately she forgot Robin. 'Oh, Ian, how wonderful! Come on, don't leave me in suspense. Tell me everything.'

He handed her the letter from his publisher. 'There's to be a launch, like for a ship. I'll have to go to London. You'll come with me, Mairi, on the train.' He grabbed his bonnet. 'I want to write to Bella but the cattle . . .'

'I'll feed them.'

'No you won't. Half an hour won't make any difference; I'm still farmer here. You stay in the kitchen, wee sister, where you belong.'

He laughed, kissed the envelope from Bella and put it back on the table to read later, jammed his bonnet on his head and went out, and Mairi was left with the letter that surely, surely would change her brother's life.

Ian, a published poet. She had never actually believed that she would see the day. It seemed the kind of thing that happened to other people but here it stated that his first author's copy would be with him shortly.

London? She would go to London with him. She would stand proudly beside him . . . Mairi stopped in exultant mid-glow. No, she would not. Arabella Huntingdon, in silver furs and sparkling diamonds, would stand beside him.

'Not in April surely,' she tried to laugh and the laugh caught on a sob. She was not crying because Arabella would be there, but because Colin would not. How proud he would have been.

She told Ian so as they ate their dinner later, after he had done his chores, read his letter, and answered both the letter from the publisher and the letter from Arabella.

Ian's face, which had been so full of life, became cold. 'Would he? I'm not sure that his feelings might have been more embarrassment, but we'll never know.'

'Ian, he did not join up because he was ashamed of you. He wanted to do his share so that it would be over for you and the boy he saved and all the other boys, sooner.'

Ian put down his spoon and stood up. He pushed his chair in to the table. 'Please, Mairi. I just don't want to think about Dad. I want to think about Bella and April and nothing else.'

She watched him as he left the room and then listened to the sound of his boots as he walked up the stairs and across the landing into his room. The door closed and she could imagine him going to his table and taking refuge in his books or his writing. Wearily she too got up and began to clear away the unfinished meal, shaking her head a little at the

267

waste and at the thought of Ian without food.

'He's a big lad and knows where the pantry is. I'm not going to worry about him.'

After she had washed up and prepared the table for breakfast she went to her father's desk where all the papers relating to the farm were kept and reread the letters about the take-over. All existing tenancy agreements would be honoured. That meant that she was safe until September. But by the autumn, if Ian married and left the farm, she would be homeless unless she was awarded the tenancy. And, she decided, she would fight for her right to stay.

*   *   *

The next few weeks were busy. Usually, in the cold months, a farmer could relax a little, take care of repairs to his house or his steading or his equipment, even go curling on the ponds with other farmers, but Ian seemed forever to be at his desk answering the letters from London and Surrey.

Bella had insisted on paying for a launch party at an exclusive London hotel and she wanted Ian and Mairi to take rooms in the hotel while she stayed with the Grey-Watsons at their London home.

'And I want you to get some new clothes, Mairi,' said Ian. 'The money from the book is earmarked for a ring for Bella but I want you to take this to buy yourself something nice. You haven't had anything since before the war.'

Mairi looked at the heavy purse he had given her and remembered the thrill she had had all those years ago when Colin had given her money to buy a dress. 'I don't need this, Ian. I'm not coming with you.' He made to interrupt and she put her hands up as if physically to stop him. 'It's not that I don't want to come but Bella will be there . . .'

'Of course she'll be there but *you* have to be there too. You *must* share it with me, Mairi.'

'I can share just as well up here. Och, Ian, take the money and get yourself a suit made. I want all those smart people in London to see that you're every bit as good as the Grey-Watsons.'

'That's got nothing to do with fancy clothes.'

'Damn it, Ian. Are you still so naive? Of course to decent people the cost of your clothes doesn't matter . . .'

'Decent people, like you and Bella, are the only people who matter to me, Mairi. I know Bella pays more for her clothes than we could ever imagine but she's sensitive.' He saw from the look on his sister's face that he had said the wrong thing. Damn it, but women were difficult.

'You have discussed me with Bella?' She was furious.

'Yes. No. Of course. Not discuss, Mairi, but naturally we talk about you. You're my family as the Grey-Watsons are Bella's. We *discuss* all of you. Mairi, it would break my heart if you weren't with me at the launch. And Bella's too. She doesn't want to come between us.'

'That's daft. She's to be your wife. Of course she has come between us'—she saw his face and changed what she had been about to say—'that's only right, Ian. Bella must come first—always.'

'You're my wee sister, Mairi. We are the same blood. That's a different tie from the one I want to have with Bella. Don't hurt me by not sharing my big moment with me.'

'Who will look after the farm?'

'Mairi McGloughlin? You know fine well any one of our neighbours will help out willingly. We can ask Jack now that his wife has decided that he's not still in love with you.'

Jack had married just before the end of the war, a marriage of necessity it was rumoured, and their first baby had arrived rather precipitately after the wedding, but they seemed to be quite happy and Jack's father-in-law, an Arbroath grocer, had been seen to smile, occasionally, at his son-in-law.

'I don't know that Jack ever was in love with me and I certainly was never in love with him.'

She turned and smiled at her brother. 'I'll come to your launch, Ian, and I'll stay at Bella's nice hotel. How could I miss your big day?'

He looked at her and he was perplexed. One moment she said one thing and immediately she said another. But she would come and his happiness would be all the sweeter because his wee sister was sharing with him.

'And will you buy something nice?'

She nodded and he should have remembered from their childhood that Mairi nodded when she did not mean what she was saying. She would buy new material but she would not waste their hard-earned money on store-bought clothes.

As soon as she could she went off to see Milly. Jean opened the door of the Schoolhouse and threw herself into Mairi's arms. Oh, the sweetness and innocence of Jean who was not afraid or ashamed to show where she loved.

'Your mum busy, Jean?'

Jean rolled her eyes heavenwards as if for Divine

guidance. 'You know Mum, Mairi. She's having a wonderful time finding things to do.'

Milly had heard their voices and came bustling out of the kitchen, her face rosy from her ovens.

'When did I ever have to look for something to do, you cheeky wee madam. Mairi, love, how good to see you. Come on in and tell me what you think.'

'Mrs Morrison used to call me a *pert wee madam*. Cheeky must be the same thing.'

Mairi looked around. Milly had been back to the farm several times since she had started working for the Dominie but this was the first time that Mairi had visited the Schoolhouse.

'Goodness what a transformation!' There were new curtains, new cushions, a rag rug in front of the fire.

Milly saw Mairi looking at it and beamed with pride. 'Would you believe the Dominie and Angus made that? My Jim showed me how to do it and I showed Mr Morrison that time we had the snow too deep for the school to open. They're making you one but you're not supposed to know. Gin they find enough old rags, there'll be everybody in the county with one of their rugs. Even Bert's had a try but he hasnae the patience. Come on, lass, come on, come away ben and tell what's up, or is this just a social call?'

'You're happy, Milly.' Mairi sat down in the old chair with its new plump cushion. It was a statement, not a question. Milly was blooming.

'Och, he's the easiest man in the world tae work for. That besom took real advantage of him and I'm sure she was skimming off the housekeeping because could we no live like kings on what he gives me for foodstuffs and the farmers that

271

generous with what they have. Mr Morrison is tutoring Angus for a scholarship to the High School in Dundee and he says he'll win it. Says he hasn't had a brain like this to work with since Ian and Robin were bairns. Bert's behaving; a stroke or two with the tawse has done him the world of good and Jean's that happy between her wee friends at school and that dopey auld horse, but come on, tell me all. Has Ian set the day? Is that it? Are there wedding bells about to peal?'

'I don't know about wedding bells but Ian has the date for the publication of his first book of poetry and they want more and even the novel he's going to write. Would you believe some manny in a big firm in London wants that from just talking to Ian and reading his poems?'

Milly sat back and basked in the reflected glow from Ian's success. 'A published writer. Well, I hope he'll never get so grand we can't talk to him—but not oor Ian. Even when he wins this noble prize that people talk about, he'll jist be Ian.'

Mairi knew exactly what Ian would say about his chances of winning a Nobel prize but she kept it to herself.

'It's about the day the book gets printed that I wanted to talk to you, Milly. It's going to be in London and Ian wants me there. But that means staying in a posh hotel that Bella has picked out. Clothes, Milly. Nightwear, underwear. I can't go into a splendid hotel in London wearing my own sewing. Ian has given me money for a new dress for the big day, a lot of money, but he doesn't realize about things like stockings and gloves and petticoats . . .'

'Trimmed with lace,' put in Milly. 'And hats and

272

gloves. And here's Miss Arabella with her silks and satins and you don't want to let Ian down.'

'I'm sure Bella won't care what I wear. She only ever sees Ian when he's in the room. It's not Bella so much as . . .'

'The maids,' agreed Milly, nodding her head vigorously. 'Now, how much time do we have?'

'Oh, Milly, you're a dear, but you're so busy here. I didn't realize you were doing so much.'

'Because there is nothing else to do, with Angus and Mr Morrison with their heads in books all evening and Bert doing his homework and bringing in the coal the way I hear Robin did when he was a lad. We'll go into Dundee on Saturday and we'll buy material and then I'll take you to meet Jim's sister, Jeanette, that has a stall at the market and we'll get trimmings from her and a decent dinner. Isn't she grateful for everything you did for Jim's bairns.'

Mairi tried hard to suppress them but in spite of her best efforts, the tears stared to fall. 'Oh, Milly, I took you in for me, not for you.'

'Ach, at first, lassie, and of course it was to help out, but God alone knows what would have happened to us if you hadn't needed me. If we were lucky it would have been ten in one room up a stair in Dundee, and my Angus would have been in some kind of trouble before he was fifteen. My boy's got a life ahead of him, thanks to you, and a few evenings sewing pretty things instead of cushion covers will be a joy. Now stop greeting. God, you're worse than Jean with your greet, greet, greet. But with her it's aye for a horse.'

'I've never wept over a horse.'

'Good. Now when's the big day, because

273

weather'll make a difference.'

'April.'

'Is that not one of the nicest months of the year? We'll probably be able to use a nice linen and do you know what, Mairi? We'll make a silk nightgown and I'll embroider roses on it. I haven't done roses in a long time. It'll be perfect, white silk with wee pink roses, and when you get back from London, you can put it away for your honeymoon. For heaven's sake, lassie, don't start again. Hasn't the Dominie had a letter all the way from Italy saying that Robin's feeling better every single day?'

CHAPTER TWENTY-SIX

Ian's book *Quietus* was published in April to impressive reviews and, whether because of its subject matter or his military history or possibly because of Bella—maybe even a combination of all three—he soon found himself courted and honoured. He thoroughly enjoyed himself—for about a week—and then told Bella he would have to head north. The farm and his pen were both waiting and the publishers were pressuring him to produce more work. But it was becoming harder and harder to leave Bella behind.

'Talk to him, Mairi,' begged Bella as they sat in the foyer of the elegant London hotel. 'He won't listen to me. Doesn't he realize that every mother with an unmarried daughter will be throwing their offspring at his feet? I don't want him to find someone prettier than me—or younger.'

Ian laughed but Mairi did not. Bella had loved

274

Ian for a long time. She deserved her prize.

'Bella's right,' said Mairi as she looked down at her silk-stockinged ankles peeping out demurely from under her lilac silk skirts. Oh, Milly was a treasure beyond all treasures. During this week of exciting happenings more than one young man had made Miss McGloughlin realize that she was not a dried-up old maid. Fine feathers make fine birds, she told herself with a smile. 'I must return to Windydykes'—for one thing she had no more lovely new clothes in which to show herself off and had in fact worn this dress to dinner the night they had arrived—'but, Ian, you need not. Why don't you marry now in London, by special licence or whatever.'

Ian was scandalized. 'Mairi McGloughlin, what a thing to say.'

'Are you sure you want to marry such an old fuddy duddy?' Mairi asked Bella. She was amazed at herself. New clothes, the admiration of young men who had not grown up with her and who had not, thank Heaven, seen her in Ian's old dungarees and her rubber boots, had been, she felt, good for her morale. She could never have spoken like this before Bella even a year ago. 'Take your pride in hand, Ian, before it ruins the best thing that ever happened to you. Get married now. You're on your way. What more do you want?'

'I want nothing more than Arabella Huntingdon,' said Ian and it was at Bella that he was looking.

'Shall I come to you in my shift, like maidens of old, my lovely poet? Is that what you want?'

Mairi got up but they did not notice her going; their eyes were only for one another. She would go

275

out, one last walk along the capital's exciting streets. Tomorrow she would return to Windydykes farm and she would put her lovely clothes away with a prayer that she might soon need them again.

Ian was not in the hotel when she returned and eventually she ordered a light meal from room service. She checked Ian's room again before she got ready for bed but still he had not returned.

He knocked on her door just before she went down for breakfast the next morning.

'I should have got a message to you,' he said and he was blushing with embarrassment. 'I took Bella home.' Then he looked at her directly. 'I stayed with her.'

'Have you had breakfast?' asked Mairi demurely.

Ian looked at his wee sister and the hot colour came and went in his face and then he laughed. 'You're a wicked girl, Mairi McGloughlin,' he said. 'Come on. We'll have breakfast and then get that train home. I'll need to get a second book out faster than ever now.' He steered her away from the lift to the staircase where there was more privacy. 'We have decided. I'm going home but I *will* get a special licence and as soon as it's granted she'll come north. Maybe there'll be time for Milly to make you a bridesmaid's dress.'

Mairi threw her arms around him. 'Oh, Ian, I am so happy for you and Bella, so happy. Bella doesn't mind not having a big wedding?'

'Mind? Can you picture the eyes of the villagers if she turned up in her petticoat, and I wouldn't put it past her, especially after last night,' he finished quietly, enjoying his memories. 'She is so wonderful, Mairi, and I don't deserve her but I'll

276

try to make her happy. Come on, are you hungry? One last big breakfast you don't have to cook.'

They went downstairs into the magnificent dining room which always filled Mairi with awe. Ian seemed not to notice his surroundings, to take for granted the elegant furnishings, the linen and china, the dutiful but not servile waiters. Oh, yes, he would fit very easily into Bella's world. But Mairi, though she could enjoy this life for a few days now and again, would only really be happy among her fields. She would only be really happy when . . . no, *O, that way madness lies* . . . she would not think of Robin.

'Are you going to ask Robin to stand up with you?' The words blurted themselves out.

'That would be wonderful but I doubt there'll be time. It shouldn't take too long to get the licence, and by the time even a cable got to Rome and Robin got leave—if it's the middle of a school term—we'll be married. Married, Mairi, can you believe it? Married, to the most wonderful woman in the entire world.'

His infatuation did not get between the lover and an enormous breakfast. Mairi, on the other hand, ordered tea and toast and had trouble forcing the toast down. Robin loved Ian and with Ian gone there would be one fewer reason for Robin to return to the village.

Her lovely new clothes were packed into her suitcase. It was a new suitcase and had looked so exciting in the farm kitchen but in the opulence of the hotel bedroom it seemed shabby.

'Never mind, little suitcase,' she consoled it. 'I think you're marvellous and I will use you every time I travel.'

277

She sat back on her heels as a picture of a nine-year-old Mairi in a flannel nightgown sitting at a window waving to the London train came into her head.

'What did I tell you I would wear?' she asked the long-ago train. 'I think I used to have a passion for red gloves but I don't remember. That wee Mairi no longer exists. And this Mairi has grown out of thinking brilliant red is a colour for redheads.'

*　　　*　　　*

Ian took out his jotter and his pen when they were settled in the carriage and Mairi tried to lose herself in a book but she was still too excited by train travel and so, until the conductor came to call the first sitting for lunch, she looked out of the window at the wonder that was England, that green and pleasant land.

Faster than fairies, faster than witches ... The poem from childhood came back, word for word. Robin had recited it so well at his Dux prize giving. She would tell ... no, she would not.

The words ran through her head as they raced through the countryside and halted for a moment when the conductor dragged Ian from the depths of Creation.

'Did you no order lunch, sir, the first sitting?'

Ian blinked at him several times and then smiled. 'Lunch, of course. My sister must be hungry.'

He was beginning to speak like Bella, if not to sound like her. His accent was Scottish but his language was different.

'I like it,' thought Mairi. 'My brother the poet. I

278

wish, I wish that Dad had lived to see him acknowledged, to read these beautiful words.'

*   *   *

Colin was not alive to read his son's words but hundreds of others were. The small leather-covered book sold out within a few weeks of publication and was reprinted. Then letters with foreign stamps arrived and yet more letters from Ian's publisher: the book was to be translated into French, into German, into Russian. Ian was asked to contribute to literary journals and even to be an after-dinner speaker.

He took it all in his farmer's stride. 'Goodness, Mairi,' he said. 'It's an awesome thing that a man can put money in a bank just by sitting at his own fireside. If I did everything these people are asking me to do I'd never have time to write. And as for being an entertainment after too many well-fed people have eaten too much food . . .'

The wedding was to be at the beginning of May and Arabella arrived, together with her maid and her chauffeur and several suitcases, and installed herself in Arbroath's best hotel. The Big House stood empty waiting for its new tenant and they drove up one day so that Arabella could say goodbye to it.

'I loved this house, Mairi,' she said. 'The best games of my childhood were played here, and here I saw Ian for the first time, my knight in shining armour. I would like to have been married from here.'

'Why did they sell?' There, it was out. It was none of her business but Mairi wanted to know.

279

Bella seemed to understand her worry. She smiled as she turned away from the house and walked towards the car.

'Oh, nothing so melodramatic as trying to thwart us. It's retrenchment, nothing more. Not everyone made money out of this ghastly war, and poor Uncle Humphrey was harder hit than many. He needed to raise some money and it was a simple choice between Scotland and England. No one really looked on this place as home, just really a little place to come to for shooting.'

Mairi looked at the 'little place'. The farmhouse of Windydykes plus the steading would no doubt fit nicely into the Ballroom.

'And your home, Bella, in Surrey?'

Bella looked at Ian who was contributing nothing. 'Well, I suppose it's a bit grander, would you say, Ian. It's older, Mairi, Elizabethan. When you come we'll go round. I don't believe I have been in every room; should be quite fun, Ian. We might find some ghosts or some treasure. He won't be able to say he has nowhere quiet to write, Mairi, and there's plenty of room for you. I shall enjoy having a sister, if you'll let me enjoy it, that is.'

Mairi had the terrifying notion that Bella's idea of having a sister was to spend as much money on said sister as possible. She abhorred the idea but she rightly interpreted Ian's warning look and said nothing. There would be plenty of opportunity to avoid Bella's well-meaning generosity. They would be married on Saturday, a simple ceremony with Mairi as maid of honour and young Angus as proud groomsman. Milly and Mairi would serve a wedding breakfast at the farm and the newlyweds, with Bella's maid, would drive off on their new life together straight from there.

Ian had asked Robin's father to act as Bella's father since Sir Humphrey had refused to participate in something he could not approve, but at the very beginning of the ceremony, just as they stood quietly waiting for the arrival of the bride, there was an interruption. A second car hurtled to a stop at the door and there was Rupert.

'I couldn't *not* be here, Bella my sweet. I don't approve, think you'll make one another miserable in a month, but here I am to give you to the poor poetic blighter, if you want me to. Maybe that's some kind of blessing that will bring you both luck.'

Bella started to cry and threw herself into her cousin's arms but as Mairi began to wonder if a weeping bride would be welcomed by her groom, Rupert stopped her.

'Come on, old thing. If he sees you with great red-rimmed eyes he might well throw you back at me and I'll have driven five hundred miles on devilish roads for nothing.'

Bella sniffed, breathed deeply, and blew her nose delicately on a piece, it seemed, of gossamer. Then she awarded Rupert a tremulous smile and took his arm. 'You don't mind, Mr Morrison,' and, preceded by the Dominie and followed by Mairi, began her walk down the aisle.

It is doubtful if Ian even saw Rupert. His eyes were on Bella's beautiful face. She had chosen to wear not white but a dress in her favourite salmon pink and a small pink hat with a tiny veil that just covered her eyes. Mairi's new dress was in pale green and she too looked lovely.

She stood behind Ian and Bella as they made their vows in strong, clear voices and she tried hard

281

to think only of them. This was their day and it would be as happy as the small family group could make it.

There, it was over, they were man and wife. Mairi heard a burst of glorious music and looked round and only then realized that the music was in her head. There was no one in the church but the small party.

'There should have been music.'

Bella had certainly given up a great deal to wed the man of her choice. Had she married Rupert or someone like him, there would have been organ music and banks of exotic flowers, rich, well-dressed guests, bridesmaids in beautiful designer gowns, but Bella seemed to be perfectly content with her simple wedding. She threw her bouquet which Bert caught and dropped as if it were red hot.

With Rupert's car there was plenty of room for the entire party and the Minister to be driven back to the farm and if Rupert winced at the paucity of his cousin's reception he gave no sign but danced with Mairi and then with Milly to the tunes played by Mr Morrison's ancient gramophone. Bella and Ian had eyes only for each other and they had to be reminded to eat and to cut their cake, made three weeks before by Mairi, and decorated with roses by Milly.

Then it was time for them to go and Rupert helped his cousin into her fur coat, since the day had grown chilly and they had a long drive ahead of them.

'You'll come and see us soon, Mairi,' begged Ian, 'and you'll keep in touch about . . . everything, the farm and everything,' he finished lamely.

'Of course, I'll keep in touch. Bella's postie will get as tired of me as old Davie got of Bella.'

'This is the worst time for me to leave you in the lurch . . .'

She stopped his worries with her hand. 'Ian, haven't I three men coming for interviews tomorrow and I have Angus and Bert as soon as the school is out? You have a whole new life ahead of you . . .'

'Which I can't enjoy to the full if I have a wee sister to worry about.' He turned her around so that they were both facing the little house where they had been born and brought up. 'It's not so easy to leave now as I thought it would be, Mairi. Part of me stays here.'

'Aye, but it's time for you to leave, Ian. I'll come to visit you both as soon as I can and I'll write to you every week. There, I can say no fairer than that.'

'After our honeymoon trip . . .' he began but she turned him again to the car where his wife was waiting.

'I know there's room and I know Bella really wants me . . .'

'And if you don't get a better offer,' he interrupted her and they both laughed.

'Bella waited for you and the look on her face says you were worth it, but this is her wedding day and you have kept her waiting long enough.'

She walked with him to the beautiful sleek motor car where Rupert was standing talking to his cousin through the open window.

'Bye, Bella, be happy,' she said sincerely as she kissed her sister-in-law.

Ian turned to Rupert and saw the outstretched

hand. 'Welcome to the family, cousin,' said Rupert and Ian could say nothing but only shake the hand that had once been withheld from him.

He hugged Mairi and then slipped in beside his wife; the chauffeur started the engine and the motor car, with Bella and Ian almost hanging out of the window waving, drew away from the farm.

Mairi was left with Rupert but there was no shyness now. 'Well, that's that,' he said. 'They make a handsome couple.' He gestured to his own car. 'Must be off,' he said. 'Staying with friends in the area.'

'Goodnight then, Captain Grey-Watson,' said Mairi.

He laughed. 'Goodnight, *Rupert*,' he said. 'Are we not family now? It's a strange new world, Mairi, and perhaps it will be a better place for us all. Make some sense of four years of carnage, I do hope,' and to Mairi's surprise and even greater embarrassment he bent and kissed her very lightly before he climbed into his motor car and drove away.

It was a lovely evening and Mairi stood for a while just reliving the last few hours—Bella's beauty, Ian's obvious happiness, Rupert's generosity of spirit.

'It's a strange new world,' she repeated to Milly who had come out with a shawl for her, 'and a better place for us all.'

CHAPTER TWENTY-SEVEN

On 21 June 1920, Mid-summer's day, Mairi woke up feeling, for some unaccountable reason, serene and at peace. She was, as far as she knew, about to lose the home where she had been born and where she had laboured, lived and loved, laughed and cried, mourned and rejoiced, during all those years. There was no reason, except that it was a perfect morning, for her to feel so happy.

The sky was a deep blue, and the fields stretched out in all directions from the farmhouse like the spokes of a particularly verdant green wheel. She could hear the hens clucking happily just outside her window as they searched in the dust for crumbs or seeds.

And then she heard the sound of the postman's bicycle bell and she ran downstairs without bothering to tie back her hair. A letter. It had to be a letter from Ian. But he was on his honeymoon and had promised postcards. Who else would write? Robin?

It had to be Robin.

She threw the door open. 'Hello, Davie, you'll have a cup of tea and a bap?'

'I won't say no,' he said, which was what he always said.

He handed her the letter. She looked at the writing and the bright day dulled. It was not from Robin. Neither was it from Ian. She looked at it as if she stared hard enough she might see through the cheap envelope to the ill-written signature. The envelope was flimsy and her name, Miss

McGloughlin, was written in block letters in a poorly educated and laborious hand.

'Are you no going to open it, Mairi?'

Mairi looked from the envelope to the old postman's honest craggy face. 'I can't think who it could possibly be from. There's an old friend writes to me sometimes when she's needing something but even her writing is better than this.'

Davie Wishart sighed and flexed his bunions inside his comfortable old shoes. 'Have you got the kettle on, lass?'

Flustered, Mairi looked up again from the letter. 'Sorry, Davie. I hoped it was from . . . my brother.'

'On his honeymoon? You'll be lucky. What a bonnie bride she must have made. You'll have a likeness somewhere.'

'The beautiful bride and, Davie Wishart, her very handsome groom had a likeness taken in London. When it arrives I'll show it to you.'

Davie made himself comfortable at the table and began to spread butter on a soft, fresh morning roll. 'A fairy story, my missus calls it, except it's the poor boy marrying the princess.'

'The princess married an up-and-coming poet,' Mairi reminded him as she poured the boiling water into the teapot.

'Aye, imagine a farm laddie writing poems. It's the war has changed everything for the better.'

Mairi decided not to remind him of the legion of farm laddies who had written poetry before Ian McGloughlin and whose poems had not stopped the worst war the world had ever seen. But it was going to be better. It would never happen again. At last the world had learned a salutary lesson. She smiled at Davie, poured the tea, and turned again to her letter. It had been written from an Arbroath address but it was not one with which she was familiar. She turned the lined piece of grubby paper over but the signature meant nothing to her and she turned back to the beginning of the letter.

Dear Miss McGloughlin,
    I saw in the paper about your bruther.

Oh, no, thought Mairi, a begging letter. Many of those had come among the letters of congratulations.

I had been sorry not to have rote before but I was woonded and in the hospital in Rooong thats in France, 25 Stayshonary. Your father was my sargint the best ever and I'm here becos he got killt for me. I wantit to say thanks but also to tell his son that the sarge was riting till him when he got it. I give him my unvilope and he was saying as how his boy was the best and he loved him and ment to say and he was proud that his boy was rite all the time and the grenade came and he yelled not him, you bastard, xcuse my french, and flung hissel on me and sometimes I wundered maybe he dun it for his boy too.
    Anyways, hope this finds you well and I will never forget the sarge and my mam too.
        Chay Maxwell

'No more bad news, lassie?' The old postman was looking at her and she became aware that tears were streaming down her cheeks.
    She smiled at him, a glorious, glowing smile. 'Wonderful news, Davie. I knew this was going to
287

be a very special day. Here, read it. It's from the boy my father saved when he won his Victoria Cross.'

Davie solemnly put down his bap, took out his glasses and fixed them on his nose before he took the sheet of paper. He struggled to decipher it. 'Well, he never spent much time at the school, did he?'

'Who cares? I'll write to him, no, I won't. I'll go into Arbroath and take him and his mam my best boiling fowl. This will mean more to Ian than all his valuable wedding presents put together.'

She would go in the afternoon when all her chores were done until it was time to feed the animals in the evening. First she would wring the hen's neck and the carcass could cool while she was working. She gave Davie another bap and a second cup of tea and tried not to be impatient while he sat savouring them. He was, after all, her life-line to the outside world.

But, at last he was gone, freewheeling as usual down the hill beyond the house to gather strength for the steep hill that led to the main road, and she put on her apron and went out to the coop to choose the hen.

No matter how often she had had to do this unpleasant task, it got no easier. But, people had to eat, and a nice plump hen would be an excellent gift for Chay Maxwell and his mother. She wanted desperately to see the boy for whom her father had given up his life.

She did what had to be done and left the rest of the, no doubt, relieved chickens to commiserate with one another and took the unfortunate hen back to the kitchen. The postman was out of sight but someone else was on the farm road, someone walking.

'Good gracious, another visitor. Who can it be today?'

She looked again at the small dark dot on the hill. Was there something familiar? No, she was desperately trying to find something recognizable but she thrust the wish away. It was a salesman, merely a salesman. But he was so thin, tall, not so tall as Ian but thinner, so much thinner even than someone who had spent over a year in a prison camp. She stood, the dead hen in her hand, and refused to hope, but she could not move from the path.

The dark speck came nearer and got larger. Dark longish hair flopping over a too-pale face. He had seen her. He stopped. He looked and then he began to walk again, a gait she recognized, a stride that she had followed from the time, oh so long ago, when she had begun to follow her beloved brother and his friend, his friend.

'Robin,' she called and then she began to run and to cry at one and the same time and he began to run and when she reached him and was gathered up into his arms she had time to notice that he was crying too, before he bent to kiss her.

He pushed her away, his face flushing with embarrassment. 'I'm sorry,' he said and his voice was hesitant and unsure. 'I have no right . . .'

She put her fingers up to his lips. 'Oh, Robin,' she began.

'Let me speak, Mairi; for so long I have been unable to tell you. I was terrified, you see. Everything had been so clear when we were small. I was clever. I would go to the university, get a good

289

degree, become a teacher, the seasons, everything in its place, following one another as the moon follows the sun. And you? You were just wee Mairi, an infernal nuisance, to be tolerated because of Ian. And then you stopped being a pest.' He was looking away from her towards the sea as if the story was written there on the waves for him to read. 'Then the war came and that was easy too, Mairi. I had to do my duty but Ian spoiled it because, next to my parents, I respected him most, loved him most, and he wouldn't fight and I knew he could lick us all. So the questions started and I went to the Front and I shot people, Mairi, I know I did, day after day, but it was my duty, wasn't it? And it was madness but you were there and I knew you were important to me, to my sanity, but that went too. Everything was so muddled, mixed up, like wire fencing that's got all tangled. The noise, that unbelievable, insupportable noise, never stopped. Even when I was in the hospital or here in my bed at the Schoolhouse, I could hear the noise and so I could hear nothing else, not Dad's voice or yours or the doctors'. I had dreams.' He looked away from her again, ashamed of his nightmares. 'The dreams made me afraid and I'm afraid again, Mairi, that it took too long. I wasted time when we were young, so much wasted time.' He looked down at her. How long had he known that he loved her? How long *had* he loved her? All his life? Since the dance at the Kirk Hall? What did it matter? She was so beautiful. Surely someone who was not afraid had come during those wasted years to tell her what a treasure she was.

Mairi put her hands up and touched his shoulders. She looked into his face, so brown from his months in the sun. His body felt strong, although it was still too thin.

'What is time, Robin? I read one of your books, one the Dominie loaned Ian. It's still here. "We live ... in feelings, not in figures on a dial. We should count time by heart throbs..." A nice poem, don't you think?'

He did not move. She kept her hands where they rested but looked deep into his troubled eyes and at last he spoke.

'I know my feelings, Mairi, but I have no right to hope I know yours. I gave you nothing ...'

'You give me everything, Robin,' she said and kissed him gently on his dry lips.

And then he moved. His arms imprisoned her and he bent his head to kiss her more deeply.

Still he could not allow the exultation to flow like warm wine through his blood. 'Mairi? I can't believe ... surely ...'

This time her lips and not her fingers stopped his words. 'Well?' she asked when at last they drew apart. 'Does that answer your question, Robin Morrison?'

The tears started in his eyes and, embarrassed, he dashed them away. 'I hoped, I prayed, but, heavens, Mairi, are all the men in Forfarshire blind?'

'Could I see anyone else with my heart full of you?' she said and kissed him again.

'My dinner?' he asked when they stopped for breath, glancing then at the poor old hen lying abandoned on the grass and they laughed again as she explained about the letter.

They were walking now back to the farmhouse and her hand was in his, naturally, happily, where it

291

had always belonged.

'I still owe it to you to tell you everything, Mairi. Perhaps I should have written but I didn't because I had to test myself, not my love for you. That has been strong and secure for a long time now, but my self, my head, I suppose. At Easter I went back to Rome and I got a job in the school where I taught before. They've asked me to sign a contract.'

He turned to her and the delight on his face sent a chill of fear through her. He was so happy. He was well and he was wanted by people whom he respected.

'That's wonderful, Robin,' she said and tried with all her heart to sound excited and happy for him.

'It is, isn't it? I'm well, Mairi. Now I can come to you with something to offer.' He took the hen which she was still holding and this time it was he who laid it on the grass. 'We'll take that into Arbroath later. Right now . . . Oh, Mairi, I do love you so.' And he kissed her again and this time as she responded she knew that she was offering him her heart, her future to do with as he chose. He understood and exulted.

'What would the village say?' he asked laughingly. '*What a hoyden that Mairi McGloughlin turned out to be.* Come on, let's get this poor old hen—hasn't it gone through enough this morning—to its new home and then we'll write to Ian and tell him we're going to be married. You will marry me, Mairi, won't you?'

Mairi looked at the little house where she had grown up. She saw the roses clambering over the doorway, the old dog asleep in the sun. She saw the fields and she photographed them in their summer dresses onto her heart and she said goodbye. For Robin she would go anywhere.

'Yes,' she said simply.

He turned to the hedgerow where the wild roses were blooming and he broke off one perfect little white briar rose.

'Roses, Mairi. I promised you roses, and maybe for a year or two wild roses are all there will be. Schoolmasters don't make a great deal of money. You won't have a home like the magnificent one Ian now owns.'

She put her hand to his lips and stopped him. 'I won't mind where we live, just as long as we are together. I'm sure I'll like Italy.'

'Italy? Well, it would be nice for a honeymoon, but I have no money left. We'd have to wait until next year and I want us to be well married by then; we've wasted so much time, Mairi, too much time.'

'But of course, Robin. We'll marry as soon as Ian gets back, before the harvest, so that you can be back in Italy by the start of the new term.'

He looked at her and then realization dawned and he hugged her to him and laughed and kissed her and kissed her and laughed again.

'What a brave woman! You thought I took the job in Italy? No, no, Mairi mine. I like Italy but I love you and . . . Mairi, I've taken a job teaching Latin and Greek in Dundee. We could live at the Schoolhouse with my father but, oh, Mairi, couldn't we live here?'

Live here? To live on the farm with its memories of Colin and Ian, the child Mairi, Milly, Angus, Jean, and even Bert. With a husband she could become a tenant. And Robin had loved occasional days of harvest; he had loved lambs and calves and,

293

most of all, he had loved sitting under trees with Ian while they read, or wrote, poetry. He had grown flowers to help him in his therapy; she could teach him how to grow other things. A farm would be a grand place for a teacher to relax, a grand place to bring up children, a grand place for a poet and his wife to bring their children. She looked at her rose, already drooping. She would take it home and press it between the pages of Ian's first pamphlet of war poems, maybe between the pages with the poems called 'Friend' and 'Mairi'.

'This poor hen,' she said, holding it up for inspection.

'Let's take it down to Arbroath,' said Robin. 'And then we'll come back and we'll talk, Mairi McGloughlin, about changing your name.'